D0360540

Dirty South

This is a work of fiction. The authors have invented the characters. Any resemblance to actual persons, living or dead, is purely coincidental.

If you have purchased this book with a 'dull' or missing cover—You have possibly purchased an unauthorized or stolen book. Please immediately contact the publisher advising where, when and how you purchased this book.

Compilation and Introduction copyright © 2005 by
Triple Crown Publications
2959 Stelzer Rd., Suite C
Columbus, Ohio 43219
www.TripleCrownPublications.com

Library of Congress Control Number: 2005929304
ISBN# 0976234955
Cover Design/Graphics: www.MarionDesigns.com
Author: Darrell King
Editor: Chloé A. Hilliard
Production: Kevin J. Calloway
Consulting: Vickie M. Stringer

Copyright © 2005 by Triple Crown Publications. All rights reserved. No part of this book may be reproduced in any form without permission from the publisher, except by reviewer who may quote brief passages to be printed in a newspaper or magazine.

First Trade Paperback Edition Printing August 2005
10 9 8 7 6 5 4 3 2

Printed in the United States of America

Dedication

I dedicate this Novel to my cousin Ernest Bryan, who I grew up with in Dufuski Island, a cousin who always had my back 'cause I was his Lil' Cuzz!!!! Also whose life of big ballin', shot Calling, and redemption has always been the inspiration of my street life prose.

Luv ya, baby boy.

Acknowledgements

Dirty South Thank You's go out to Ms. Vickie Stringer, it feels great working with the Queen of Gangsta Lit herself!!! Tammy, Chloé Hilliard, and the entire TCP family, the world is ours!!!! TCP 4 ever!!!!

To my wifey Sonya a.k.a Redd and Carrotcake. My children India, Darrell Jr., K'linn, Peolandria, and Angel, I love you all. Dad and Mom do a lot to make you happy and comfortable with this incredible life we live each day.

To David & Tracy Belton, Lil' David, Dawn, and Danielle, you guys always keep it real with us, even when it hurts, and that is a true friendship, God Bless you!!!! To my Number 1 buddy, Carlos Gonzalas, words can't express the way our family feels about you, you have been a brother to me, and a great godfather to my girls, they luv you very much, man you have inspired me from day one, and that means so much to me, Papa Dios put you in our lives as a guardian angel, and I thank God for you, be blessed!!!!

To my Mom Delores Bryan, and my Dad Allan King, thanks for having me, because if it where not for you two, there be no me!!!! Thanks!!!!! My two brothers, Byron & Robert. My step-mother Linda, be kind to my pops!!! Always make him happy!!!! My Mother-in-law Rev. Ruby Burgin a.k.a. Ms. B, you have been a great mom to me, and I thank you for producing my wife with the help of my Father-in-law David Burgin Sr. cause I have a beautiful family!!!! My step mother-in-law, Cathy Burgin, keep my other pops happy!!!! My Sister-in-law Kimberli, Brandon, Big John, and Lil' John Douglass, don't forget your sister Patrice Douglass, and Charmaine, oops I forgot Mr. Donnie.

Giving props out to all my Piceses people, Lia Brice, Nadine Nicoles, Tim Owens, Ronnie Duncan, I am sure there are more, so I give you props too. My Brother-in-law David Burgin Jr. and family Keisha, Amira, and Layla, My cousins Eric, Joseph, Rebecca, Lisa, Kenneth & Tyrone. My aunts Ja Nay, Emily & Patricia. Patsy Coton, Adrian Johnson, Nadine McCall, Freddie Cook, who my children adore so much!!!! Big B (Bryant Bethea, the head banger). Michel Byrd & Tasha Williams, thank you for all your support!! The Ratpack; Erik, Hal, Chris & Brian, you cats are the absolute best!!! Angie Koch, to a magnificent athlete & friend… "All blacks Rock!!!

Tonya Powell for taking my family in when we where homeless, and had no one to turn to, you are the absolute best, God will truly bless you for what you did for us.

To Pastor George & First Lady Sharlene Hawkins & the entire HCM family, Thank you for keeping me spiritually grounded. To every Southern Hip Hop artist who has represented for the Dirty, Dirty keep it crunk baby!!! To Daufuskie, Hilton head, Charleston, & other island of the South Carolina Low Country Holla at ya boy!!!!

To my second home, Washington D.C., I ain't never gonna forget about the Chocolate City wait till my next novel. We gonna punish these literary bamas, and finally to all y'all haters out here, remember this…The game is meant to be sold, not told!!! See this is a head banger!!!! Run tell dat!!!!!!!!!!

I am rich beyond my wildest dreams, I am, I am, I am. Words that come from some important people. I am Rich Beyond my Wildest Dreams. Thomeas L. Pauley and Penelope J. Pauley, give and it shall be given back to you. Amen, selah to all my Mystism Gorus. Oh and Roslynn Beckmon if you are out there and come across my book, we love you!!!!!!!!!!!!!!!!

South Carolina raise up!!!! peace and Luv!!!!!!!

INTRO

As I look back on my past, you know, I never really wanted to do most of the things I did. I didn't like drug dealing. I had to witness too many murders—those of my friends and a whole lot of innocent folks. I just was a poor country kid growing up in Peola, Georgia trying to belong to something...anything that would elevate me from a life of hardship and poverty. That's when I found out about drugs, money, and power, not to mention the intoxicating feeling each gives you.

During the mid-eighties, during the height of the crack-cocaine epidemic, I was a 16-year-old junior at Cayman Senior High in West Peola. I had pretty decent grades back in '85, even made the honor roll twice that year. All the teachers spoke highly of me. I was captain of both the varsity football and basketball teams. During my senior year in '86, as quarterback of the Fightin' Crusaders, I passed for over 1,000 yards and 63 touchdowns. We went undefeated that year and knocked off Savannah Union 24-3 in the Peach State Championship played at the Atlanta Georgia Dome. I also received honors for my outstanding contribution on the basketball court, however, as a team we didn't fair as well as our football squad.

Although I received honors, awards, recommendations and

trophies during my last two years in high school, truthfully I wasn't really that impressed with all the small town attention I was getting or with all the recruiting letters from top division 1-A universities that flooded my mailbox each week. I'd only played high school sports as a break from the monotony, a diversion, something to do...that's all. It kept me busy and in school. But my mind was made up; I had no interests in living out any hoop dreams or gridiron fantasies beyond Cayman High School. I wanted that fast money, I wanted to hustle because it would get me out of the hood and give me the type of lifestyle I felt that after so long I deserved to have. Little did I know it would come with a price and teach me a valuable lesson in the process.

I

Troubled Son

I was born Rae Kwon Lake on January 5, 1970, to Selena "Katt" French and Smithfield "Smitty" Lake. My mother was an ex-stripper turned porn queen from New Orleans and my father, also originally from the 'Big Easy', was an amateur prizefighter and loan shark. The only thing that bothered me about my mom and dad was that they were always away from home. I was constantly being watched or cared for by someone other than them, sometimes even for weeks at a time. Whether my babysitters were relatives, neighbors, or the occasional nanny they were all paid handsomely by my father.

Once while my parents were away, I stayed out all night and came home the next morning. The chick that was babysitting me freaked out and almost beat me half to death. When my folks got back in town, I couldn't wait to show my bruised back and welted behind. Although my father felt I deserved the spanking, my moms was furious. Determined to find the woman who had beaten her only child, she and I stalked the back alleys, projects, and side streets of New Orleans' seedier sections within the plush confines of a hunter green Chrysler Le Baron, which my mother adored. Upon finding ole girl, my moms literally snatched her up off the street and commenced to whoopin' on her ass to the delight and amusement of all who passed.

"Come on Rae-Rae," my mother said panting from exertion, "I reckon she's been whooped enough." She yanked my arm, pulling me back towards the car with her.

Remembering that day, my mother punching, hair-pulling, clawing and kicking that unfortunate woman into bloody submission, while the rapidly growing group of onlookers cheered her on like a demented group of Roman gladiator spectators, I felt even at that tender age (which couldn't have been more than eight or nine) an exhilarating sense of power. Everyone knew my parents in New Orleans, from the mayor down to the vagrants hangin' out on the corner sippin' on cheap booze.

A path cleared for us as we quickly made our way back to the car parked on the curb. A big, dark-skinned bald man opened the rear door for me and the driver's side door for my moms. My mother smiled at him, whispered 'Thank You', and sped away into the New Orleans' night. It was the first time that I'd witnessed an act of violence in my young life, but surely it wasn't my last.

I lived with my parents until I was ten years old. Then, in 1980, I was sent to live with my father's mother in Baton Rouge. Living with my grandmother, Ella Mae Lake, was quite boring. All she did was make me go to church every evening, and all day Sundays. School and church, church and school; that's all I ever did.

Grandma and I had a pretty decent relationship, but I was one hardheaded lil' thug out on the street and in school. The product of two hot-tempered parents, it was only natural that I too would be prone to violence and unruly behavior. It was but a matter of time before that violent streak would surface-much to the torment of my childhood peers and teachers. At Amherst Middle School, I became a bully who relished in picking fights wherever I went. Most kids feared the very name of Rae Kwon Lake. Playgrounds, schoolyards, and buses were my hunting ground; no kid, male or female, was exempt from my harassments. Many wore the black eyes, bloody noses and swollen lips attributed to my flying fists. I could always find a seat on the crowded school bus, or easily break in front of the lunch line and no one said anything at all. I had kids bringing me their lunch money, their allowance, and their snacks.

Once, this white kid named Jarrett Leavey even gave me a go-kart to try and stop pickin' on 'em every day. I graciously accepted it and still knocked his ass out for fun. Teachers found me to be a menace to the other students and a highly disruptive presence in the classroom. "Rae Kwon is always picking fights, and teasing the other kids to no end," one frustrated Amherst teacher informed my grandmother. "Sometimes, when I leave the classroom for a second, I return to a scene of absolute chaos caused by your grandson," she concluded with a sigh.

My grandmother was a half-hearted disciplinarian who'd rather pray for blood of Jesus to save me than give me a sound ass whooping, which at that age I surely deserved. When that didn't seem to quell my 'thugged-out' behavior, I was told on a regular of the torments of hell and how it would be my home in the afterlife if I didn't make a change for the better while I was still young. The "thou shalt not sin" thing went in one ear and out the other. On rare occasions, Grandma Lake had no choice but to go out back into the yard, cut a nice twig branch off the dog wood tree just outside the picket fence, and wail on my hind parts for a bit. She always wound up feeling sorry for me and made up by preparing me peach cobbler and ice cream or some other delicious, kiddie-lovin' dessert. Shit, soon I was actin' out simply for the post-ass whoopin' treats.

The only thing about my four-year stay with Grandma Lake that I can really say was enjoyable was her cooking; she could throw down in the kitchen for sure. Crab cakes, jambalaya, seafood gumbo, fried chicken, candied yams, collard greens, cornbread, fried catfish...and that was usually the appetizer. When I came back home to New Orleans in '84, I was 14 and pretty big for my age—5'11"-190 lbs and still growing. By the time I turned 18, I was 6'3" and 245 lbs. I attributed my growth spurt to Grandma Lake and her hearty Cajun dishes.

Triple Crown Publications presents

II

Homeward Bound

By the time I turned 13, in 1983, I was a true teenager. My voice deepened and the first sign of facial hair appeared, I was totally outta control, off da hook. Before I could even think about enrolling in Amherst High, my grandmother could take no more of my violent behavior and boorish manners.

Surprisingly, I had passed all my classes. It was amazing to everyone including myself, with all the suspensions, parent/teacher conferences, and in '82 a near expulsion for threatening to kill a math teacher. But nonetheless four years of me was more than Ella Mae Lake could handle. She informed my mother that I was just like my father, "nuthin but a dog-gone hoodlum." My mother, always my #1 supporter, assured my grandmother that she'd get me off her hands within the week. That week never came.

My parents owned a private plane, a little ole Cessna that my dad got from one of his 'clients' as collateral on a loan. He'd always had a thing for planes and collected dozens of radio con-trolled and gas powered models. Whenever and wherever they went across country, he flew that plane. He began teaching my moms to fly shortly before they shipped me off to Grandma Lake's. My folks got caught in a windstorm that summer. I've no clue as to why my old man needed to fly at night in inclement weather, but it proved to be his undoing. On July 3, 1983, my parents Selena French and Smithfield Lake crashed into a bayou right outside of Ballston, Louisiana. My dad was 31 and my moms was 28.

I was somewhat indifferent to my dad's death. I mean, we didn't have the typical father/son relationship. He was always gone and when he was at home there was no bonding; I didn't really care if he lived or died. But my mother was my boo, that was my heart right there. Even though she would be away often herself, shooting porn films out in California or Nevada, she always made up for lost time when she got home. We went all over the city—the zoo, museums, and aquariums, all that educational shit, we did it. We laughed and joked with one another and she always made a big deal over my birthday and made sure that it was a big time party that sometimes lasted well after I'd gone to bed. My heart was crushed; it took me some time to recover from my mother's untimely death. For a long while I cursed the name of my father for taking my moms up into the air with him that fateful night. The very next day was the Fourth of July and to this day I have no love for that holiday. My grandmother came around shortly after my parents' burials. Our deteriorating relationship vastly improved, and now with my folks being dead, I had nowhere to go and my grandma knew it. Being the gentle soul that she was of course she allowed me to stay only this time it would be different. Different in many more ways than one, for I was to meet the individual who would single-handedly change my entire life.

III

Snookey

By September of '83, I was enrolled in Amherst High. Unlike my previous two years in middle school, I wasn't the same ornery asshole I'd been before. My grandmother told me that in order for me to remain in her home I'd have to make a change in attitude, which I did...to an extent. I mean, I didn't bully everybody like I did in middle school, but I was still feared by most of my peers and found the teachers very wary and prejudiced against me. I was blamed for actions I wasn't responsible for and given a hard time by everyone from the school janitor to the principal; during the first grading quarter I failed two classes for the first time in my life. I knew it was bullshit, I mean here I was bustin' my ass to work hard at my studies, not fucking with anyone like before and I'm getting' fucked over by school administrators left and right. I just guess what goes around comes around, and I was getting back what I deserved for all that dirt I'd done in middle school. Being the tough guy that I was, I took it in stride; I had to have a roof over my head and I knew that Grandma Lake wasn't fakin' when she said I had to change or get the fuck out.

By October, things had gotten so bad in school I felt like just sayin' fuck it and dropping out. I didn't feel that I'd use any of that academic garbage after high school anyway. Besides, I had no friends, no girlfriends, and no plans for college; so what was the point? I figured I'd find something to do with myself other than sitting in some dumb ass classroom all day. That's when my life changed forever.

During the Thanksgiving Day school break, my uncle, Marion Lake, also from New Orleans, paid grandma and me a visit. I'd never met my uncle, but always heard stories about him from my mother and her two sisters. My father never talked much about his brother 'cause, according to my moms, my father was the black sheep of the family and always envied and hated his younger brother because of his height, athleticism, and strikingly handsome looks.

Now my pops wasn't an unattractive cat by any means, but Marion had him beat looks wise by a mile. Standing approximately 6'11" and weighing in at about 270 lbs, his was an intimidating presence to say the least. My father was much shorter, only about 5'11" and slightly overweight. My Uncle Marion had been a professional basketball player during the early '70's. He'd played power forward for two and a half years with the Virginia Squires of the now defunct ABA. Grandma Lake even had an old photo of the team with Uncle Marion standing beside Dr. J at the very top of the picture. This was encased in glass with several other photos and ABA memorabilia, including an orange and white basketball bearing the signature of every Virginia Squire ballplayer. My uncle Marion was known as "Snookey" amongst family and close friends, a moniker he was given many years ago due to a childhood mispronunciation of the word "Snoopy" which was his favorite cartoon character as a toddler.

We had a wonderful holiday with Uncle Marion, his wife, Melissa, and their twin son and daughter, Shawn and Dawn. It was a pleasant surprise to some kids my age over to kick it with; I'd long alienated myself from half the teen population of Skye County, LA. My cousins and I had a lot in common. We were all 13, quite temperamental and troublesome. After Thanksgiving dinner, the three of us decided to retire downstairs while the three adults conversed and watched the game.

Once downstairs, we began playing gin rummy and while doing so we began sharing our experiences with one another.

Man, I thought I was a juvenile delinquent. Shit, I was a saint compared to those two! Robberies, assaults with deadly weapons, vandalism, burglaries to name but a few of the criminal activities the twins were involved in.

"We never got caught" Dawn said, shuffling the glossy playing cards, "We were just too smooth and at the time we were only 11, 12 years old!" Shawn would look at his sister and smile broadly, nodding in agreement. After playing several games, we got tired of it and went outside on the deck. As the evening sun went down behind the Spanish moss tangled trees of the bayou, we sat on the porch and listened to the low rumble of alligators stalking the murky waters in search of prey.

Uncle Marion and his family stayed the week with us to both the delight of Grandma Lake and me. The Sunday before Uncle Marion left for the Big Easy, he pulled me to the side, "Listen Rae, Mama done told me that you been having some trouble in school out here," Uncle Marion lit a cigarette and patiently awaited my answer.

"Yeah…I guess so," I answered reluctantly.

"Well, don't worry 'bout dat, ya see Mama's getting' up in age and I done told her dat she kin come to N'Awlins wit me, 'Lissa and da chi'ren. But she don't wanna do dat dare, so's I can't be makin her, ya heard me? But since she's getting older now she don't need no drama, ya heard me?" I looked up at my towering uncle and asked him what he was trying to say. "What I'm sayin' is dat you be a young strappin, nigga, why you wanna live wit an ole lady and go ta school out here on da outskirts of Baton Rouge? Ain't no happenings out here boy. You come on live with ya Uncle Snookey and I'll make sho ya pass school and make something of yaself, ya heard me?" I smiled and nodded with approval, as my uncle embraced me tightly. "Now don't say ya Uncle ain't never done nuttin for ya stinkin' ass, here boy." I could hardly speak as I stood mouth agape and eyes wide in amazement as Uncle Snookey handed me a cash stack. "Well, whatcha gonna do, just stand dere lookin' stupid or put that cash away and help me load the bags in da car?"

"Yeah Uncle Snookey, no problem," I answered snapping out of my dumbfounded state. As I ascended the rickety old spiral staircase I quickly removed the rubber band from around the wad of money in my hands and slowly began counting. By the time I'd reached my room I'd counted nearly $900. When I entered my room I placed $1,000 on my bed and simply gazed at all that money, once again dumbfounded.

I placed the grand in an old shoebox that I kept under the bed, I then quickly went downstairs and assisted with the packing. Before they left, Uncle Snookey left me phone numbers to reach him at home and at work.

"Don't spend it all in one place, ya heard?" Uncle Snookey remarked before leaving.

"Awright," I remember saying with a smile. Grandma and I waved and shouted our goodbyes as the big Buick Skylark melted into the distance leaving a cloud of dust down the old country road.

After the Christmas holidays Grandma Lake fell gravely ill. She was admitted into Amherst Community Hospital Center and was diagnosed with breast cancer. Although Uncle Snookey offered to fly her back to New Orleans, she refused. She also told him that she wasn't going to take any of the chemotherapy treatments either. Everyone in our family knew that Grandma had already prepared herself and everyone else for her impending death. All that Uncle Snookey could do was fly out to her old farmhouse and pay for a hospice worker to care for her until the inevitable happened.

When Grandma Lake died, her son, daughter-in-law, grandchildren and most of her church family surrounded her. She went peacefully on April 1, 1984, the same day Motown great, Marvin Gaye, was shot to death by his father. Her funeral was bittersweet. We would miss Grandma Lake, but she lived a full life and had many community leaders as well as Amherst Baptist Church members speak highly of her lovely personality and her many civic works during her 81 years on the earth.

After the funeral and burial ceremonies, Uncle Snookey began the task of taking over Grandma Lake's estate. There was the farmhouse and approximately 77-acres of land, mostly untamed woodland. When this was completed, Uncle Snookey agreed to pay Pastor Mamie Budge of Amherst Baptist Church, $2,500 a month, to have the members of the church tend to the land and upkeep of the farmhouse while he was away. Livestock were donated to local farmers without cost.

By the end of April, I was back in New Orleans with my uncle, aunt, and cousins. However, we didn't stay there very long after we returned. It soon became obvious to me that Uncle Snookey was no ordinary working stiff. He kept big loot on him at all times and spent money on himself and his family like it was running water.

When we arrived back to the city, my uncle had us living out of hotels. The hotels were always five star accommodations and we were always treated roy'ally, but I couldn't understand why he had us bouncing all over New Orleans. One night when Uncle Snookey and Aunt Melissa were away, I inquired about our nomadic lifestyle and wasn't prepared for what I heard.

"Oh, our dad's a baller," Shawn announced casually as he and I sat on the floor played video games in the lavishly furnished Montpelier Hotel suite in which we were residing at the time.

"A what?" I asked in ignorance of the soon to be oft-used slang for drug dealer.

"A baller, fool," Shawn answered lowering the joystick while staring at me curiously.

"Look here nigga, I don't know what in the fuck a baller is, ya heard?" I replied.

"Dad's a drug dealer," Dawn said as she lay on the bed eating pizza. I was totally shocked that Uncle Snookey was into that fast and dangerous life...but then again it was all clear now. No wonder Uncle Snookey kept large amounts of cash on him at all times and he was constantly on the phone. But more than that, the calm, nonchalant attitudes of the twins took me by surprise. After some thought, I concluded that any kids who were as thugged out as these two considered it the norm, honorable even, that their pops was a real life Nino Brown/Tony Montana type of gangsta.

I never did bring up the topic again. I just went with the flow. Soon, I was about to find out that going with the flow reaped hefty benefits for me. Uncle Snookey wasted no time in having me drop off packages of marijuana and cocaine to his customers.

Most of his customers were rich white folk and a few affluent blacks. Many lived in plush communities on the outskirts of the city. All of them paid handsomely for their products; plus in addition to their tips, Uncle Snookey was tipping me, too. Once I made $2,200 in tips in one week.

Although Uncle Snookey and Aunt Melissa never hid the fact that they were selling street drugs, they never let their own kids drop off dope unlike me. Not because they had morals or anything, but they knew their twins were too unstable, temperamental and immature to deal with their high-end clientele. They trusted me and I never let them down. They allowed Shawn and Dawn to help me bag up dope and weigh it, but it was always me who distributed it.

Money, power, prestige and more women than any man could possibly handle. My uncle had all of that and more and now I was about to join the ranks of the big ballers of New Orleans. I could taste my rise from an orphan to becoming "the man" and maybe even "The King of New Orleans." Little did I really know how much power I'd eventually possess.

IV

Baby Ballers

By years end, Uncle Snookey, Aunt Melissa and I had flipped enough dollars to move up outta New Orleans. Uncle Snookey did all the networking with his suppliers down in Miami. Aunt Melissa utilized her catering business as a smoke screen to elude the Feds for the better half of the summer of 1984 and I took care of the distribution of dope.

My twin cousins assisted me in bagging the drugs and cooking the left over powder, which would later be chemically changed into "crack." Many a time I felt like a mad scientist or some medieval alchemist at work in the lab. Dawn, Shawn and I would slave over a hot stove, sometimes for hours, producing dozens of bags or sometimes vials of tiny, hardened pebbles of cooked coke, which disappeared as quickly as it was produced.

Weekends were our time to unwind. I spent most of my time observing my uncle and his method of doing business. Little did he know that occasionally I'd skim a little dope for myself and flip it in my spare time. My alibi would always be a trip to the movies or I'd say I was gonna go play basketball with some local kids.

From the time Grandma died until the next year, 1985, I didn't attend school. Dawn and Shawn had long since been expelled from at least three New Orleans high schools for unruly behavior and the one co-ed private school that they were place in kicked them out for marijuana possession and vandalizing the principal's BMW. I'm sure that one prompted their parents to greatly limit their involvement in the family business.

From that point on, private tutors hired by my uncle and aunt educated the Lake twins. Although full of mischief and attitude, both Shawn and Dawn terribly feared their father and therefore knew better than to waste his money goofing off. So, my uncle got his money's worth and the twins ended up passing after all. One thing I could say about my uncle…whatever he said he was going to do, he did.

As August approached, the heat was on and I don't mean the temperature. The Feds started getting wise to our family-run dope business. Soon even the local cops began harassing my uncle and aunt.

From August to October we had to chill. Uncle Snookey was in court almost every other week for one various charge or another ranging from petty to serious. He knew the District Attorney was trying hard to bury him. Although the D.A. failed to produce enough evidence to indict him on homicide charges, he did manage to convince a twelve-man jury to convict him on several narcotic charges. Uncle Snookey spent approximately two days in a New Orleans jail cell before he was released on a $50,000 bond.

By October, Uncle Snookey had beat all the charges levied against him and had once again escaped the clutches of both federal and local authorities. Those trials, which went on from August to October, were newsmakers throughout New Orleans and much of Louisiana.

Marion Lake was well known in the Crescent City, loved by the have-nots for his generous financial gifts to the underprivileged youth, elderly and single mothers of the projects. Yet, at the same time, he was despised by the red-necked southern aristocrats of the Big Easy because of his great arrogance, glamorous lifestyle and celebrity appeal to the masses.

On the day Uncle Snookey was acquitted of all charges, it was a media circus outside the New Orleans Superior court-house. Flanked by his two lawyers and embraced by Aunt Melissa, Uncle Snookey stepped outside the highest court in the city to be almost instantly mobbed by an anxiously awaiting throng of reporters and television cameramen. Marion further angered the already agitated group of local lawmakers and cops by being boastful and cracking jokes on his way down the seem-ingly neverending steps towards the street below.

"What can I say? I'm young, black, good-looking and got plenty money. I got a successful caterin' bidness, I own real estate in different parts of Louisiana and sometimes...hell, I like to get high. Ain't doin' nothin' no different den dem dere white boys do who make all dese here laws. See all dem people down dere on da street, dey loves me and I loves dem back, ya heard. So tell da mayor when he done finished his last term in office and he don't have a job no mo', come see me." Uncle Snookey flashed a gold-toothed smile for the flashing cameras and calm-ly brushed past the swarming journalists who trailed him down the steps hounding him with further questions.

As he approached the bottom of the courthouse steps, he was nearly lost in the sea of wildly cheering (mostly black) peo-ple who had gathered outside the courthouse since the start of the proceedings. That morning many had stood outside in the rain simply to get a glimpse of their beloved Snookey.

We partied all weekend long, wining and dining all over the city at most of New Orleans' most exclusive restaurants and bought up a shit load of gold jewelry and diamond encrusted watches and rings. We took in a Saints' game at the Superdome, where we enjoyed the contest between the Saints and the 49ers in the luxury seated skybox while sippin' on Moët and eatin' Jambalaya. Here I was, a 14-year-old fuckin' hangin' out with known con men, drug dealers, pimps, mob guys and other shady characters.

My wardrobe filled over five closets not to mention my ten-nis shoe collection, which numbered over 30 pairs of brand name sneakers. I had more jewelry than a pawnshop, yet, even though I possessed all these costly material items I never lost focus on the objective—making as much money as I could and invest it into purchasing my own dope, flippin' it for myself and pocketing all the earnings.

I approached Dawn and Shawn about my idea. They were excited about the prospects of earning their own loot though I cautioned the twins that unless they were serious I had no time for them. Both of them assured me they were serious and that their parents never gave them a chance to redeem themselves from their earlier fuck ups in school and elsewhere. We decided that we were going to begin our own drug operation, I would make the connections with the proper sources in order to have a constant supply of coke and weed. The plan was quaranteed to work, even with hotheads like the twins. But the game always has, and always will be filled with a certain degree of danger, violence, and, of course, death. I'll never forget the lesson I learned along the bloddy and danger-filled roads to riches.

V

Bloody Bayou

By March 1985, the entire Lake clan had relocated to the state of Georgia, settling in a medium size South Georgia town outside Savannah, known as Peola. Coming from New Orleans to a slow paced backwater place like Peola reminded me of the years I spent with Grandma Lake.

Uncle Snookey had one last major incident with the New Orleans police department in January 1985. Two homicides were attributed to him and his close associates along with an ex-con from Houston known for his violent temper and fetish for prostitutes and sleazy strip clubs. Two strippers Janet Cross and Renee Folsom were found bound and gagged in the burned out, blackened frame of a Jeep Cherokee. Their charred remains revealed that both women were shot twice in the back of the head.

Uncle Snookey was very cooperative with the police who questioned his whereabouts on the January weekend of the grisly murders. Uncle Snookey was a thorough con man and an accomplished liar. He boasted to us how he sat cool as a cucumber through nearly two hours of hard-core police interrogations that yielded the cops about as much info as they had before they pulled him in for questioning.

"Fuckin' bitch ass cops, always fuckin' wit a nigga," Uncle

Snookey told us the next day. "We gots ta get the fuck from around here. It's done got too hot, ya heard me?" As Uncle Snookey snorted a line of coke we all agreed in unison with his decision to move. "But first, dat stupid ass muthafuckin' Phil has gots to be dealt with, ya heard? He da fuckin' reason dem fuckas is fuckin'wit us!"

I knew full well what that meant. Phillip was a fool for fast women and sleazy sex. He had, on several occasions, gotten into some serious trouble for assaulting some call girl or street hooker. Only this time two of his weekend hoes had gotten him caught up in some shit. Phillip was my Uncle's enforcer and drug smuggler of international deliveries. Phillip would pick up dope from as far away as Columbia and Mexico, drop the packages off in Texas with some old homies, who then arranged for the illegal cargo to be transported cross country to Louisiana. Uncle Snookey would then have the narcotics broken down, prepared and bagged ready to be dispersed throughout the South's major cities.

Janet and Renee were two of Phillip's accomplices whom Uncle Snookey had long ago warned Philip about dealing with. Both women were girlfriends of Phillip's and he frequently had them hold money, bag drugs and even pull drive-by shootings at his request. But recently, they'd been caught stealing money and drugs and quickly sought the police for protection form Uncle Snookey and his hoodlums. Knowing that Uncle Snookey was a prime suspect in a wide variety of drug related crimes the exotic dancers offered to testify in court against both Uncle Snookey and their sugar daddy, Phillip Moss. In return they would both become part of the witness protection program. But once my uncle got wind of their plot in December '84 those two broads days were numbered.

In February, Uncle Snookey took Aunt Melissa to the Cayman Islands for Valentine's Day. They stayed there a week. During that week, Uncle Snookey had asked Phillip to hold things down for him until he returned. Things were so unstable that nobody did anything for fear of the Feds. Even I cut back my little side hustle for the time being and just chilled with the money I had accumulated from earlier in the year.

When Uncle Snookey and Aunt Melissa returned from their Valentine's Day vacation, we all went out to dinner in the French Quarter. After dinner, Uncle Snookey dropped off Auntie and the twins at the Gold Dust Hotel, but asked for me to remain with him while he dropped Phillip off at home.

We drove for what seemed like hours, until we eneded up at a little, seedy strip club on the western tip of the city, called the Snake Eyes Burlesque Bar. Inside were a number of worn out, skanky-looking strippers who reeked of cheap perfume and wore too much make-up, and a few, lonely, red-neck truckers who seemed to cherish their company. Uncle Snookey, Phillip and I immediately ordered several rounds of "Hen Dog" on the rocks. Three of the clubs better looking dancers approached us soliciting lap dances. Both Uncle Snookey and Phillip obliged, but I gracefully refused and ordered another glass of the smooth Cognac. Phillip spent the next hour and a half getting drunker and drunker, nearly oblivious to the half-naked women competing for his attentions. He just kept emptying glass after glass of Hennesey.

As Phillip drank that last sip from the glass, which he held unsteadily, his slurred speech and liquor-reeking breath spoke volumes to my family and I about his condition. Heavily inebriated and oblivious to the fate that would befall him, the tall wiry gangster staggered toward the awaiting Cadillac. Inside, my uncle and I waited. I observed my Uncle Snookey as he sat behind the steering wheel of the big Cadillac, the leather upholstery seeming to embrace his massive frame as he reclined in a sort of gangsta lean. Uncle Snookey pulled open the glove compartment and pulled out his chrome plated nine millimeter. Slowly shutting the glove compartment he ejected the weapon's clip, checking to see if it was fully loaded...it was.

Uncle Snookey took a sip from a cup containing a pungent smelling drink and then took a long drag on a half finished cigarette soon after. "You know Rae-Rae, it shouldn't have ta be like dis, but in dis here bidness ya gots ta cut ya losses and keep on goin'. I been done told dat nigga ta stop fuckin' wit dem hoes. But no...dis nigga done fucked around and let dem turn 'round and play us both for a fool." Uncle Snookey crushed the cigarette butt into the black ash of the ashtray beside him and tucked his gun in his waist.

"Fuck's up my nigga!" Phillip exclaimed loudly as he swung open the back door.

"Ain't shit...sit yo ass down, nigga, witcha drunken ass!" grinned Snookey waiting for Phillip to shut the door. When he did the two old friends smoked a blunt, which they shared with me before pulling out.

As we cruised through downtown New Orleans laughing and cuttin' up, it didn't even seem as though my uncle was going to take Phil out. But then we pulled over near Crescent City Manor, a quiet little senior citizen community about 50 miles west of the city. By the time we stopped Phil Moss was so drunk he could hardly make it out of the car without help.

"Rae-Rae get behind the wheel...got some funny ass Dolomite cassettes in the glove compartment; check out the black cassette, side one, the 'Signifying Monkey.' That shit will split ya fuckin' sides. And, oh yeah, there's another joint already rolled up, you can fire it up as ya listen ta brother Rudy Ray Moore." With that said Uncle Snookey slapped my head playfully and assisted his drunken partner from the rear of the big burgundy Caddy. I watched as both men disappeared down a lonely dirt trail leading into a dense thicket of cattails and other aquatic weeds bordering a murky swamp known to natives of the area as Pirate's Bog. Supposedly, back in the day, the pirate Jean Lafitte buried treasure and killed enemies there.

About thirty minutes later I sat puffing on what was now a roach; there was a tapping sound on the driver's side window. Quickly, I turned to see who it was, I'd been listening to the Dolomite tape so intensely I had lost track of time.

"Dat's some funny ass shit ain't it?" my uncle exclaimed opening the door and motioning for me to slide over to the passenger seat.

"Where's Phil, Uncle Snookey?" I asked feigning ignorance.

"Where the fuck do you think he's at boy?" Uncle Snookey snapped back, flashing me a quick glance of anger. "Dat skinny muthafucka is back dere in dat swamp, dat's where he's at."

Uncle Snookey removed his leather gloves as he spoke to me. He then opened up the glove compartment, placed the gloves inside and neatly placed the nine-millimeter on top of the gloves. I could see that the clip was missing three shells as he removed it from the handgun.

"I asked because I was wondering how you were gonna get rid of the body?" I said tossing the roach out the window. Uncle Snookey gazed at me piercingly then ever so slowly smiled, looking sort of like a sadistic Cheshire cat.

"Oh, don't you worry 'bout dat nephew" Uncle Snookey announced. Shaking a pack of cigarettes in his left hand, Uncle Snookey removed one and bent down quickly, lit it and took a long drag as he turned towards me and blew a billowing cloud of smoke into my face while laughing. "You ever been back up in da cut, back dere in Pirate's Bog Rae-Rae?" Uncle Snookey asked.

"Now when I was little, people said there were ghosts back up in dere, so me and my homies never hung out back dere."

Uncle Snookey took another drag, this time exhaling his second hand smoke out the open window. "Well let me tell you somethin' 'bout that swamp back dere…don't nobody goes back dere, ever. Dere's gators a plenty back up in dere as well as poisonous snakes and all kinds of other creepy crawlers. So you don't have ta worry 'bout no police or anybody else fuckin' 'round back dere. Shit, during da daylight hours skeeters and horseflies so bad back dere they'll tear ya ass up by demselves. But dere's and old dock next to a swamp tree in dere so I just took Phil over dere to da dock put three hot balls up in 'em and let his lanky ass fall into the water below. Didn't take long befo' dem gators got to em."

Uncle Snookey finished up his cigarette and asked me if I was hungry. I answered hell yeah due to the munchies, which had kicked in as my high slowly began to dissipate. Uncle Snookey ejected the Dolomite cassette and popped in Teena Marie. The midnight chorus of frogs and crickets were accompanied by the up-tempo, pulsating melody of "Square Biz" as the huge Cadillac squealed away from the dark foreboding crime scene.

Before we left town for Georgia, in March, Uncle Snookey and I made four more trips back to Pirate's Bog where we off-ed four more associates of his, whom he feared could possibly fold under police questioning or whose loyalty he questioned. I learned from not only Uncle Snookey, but also his own children, Shawn and Dawn, that Pirate's Bog had long been a dumping area for the remains of individuals murdered by their father and his henchmen.

I watched my uncle kill many people during my young life and even though he was my own flesh and blood I didn't trust him as far as I could throw him. Marion Lake was a cold and calculating criminal and when it came to dollars and cents he was all business and no bullshit. Disloyalty was not tolerated even among his own family.

Being a highly attractive man and very vain, he was quite a player as well as a hustler. His womanizing ways were well known throughout New Orleans. There probably wasn't a woman with beauty and sex appeal within the 504 area code whom he hadn't fucked. He especially loved preying on the wives, girlfriends and even daughters of cops, lawyers, and civic leaders of the city. He kept birthday cards, letters, phone messages and even lingerie, which these women had given him in secret. He'd show me nude pictures taken of some of New Orleans' most respected and well-known daughters. He even had in his so-called "archives" a thirty-minute tape of him having sex with Patricia Rossum, then wife of Leon Rossum, New Orleans City's Chief of Police.

"Now dat white bitch wuz a masterful dick sucker. Good

God Almighty, could she gobble a dick!" Uncle Snookey would reminisce with fondness.

Uncle Snookey owned two riverboats, which he sold upon his departure from the Big Easy. He always used "Rump Shaker," the larger of the two, to entertain his crime buddies and more prestigious clientele with strippers, who performed all night long, pleasing the men with nude lap dances and full service sex. There were also many orgies that went on aboard the "Rump Shaker." Now the smaller of the two, "The Big Baller" was strictly for casino gambling and drug transactions. It was rumored that even key members of New York's Genovese and Gambino crime families visited "The Big Baller" on several, separate occasions gambling and discussing drug business.

Now, Aunt Melissa was a strong supporter of Uncle Snookey's illegal operation. In fact it was her catering business, Melissa's Cajun Catering, which helped Uncle Snookey get by during some truly close calls with the cops. She was also fiercely loyal to her husband and had even shot several enemies of Uncle Snookey's herself. Tall and shapely with a hazelnut hue complexion, Melissa Lake was a shrewd businesswoman and dangerous when provoked. Even Uncle Snookey felt the sting of her wrath on more than one occasion.

The Lake's had a picture perfect marriage with the exceptions of Uncle Snookey's infidelities. Several of Uncle Snookey's mistresses were approached and even attacked in broad daylight by an enraged Melissa Lake. One jezebel, a certain Claire "Coochie" Haughton of the Magnolia Housing Projects was never seen nor heard from again after one such encounter with Aunt Melissa. There was often arguing and yelling going on between Aunt Melissa and Uncle Snookey, yet somehow they always knew when to simmer down since we were always on the run living out of hotels. Dawn said Uncle Snookey had hit her mother only one time and had nearly paid for that mistake with his life. He still to this day bears the scar on his upper torso where his wife, in a blind rage, slashed him with a straight razor blade.

Toward the end of February, the Feds were on the move again and this time they caught on the fact that we had been living out of hotels all over the city. One of the concierges at the posh Gold Dust Hotel, where we were currently residing, had been a love interest of Uncle Snookey's as well as a drug client. She was prompt in alerting him about the Feds snooping around asking questions and requesting to look at hotel records containing customer reservations. That was good looking out on her part because it gave us ample time to lay low at Grandma's old house, in Amherst. So while the city of New Orleans was being turned upside down by federal and local police officers, we were contemplating our next move.

Uncle Snookey decided on moving to Peola, Georgia. At first he wanted to relocate to Atlanta, but quickly scrapped that idea when he realized large cities had brought him nothing but grief. So two hectic months into 1985, we left the Big Easy and its non-stop drama behind for the rustic tranquility of Peola's down home surroundings. However, lil' ole Peola was about to meet Louisiana's most infamous crime family.

VI

Drama in the Peach State

When we arrived in Peola in March of 1985, the first order of business was to get myself and the twins enrolled in school. Uncle Snookey enrolled the three of us in Cayman Senior High School in West Peola. West Peola was the upper middle class section of the South Georgia town where the residents were mostly white-collar black professionals and young white yuppie couples. Although we lived in West Peola and attended school there, my cousins and I soon grew tired of the inflated egos and shallow personalities of our aristocratic neighbors both young and old alike. Their expensive sports cars, lavish weekend parties and six-figure incomes did nothing to impress us. As a matter of fact we found these rich folk some of the most laughable and boring people we had ever seen. To us they were to be preyed on.

Uncle Snookey had moved us here because one of his most loyal clients, Cecil Lattimore, was the mayor of Peola. Mayor Lattimore had a thousand-dollar-a-day coke habit, and he wasn't the only one. Several other high ranking officials such as Peola Fire Chief, Maurice Whitfield III, Peola City School Superintendent, Oscar Ashcroft, and Peola's premier entrepreneur, Leslie Thornton, who owned the town's three auto dealerships and two country clubs made sure my uncle's business thrived.

We often traveled across town to South Peola, whose drug ridden and violent neighborhoods such as Hemlock Hills, Geneva and Badlands Manor gave us the excitement, challenge and thug appeal that we sought so desperately. The kids from South Peola were hard-core and aggressive, just as we were. Most of those project kids attended the rowdy Mash Burn Memorial High off Route 1 in South Peola. Known for its violent, sometimes deadly student body, it was the norm at Mash Burn to pass through metal detectors and observe armed security guards patrolling the halls and exterior grounds.

It didn't take us long to make friends with some of the kids from Badlands Manor and soon we were selling weed right outside Mash Burn High. That is until we got busted by the school's security and detained until the cops arrived. We spent about two hours in a downtown Peola holding cell until Uncle Snookey could come get us out. We left on our own recognizance. However, our skipping school and landing in jail didn't sit well with Uncle Snookey, who not only cussed us out for at least twenty minutes but made us cough up all the extra money and dope we had in our little stash around the rear of the house.

Dawn and Shawn were highly upset that their father had taken their dope and money. I, on the other hand, had at least fifteen hundred dollars of my own left in a safe inside my closet along with about an ounce of marijuana and a half an ounce of coke. I went to school the next day and quickly sold all of it.

On Friday and Saturday nights my cousins and I usually hung out at a spot called Da Juke Joint, a teen nightclub in Hemlock Hills, which drew kids from the surrounding projects of South Peola. Thugs from Geneva, ballers from Badlands Manor, and Hemlock Hills own self-proclaimed "Wreckin' Crew" were all over the place. Crowds were dense, especially on Saturday nights when there was open mic night for any amateur rapper who felt they could flow. The age range was about age 18 to 28 although kids as young as 15 and 16 could slip through. There were no alcoholic drinks served at the bar to anyone under 21, however there were those of us who found ways to sneak booze into the parking lot and drink there. Monday morning, the parking lot of JJ's was usually littered with empty liquor and beer bottles.

My cousins and I were famous in Peola long before our arrival in town, due to Uncle Snookey's widespread notoriety throughout the south. It didn't take long for me to make the contacts that I'd promised Shawn and Dawn. We'd met with a cat named Wallace Minter who along with his brother-in-law Gerald Huggins owned Da Juke Joint. Minter was a thirty-something Jheri-Curl wearing ex-pimp who always dressed in the latest athletic wear and usually completed his urban ensemble with gaudy oversized gold chains with a huge diamond encrusted medallion the size of a small clock. He used to do business with Uncle Snookey back in the day, but had broken off contact with him since the murders of Janet Cross and Renee Folsom, who had worked as prostitutes for him in New Orleans before they became strippers. Minter who once stated that his "hoes were family" never forgave my uncle for the murder of the two women.

I was able to take my uncle's loss and make it my gain. Not only was Minter co-owner of the popular nightclub, he also owned a fleet of shrimp boats down in Key West, Florida which kept illegal drugs coming up from Florida to Georgia. It was he who supplied me with the bulk of my dope. We made transactions every Saturday night.

After the little schoolyard incident neither I nor the twins trusted Uncle Snookey so we had Minter set us up a little spot in Hemlock Hills where we were able to prepare our dope for distribution. Apartment #313 at 6606 Hemlock Hill Complex was our spot where we cooked up crack, weighed and bagged weed and occasionally prepared heroin when it was available. Everybody knew us and knew that it was Minter who'd set us up in the apartment so we never had to worry about stick-up kids or getting fucked with at all. Hemlock Hills was the most violent projects of the crime-infested South Side. Even Peola's finest dared not venture into The Hills without adequate reinforcements.

Soon, business got so busy on the weekends that we needed assistance in our operations. We had four Hemlock Hills Wreckin Crew members helping us out. There was Big Tate, who was the leader of the gang, Whiskey, Lil' Shane and Domino, who sat on top of the roof with his three brothers acting as snipers just in case some shit jumped off.

Pretty soon we were over in South Peola every weekend. It was never a problem because during the week I made sure that we attended classes at Cayman and there were no traces of drug paraphernalia in the house whatsoever, except for Uncle Snookey's own dope and cash. Uncle Snookey was always away from home anyway, making his usual drug transactions throughout the Mid-Atlantic region and many times he took Aunt Melissa along for the trip. However, when she was home she was a much easier individual to deal with than her husband. She didn't question our every move and go ransacking our closets and clothes in search of dope or extra money. Uncle Snookey was a great father and uncle, but when it came to the game he was cold, suspicious and vindictive.

I began to find him somewhat hypocritical in his viewpoints. He turned me on to the drug game then expected me not to flip dollars any more once we arrived in Peola. He constantly got high and counted along with his wife huge amounts of cash right in front of the twins yet expected them not to use or sell drugs at any cost. And after the degrading way he spoke to us when we got busted hustling outside of Mash Burn High, I lost some degree of respect for the man myself. He never did approach me to deal drugs with him again, which was fine with me. Hell, for all he knew I was clean, just like Shawn and Dawn...man, was he mistaken.

Even though Minter was cool with us three and we got into the club for free with VIP status anytime we wanted, his brother-in-law Gerald would stare at us with suspicion and dislike. He was a stumpy dwarf of a man with a receding hairline and a pot-belly complete with love handles. He was part owner of the club along with Minter, but he was not popular with the area youth unlike Minter. Nor was he gangsta like his cooler brother-in-law.

When Minter was around, which was most of the time, Gerald was subdued and quite, though he seethed with anger anytime he saw myself, Dawn or Shawn in the VIP sections or at the bar ordering alcoholic drinks on the house. But the few times when Minter was away, Gerald's Napoleon complex would kick in and he'd order the bouncers to kick us out. Once, when we'd been getting blasted, he approached us from behind as we sat accompanied by friends.

"What the hell are you little hoodlums doing in here? And why the fuck are you smoking pot in this establishment?!" the little man asked, his jaws tight with anger. We hardly looked in his direction as me, the twins and a few "Wreckin Crew" homies passed "the funk" between us and kept on puffing. As I raised a glass of Dom P. to my lips this little fuck comes charging over and snatches it from my hand. "Get the fuck outta here right now or I'll have my bouncers come up her and toss you all the fuck out on your fuckin' heads!!!"

My first thought was to drive on his ass right then and there, but because he was one of Minter's folks, I restrained myself, but my cousin Dawn did not. Without a moments hesitation Dawn had pounced on the little man and was punching him in the head and face repeatedly before Whiskey and Domino could pull her off of him.

"Fuckin' disrespect my cousin again and ya little bitch ass is dead, ya heard!!!" Dawn shrieked, while struggling to break free from Whiskey and Domino so she could go at Gerald again. The startled man slowly picked himself up off the floor and stood briefly on wobbly legs before grabbing a rail for support. His face was a mess. Dawn had blacked his right eye, bloodied both his nose and mouth, and had knocked off his designer gold rimmed glasses and trampled them. Gerald steadied himself while removing a handkerchief and wiping the oozing blood from his nostrils and mouth. Quickly, I noticed that Gerald was reaching down his pants, but before I could warn anyone the barrel of a glistening black Desert Eagle was pointed at my cousin Dawn who stared defiantly into its barrel and then toward Gerald. "Whatcha gonna do? Shoot me?" Dawn asked sarcastically. Gerald gritted his teeth in rage and swiftly cocked the hammer of the handgun back, which placed a slug into the chamber with a loud metallic click. Gerald was perspiring noticeably across his brow and his hands were shaking. Dawn was provoking the gunman by showering him with insults. Me, Shawn, and our Hemlock homies could do little but look on in silence as the little guy nervously leveled the semi-automatic on each member of our small group one at a time.

"Get your shit and get the fuck outta my club. Don't ever bring ya stinkin' asses back in here again. For when and if you do I'll shoot every fuckin'one o' you lil' nappy headed muth-fuckas dead where you stand and tell five-o that you all were trespassing." Gerald grinned through bloodstained teeth as he forced us at gunpoint toward the rear of the club. "Get your fuckin'hands on your head muthfuckas!" he barked at us as we shuffled along down a steep stairway towards a door at the bot-tom step. As we approached the door we were told to open it and depart without looking back, but before we were through the door Gerald swung and caught Dawn with a haymaker in the left side of her face, a blow which rendered her briefly uncon-scious as she fell into the dirt and trash of the backyard. Shawn and I both charged towards the door with fury only to have it slammed in our faces seconds before we could bum rush inside.

"You's a dead man you bitch ass nigga! Nobody hits my sis-ter, muthafucka!" Shawn yelled outside the locked door, his face noticeably contorting in anger and frustration. We couldn't take long in reviving Dawn, who bore a wicked shiner under her eye from Gerald's sucker punch. We'd heard growling and barking toward the far right of us, which grew louder as the rapidly approaching footfalls of dogs neared. As they rounded the cor-ner we were off and running. With me being rather big for my 15 years, I was able to lift Dawn's 110 lb. frame and hurry her along to safety beyond the fence. Domino was the last to make it over the fence nearly getting bitten in the process.

The five huge Rottweilers barked ferociously behind the rick-ety old fence, which threatened to collapse under their power-ful weight. We disappeared into the night, exhausted and furious as we arrived on the other side of the woods nearing the train tracks outside of Hemlock Hills Subway Station.

By the time Minter returned from his business trip early the next morning we had an immediate meeting at apartment #313. "We got a big fuckin' problem Mint, ya brotha-in-law done fucked up, ya heard? An we gots to do something 'bout it." I relayed the entire club incident to Minter who also heard Shawn and Dawn's testimonies as well. He also saw that Dawn sported a bruise under her left eye. Minter shook his head while setting up a long line of coke on the glass table top before him.

"Lissen here, ya'll know ya'll are like my own chillen, and God knows I hate dat little bitch ass nigga mo den anything, shit...I woulda peeled his fuckin' cap back a long time ago, but he is my brotha-in-law and if my wife knew that I had anything to do with hurting him it'd kill her. Plus da little bastard done gone and snitched to my parole officer on me 'bout my trips outta state, so I can't be involved in no bullshit for at least a month or so until I can clear up dis here trouble wit my P.O., ya heard?" We shook our heads dejectedly and arose from our seats, while Minter deeply inhaled the line of powder into his left nostril. Minter threw his head back from the coke line and pinched his nose briskly. He didn't even see us to the door nor did he bid us goodbye. I stood at the doorway briefly eyeing him angrily as he dipped his Jherri-curled head back down to snort up the remaining coke. Dawn took me by the hand and I slammed the door shut.

By the time we emerged from the subway at West Peola's Cayman Subway Station, we noticed the familiar gargantuan figure in the distance sitting on a subway bench near the parking lot entrance. "Well, well, well what do we have here? The Three Stooges or The Three Musketeers?" Uncle Snookey asked jokingly as he sat there on the bench legs crossed in the cool of the early May morning decked out in a rust colored custom tailored Armani suit. The two carat diamonds in his Cartier watch caught the sunlight and gave off a sparkling brilliance, which matched the bling-bling coming from his ice, covered rings. We braced ourselves for the worst yet surprisingly this time around we were treated with much love and concern.

"Ya'll little niggas wanna eat," Uncle Snookey asked hugging each of us, one after the other. We nodded and with that Uncle Snookey placed his sunglasses on and we followed him towards the luxurious Cadillac waiting at the end of the parking lot. Uncle Snookey told us that he knew where we'd been hanging out for the last two months and that he had friends who secretly kept tabs on our whereabouts. "At first I wuz gonna straight up whip ya little asses, but then I thought long and hard…if ya gonna be out here tryin' ta stomp wit da big dawgs, ya might as well start at home. Ya see da game is not for beginners and I'd never forgive myself if ya fucked 'round out here an got ya caps peeled or ended up in jail fo da rest of ya life behind dis here scrilla." Uncle Snookey flashed a huge wad of hundreds as he continued his speech while cruising down Century Boulevard en route to IHOP.

Uncle Snookey continued his discussion over breakfast and told us exactly what it was that he expected from us. First of all, he wanted us to stop hanging out over in South Peola. "It's too hot there to hustle and everybody out here knows this."

Dawn whined softly and interjected, "But what about all of our peeps? We'd miss them and they'd miss us. We have a lot of fun over there, and besides that we hate these spoiled ass kids out here in West Peola, they're some straight suckas."

Uncle Snookey grinned slightly as he listened to the emotionally charged words of his little girl. Then as he finished off his western omelet he leaned over the table to get a closer look at his daughter's face. "Dawn, what happened?" Uncle Snookey asked as he inspected the bruise more carefully. Dawn sat silent occasionally looking at her twin brother, me, and then finally up at her father. "I got sucker punched," Dawn sighed.

"By who," her father asked inquisitively.

The breakfast table fell silent. We knew that Uncle Snookey had known where we were and we also knew that he had seen Dawn's bruised eye earlier, he had just patiently waited until the right moment to ask us what had happened. Uncle Snookey was famous for putting niggas on the spot like that. As Dawn reluctantly began to tell the tale of what happened on Saturday night, Uncle Snookey stopped her in mid-sentence.

"Hold up, ya'll mean ta tell me, ya'll go up into some joint co-owned by stinkin' ass Wallace Minter and ya'll don't think nuthin 'bout it!" Uncle Snookey barked his face now crimson with anger. We could only look on, dumbfounded, as Uncle Snookey continued his renewed tirade. "Let me tell you little mutafuckas somethin'...do ya'll know who da fuck Wallace Minter is!?" We shook our heads sheepishly, trying not to make direct eye contact with Snookey. "Well I'll tell you who dat muthafucka is, dat's one no good, low down, bitch ass nigga and his fuckin' brotha-in-law Gerald Huggins is worse than he is. Ya lucky ya little asses came up outta there in one piece!" Uncle Snookey's angry outburst startled several nearby diners who became uncomfortable and quickly left with their food half-eaten.

When the restaurant manager came over Uncle Snookey pulled her to the side, apologized for the inconvenience and slipped her $250.00 for herself, paid for our meals, he then left $100.00 tip for the cute little waitress as well as his new cell phone number (the bulky, sky blue phone that sat on the floor between the driver and passenger seats as a symbol of his wealth and power in addition to being the latest in communication technology). He hadn't noticed that I'd caught his mack move from the corner of my eye. As we made our way from the restaurant towards the car, Uncle Snookey didn't mention a thing. He just put on his designer sunglasses, lit up a cigarette and preceded toward the car while making a quick call on his cell phone.

Uncle Snookey silenced the car alarm allowing us to enter as he sat on the hood of the Cadillac engrossed in conversation. Dawn and Shawn argued with each other as they slid into the back seat. As I took my place in the front passenger seat, I overheard bits and pieces of Uncle Snookey's conversation. He was setting up a hit on both Minter and Huggins. I'd been a witness to several of my Uncle's preplanned killings; they were always swift and brutal. Dawn and Shawn also knew what time it was as they silenced themselves in an attempt to hear the remainder of their father's conversation.

Uncle Snookey concluded his conversation and finished his cigarette as he took the driver's seat. Being as vain and glorious as he was, he admired himself in the sun visor's mirror before flipping it up and starting the engine. "Ya'll won't have ta worry 'bout goin' to Da Juke Joint no mo'," Uncle Snookey smirked while pulling out of the parking lot.

"What do you mean?" I asked curiously.

"Oh, don't worry. You'll see soon enough what I'm talking 'bout." With a mischievous grin spreading across his face, Uncle Snookey wheeled the big luxury car from the IHOP's parking lot and back onto Century Boulevard.

From that morning in May until my cousins and I got out of school on June 9, 1985 we didn't hang out in South Peola anymore. On May 25, 1985 the Juke Joint was fire bombed. The incident made the headlines and was the hottest topic of discussion in the rather laid back town of 95,000. The front page of the Peola Gazette read: "Popular Teen Nightclub Firebombed on Peola's Southside...Criminal Investigation Probe Forthcoming." The local news broadcasts headlined the blaze for over a week.

About two weeks after the bombing, the badly decomposed corpse of Wallace Minter was discovered near the muddy banks of Sik-Sik Creek outside of Pemmincan, another posh upper middle class neighborhood in Western Peola. Fish, crabs and other aquatic creatures had eaten away most of his face until there was nothing but a grinning skull left. He was also bloated to about three times his original size, which made it nearly impossible to identify his body until forensic experts near Savannah could be contacted. Gerald Huggins disappeared and was never heard from again. Uncle Snookey claimed that one evening after he had Huggins snatched from his truck right in front of the South District Police Precinct one evening, he drove him to an undisclosed spot in the Badlands Manor housing project. There, he subjected Gerald to two days of excruciating torture before shooting him execution style. He then had his hired henchmen take the corpse to a crematorium in Savannah, whose owner was a client of his, where Huggins' remains were reduced to ashes.

With that, Uncle Snookey had avenged us in the worst possible way. It brought back a certain amount of respect for my Uncle, which I had previously lost. But for the remainder of the summer '85 we did little except attend summer school (because all three of us had failed the regular school year). When September came around, there would be no hanging out down in South Peola due to our poor school grades earlier in the year and now since both Minter and Da Juke Joint were history there was nothing to do down there anyway, except get into trouble and Uncle Snookey made it clear that he'd have no foolishness from us at all. I, for one, understood that Uncle Snookey was not the kind of man who you'd mess around with, even if you were kin. But it was all good though, because I began to find activities of a different nature to indulge in during the coming months in our new hometown.

VII

Donita Grimes

During the fall of '85 we buckled down in school. I improved my GPA from a 2.15 to an outstanding 3.0 by January of the following year. My cousins Dawn and Shawn's grades also improved greatly, which was a plus because this progress kept Uncle Snookey pleased.

Dawn began playing softball for Cayman High in March and she always had a number of her teammates over at our house after practice or before the games on Saturday. One of her teammates, shortstop Donita Grimes, had a crush on me...and boy did she have it bad. She was a damn good looking girl with hazel eyes, wavy shoulder length hair and a beautiful coco brown complexion with the loveliest smile ever, but she was a tomboy and all I ever saw her wear were t-shirts, jeans, and sneakers. I never gave her that much attention although she was certainly seeking mine. I'd find little notes attached to my locker or little secret admirer love letters inside my desk in math class, which we both had for 2nd period. Or she'd always try to strike up a conversation with me whenever the team was over at the house on one of their post-practice or pre-game visits.

One day Dawn approached me about Donita. "Rae Kwon, why don't you like Donita? The girl is a fiend for you and you act like she doesn't exist!" I continued doing my homework, pretending not to hear my cousin who only got even more verbal.

"What is it with you nigga, you scared o' pussy or what?" Dawn asked sarcastically slamming my textbook shut and plopping on my bed.

"Girl you 'bout to get knocked the fuck out! Now get yo ass up off da bed," I growled as I yanked my book from beneath her. "Look here hooker, I ain't scared of no pussy, ya heard." I snapped back, "Donita just ain't the type of broad for me that's all."

Dawn smiled knowing she had gotten under my skin just that quick. "What's wrong wit my girl Donita. She's a fuckin' pretty girl, Ray-Ray. I mean yeah, she needs a makeover for sho,' but other than that she ain't no bad-looking chick."

"What the fuck is you up to?" I finally asked knowing my cousin and how she loved playing matchmaker. Dawn smiled her usual mischievous smile whenever she had the wheels turning in that little head of hers.

"Our last game is next Saturday at 8:45 am. Our coach is holding a luncheon for the team after the game and we can invite anybody we want. I know you'll be there along with Mom, Dad, and Shawn...but after the luncheon is over Malik is taking me out to dinner and then to the movies and I was just thinking..."

Immediately, I put my head down and sighed in disbelief. "You are a muthafuckin' trip, I can't believe that you'd just volunteer me like this!"

"Aww nigga chill out. It ain't like you're goin' to the dentist! Damn, all Donita wants is for you to go out with her this one time. That's it!"

Reluctantly I agreed to go after Dawn's long drawn out luncheon in which she received a trophy and letters for her athletic achievements. When we got home, we got dressed to go out. I threw on a slick Versace outfit with a pair of patent leather alligators and stepped out in the living room.

"Malik sit down and play a few hands cause if you're waiting for Dawn you're gonna be waiting for a while." Shawn said looking in the direction of his twin sister's room. Malik, who was waiting for Dawn, sat down and played a round of spades with, Shawn, Uncle Snookey, and me. Finally she emerged in full Fendi regalia.

"It's about time," Malik said looking at his watch and feigning irritation.

"Nigga please," Dawn remarked blowing off her boyfriend's statement. "Ya'll ready to go, we gots ta pick up Donita." All the guys in the room could do little but smile and shake their heads at Dawn's urgency when only minutes ago she'd just arrived out of the bathroom. The three of us climbed into Malik's Jeep Cherokee and off we went to Danita's.

By the time we arrived, Donita was sitting patiently on the porch of her parent's Texas-style Rambler. She excitedly waved as she ran over to the curb awaiting us. As she came off the porch, I'd never seen Donita look so beautiful. She was a good-looking girl, cute and all, but I'd never really paid her any mind. The slinky sequined skirt that she wore clung closely to her shapely physique accenting curves, which were kept hidden under her usual baggy jeans and sweats. Dawn smiled and winked at me knowing that at last her best friend had my undivided attention.

"Wuz up!?" Donita announced plopping down beside me and playfully pushing my head to the side.

"Oh, so all you see is Ray-Ray?" Dawn asked in mock irritation.

Donita leaned up to the front seat to give Dawn a quick hug and kiss. "Hi Dawn." Donita also greeted Malik before she sat back down, this time in my lap. All night long we were hugged up and after the movies we had to be pried from each other in order to leave the theater.

As we rode back towards our homes in West Peola, Donita

and me tongue-kissed passionately in the back seat of Malik's jeep.

"Oh baby I want you inside me," Donita whispered sensually in my ear as her moist tongue slowly snaked its way into my ear canal. My dick was stiffening with every second of our brief, but steamy make-out session.

"Damn girl, I wanna fuck you right now," I murmured now drunk with lust.

"Damn ya'll two ain't bullshitting, huh?" Malik snickered peering at us through the rearview as we intertwined in a heated embrace behind him.

Before long Donita had pulled her lace panties to the side and slightly hiked up her hip-hugging skirt in order to straddle me. I let out a deep groan as Donita guided my thick 9-? inches inside her dripping wet pussy.

"Ohh...Ohhh...Ohhhh...G...G...God!!!" Donita moaned as she took in the length of my johnson.

"That's right baby, ride this dick! That's right come on ride this big dick baby!" At this time I hadn't even noticed that we were pulled over outside of Dunn Park, a lover's lane of sorts where all of the West Peola cats went to get their fuck on late on Friday and Saturday nights.

I could hear Malik fucking my cousin Dawn in the front seat and occasionally I could see her legs sprawled wide in the air and his naked torso, dripping with perspiration, as he laid pipe in her missionary style. Donita was moaning heavily now as I bounced her up and down while cupping her firm round ass checks in my hands.

"Make me cum Ray, please make me cum!" Donita pleaded as I gently nibbled on her erect nipples.

"I wanna hit it from the back," I said wiping the sweat from my eyes. Without saying a word Donita hopped up off the dick, which popped out with a nasty sucking sound. Donita backed out of the Jeep buttass naked bringing me along ,by the dick. When she got outside the jeep she kneeled down on the soft grass of the roadside and slowly swallowed my gooey cum drenched penis until it bounced off the back of her throat as she vigorously bobbed back and forth. I felt my meat throbbing within Donita's warm mouth warning me that the inevitable "point of no return" was near. I grabbed Donita by the back of her head and gently removed my dick from her mouth which hung suspended before her like a black polish sausage link with strands of saliva and vaginal secretions stringing from it to Donita's juicy lips.

"Get up against the Jeep," I commanded Donita while circling her full lips with the head of my manhood. Donita eagerly complied spreading her shapely legs wide so that I could get an up close and personal view of her rounded apple shaped booty and swollen pussy lips which opened slightly revealing the pink slit in between the curly black bush surrounding it.

"Come on baby, put it in me please don't make me wait!" Dawn was on fire and so was I. This time I had full leverage on her from the back and I commenced to beatin' the pussy up for her.

After about ten minutes of intense, sweat-soaked, booty clappin', ass smackin', nuts swingin', Doggie-style fuckin' I pulled out of her and fired off a volley of thick white semen which sprayed into her luxuriously long hair and onto her back. I wobbled slightly as my dick spasmed spitting out several more globules of cum on her jiggling ass checks before I backed away, collapsing on the backseat breathing heavily.

Malik and Dawn, who had finished fucking long before we had, gave us a comic round of applause. Dawn even made two fake score cards penciled in with a red lipstick #10 on both.

"Now that's what I call fuckin', ya heard?!" Dawn laughed.

We all had a hearty laugh from our little wild romp in the

park then we got dressed and went over to Malik's where we showered, ordered pizza, and smoked some weed for the remainder of the night...and oh yeah, we all fucked some more too.

By June 1987, I'd graduated with honors along with my twin cousins. I'd had a successful run as a high school athlete excelling on both the football field and the basketball court. Uncle Snookey sang my praises, as being an ex-jock himself, I made him proud. He wanted Shawn to participate in high school sports, however Shawn showed more interest in auto-mechanics and girls than sports.

"I only get sweaty and grimy up under a car or on top of a bitch." was Shawn's motto. His father couldn't find fault in him. He was studious and he got his womanizing ways honestly from dear old' dad, nuff said.

Over the summer, Uncle Snookey sat us down and explained to us in detail what it was to operate a "real" drug business. After lecturing us on shit we all ready knew for real, he told us about a shipment of coke coming in through Atlanta.

"Melissa and I are going to be gone for about a week. All three of you are mature enough to watch things here until we get back. If you need to reach us for any reason hit us on the cell phone. We'll be calling here every day to check on ya'll." Uncle Snookey left us with $1,500 each and he and Aunt Melissa bid us adieu.

As soon as our guardians were gone we couldn't wait to make our way back to South Peola. We had our licenses at the time and each of us had vehicles. Dawn had a new '87 Ford Bronco that Snookey and Melissa bought her as a graduation present. Shawn, who had found work at one of the several junk-yards in Peola, restored an old '72 canary yellow Roadrunner from scratch. When he first started work on it, it was simply an old partially rusted frame, within a month an a half and $3,000 later it was a mint conditioned masterpiece which drew stares and compliments almost everywhere he drove it thorough out the town. I myself pushed an '86 Silver BMW. Jazzed up with a spoiler kit and ultra dark tinted windows of course. I had $1,000 20-inch chrome rims just to top off the baller-look.

Dawn insisted that she had someone for us to meet so she drove us around Badlands Manor where we met up with two older cats, probably in their mid-twenties, who warmly embraced Dawn as she approached them from the car. After introducing us to them they hopped in the truck and we went down Swilling Street eastbound for about five miles until we came to an old warehouse where one of the guys got out and went around back. Coming around nearly five minutes later with a long box upon a handcart as he neared the truck, he motioned for us to get out. We obliged and I went over helping him with his bulky cargo. When the box was pried open, the contents brought a smile to our faces; the box contained an assortment of automatic and semiautomatic weapons.

"Here ya go, Dee-Dee, everything a nigga needs to put in work out in dese here streets." One of the guys said smiling while showcasing the deadly hardware displayed before us.

"I want all of it," Dawn said without hesitation. The bandanna-wearing thugs smiled in acknowledgement of Dawn's decision. As the men went about the task of reattaching the heavy lid onto the oblong box and placing it into the rear of Dawn's Bronco, Shawn questioned his twin sister about her ability to pay for the smuggled weapons.

"Don't worry 'bout it boy…I got dis!" Dawn seemed overly confident as she assured her somewhat unsure twin. "All right Jay-T give dis ta Mike-Mike, good lookin' out," Dawn said hugging the tall muscle bound gunrunner.

"You got it baby girl…if you need me, hit me or Mike-Mike up on the pagers."

I observed Jay-T walking off over to his homie and heard them laughing lightly as they began counting their money near an alley on the opposite side of the warehouse. Soon they disappeared from sight altogether leaving only us three within the open space of the empty loading dock.

"What the fuck are you up to now Dawn?" Shawn asked his sister while suspiciously observing his surroundings.

"Just sit back and chill da fuck out nigga…damn! Come on let's get in the ride and bounce."

Shawn stared at me in total bewilderment.

"Hey don't look at me partner, dat's yo sista." Shawn smiled at me and then shot me the bird as he and I climbed in the Bronco.

"I know ya'll two peazee head muthafuckas can't wait ta ask me bout what's goin' on."

"Ya damn Skippy!" I blurted out from the backseat amidst the hearty laughter of Shawn who sat beside his sister.

"Well if you two would just let a sista tell you what da fuck's happenin' instead of being so damn fast ya just might learn something." Dawn put the truck in drive and squealed out of the loading dock leaving tire tread marks in her wake.

Dawn told us of a weapons connection she'd made awhile back when she was playin' softball last spring during our senior year in high school. She'd saved up money given to her by her parents as well as her boyfriend Malik and quite a few stupid little rich boys at Cayman who were dying to fuck her, but never got the chance.

"Shit, I played a whole bunch of dese little simple niggas out here in Peola," Dawn snickered, "they gave me gees like they's givin' away candy. Dumb muthafuckas thought they wuz gonna get some of my pussy…shhiiiit. Dem punk ass niggas musta bumped their heads." Dawn handed Shawn a sandwich bag filled with strong smelling marijuana. "Shawn, baby, can you roll me a blunt or two or three?"

"I can if you give me some blunts." Shawn answered through a constant stream of chuckles.

Dawn sighed while shaking her head. "Boy...how is it dat you never have any blunts, but you always get high?"

"Man, fuck dat bickerin' shit you talkin', pull over to the nearest liquor sto' and let me out. I'll buy da fuckin' phillies...damn!" I barked, tiring of the twins' mouths and wanting to hear more about the deal with the guns.

After purchasing the phillies, we got on the highway en route towards Hemlock Hills. About two blunts and a fifth of Hennessey later we arrived in Hemlock Hills, our old stomping grounds. We hadn't been there in almost a year; however, everything remained the same. The same shot callin' ballin' niggas was on the corner of 13th and Fenris Streets clad in either tank tops, stocking caps and baggy jeans, or totally shirtless showing off their prison hardened physiques and homemade tattoos.

"Goddamn, these niggas is fine," Dawn said excitedly rolling down her window as she pulled up into the open-air drug market.

Soon we were surrounded by scores of mean looking drug peddlers seeking a sale. We were immediately recognized and warmly greeted by nearly half the block. Among the hot boys were Whiskey, Domino, and Lil' Shane who made their way through the crowd trailed by several members of the Wreckin' Crew. Dawn pulled over to the curb and the three of us exited the vehicle. We again were greeted with much laughter, hugs and mutual pot smoking. Shortly thereafter we had Whiskey, Domino, and Lil Shane peek inside the rear of the truck where Shawn pried open the pine chest. The eyes of the three teens grew large and their mouths fell agape.

"Yeah...nigga dis here is da shit, ain't it?" Dawn said admiring the weapons she'd just recently purchased.

"Hell, yeah Dee-Dee, dis right here'll git a nigga's mind right, ya heard!" acknowledged Domino holding up an AK-47 assault rifle.

"Whatcha tryin' ta let dis here go fa?"

Dawn smiled her usual devilish smile. "Nuthin'…but what I wanna do is talk some bidness. Let's go ta 313, every muthafucka don't need be hearin' our bidness out here."

"Dat's a bet. But ya know faggy ass Chauncey rents dat place right now" Domino answered inhaling a deep drag on the thick blunt before passing it to me.

"For real…hmmmm, awright, no problem…let's roll."

Piling into Dawn's Bronco we drove down the block a little ways up then parked near complex 6606. Rain began falling as soon as we exited the vehicle, so we quickly made our way over to the complex, up the stairs and knocked on the door we once called our home away from home. The door opened slightly due to a chain lock attached.

"Who the hell is it?!" said a high-pitched pseudo-feminine voice from inside.

"Open up da do' you faggy ass nigga!" Domino barked from outside.

"Well, you can keep yo' dusty behind outside!" Chauncey slammed the door in our faces as we all stared at Domino in anger.

"Get outta da way boy." Dawn spat brushing in front of Domino, "Chauncey!, Chauncey it's Dawn, girl open up…don't worry about Domino's dumbass. I got him in check."

We waited around about a minute, now wet from the brief soaking we'd taken in the rainstorm, before Chauncey finally opened the door and motioned for us to enter. Now Chauncey had been in the neighborhood ever since he was a baby, and was the only openly gay nigga I ever knew in anybodies ghetto. He had tons of relatives in Hemlock Hills including two hustlers who were his nephews, Marion and Paul Ballard. Chauncey would cross dress and go to gay clubs across town in West Peola and sometimes it was rumored that he ran a sort of gay whore-house up in the apartment. But I never did see evidence of that. Dawn and I spoke to Chauncey about using his crib occasionally to operate our drug business. He was all for it except he wanted no parts of Domino's presence within his home. Domino hated homosexuals and Chauncey knew it, so we had no choice but to agree. We agreed to pay Chauncey 10% of our earnings and to relinquish occupation of the apartment on weekends, which was when he'd have his all gay parties and the like. Chauncey allowed us to unload our weapons at his home where he stored them in the guest room. It was there that we conducted an armed robbery scheme that I came up with after Whiskey told us about a huge shipment of heroin coming into the "Decatur Street Mob," a violent gang out of Geneva by way of Kingston, Jamaica. It took a week to plan the robbery so that it would run smoothly. We had a stroke of good luck cause Aunt Melissa called and told us that she and Uncle Snookey decided to stay until the end of July.

"Snookey and I, we're goin' ta Disney World!," Aunt Melissa giggled over the phone, "And Epcot center! You kids can handle the house for two more weeks, can't ya?"

"Sure can Auntie," I sipped on gin and juice as I spoke to her.

"Okee Dokee, tell the twins Mommy loves em, kay? See ya!"

Great, we had the remainder of July ta handle our business. On July 15, 1988 we amassed a large group of armed youths, most of whom were members of the notorious Wreckin' Crew gang of which our three accomplices belonged. We supplied our little stick up boys with the firearms necessary to do the job, and do the job they did. The Wreckin' Crew robbed the Decatur Street Mob at gun point coming away with a huge amount of heroin, which Uncle Snookey later estimated to have a street value of about $70,000. As for the other drug money and dope taken off the Jamaican traffickers, we allowed the Wreckin' Crew to divide the spoils amongst themselves. We told Uncle Snookey and Aunt Melissa what we had done during their "business" trip when they returned. Now at first, Uncle Snookey was none too happy that we'd once again strayed into the mean streets of South Peola, however never one to turn up his nose at a chance to make a profit, he was very pleased to see the amount of heroin that was seized from the Jakes in that successful robbery and he was elated that the three of us had come to him seeking his assistance and advice.

"Well first of all I want to congratulate the three of you for being honest wit me 'bout ya extracurricular activities...now, normally y'alls asses woulda been in mo' trouble than a little behind dis shit, but since ya'll done went out and planned dis shit here so damn perfectly...shit, I gots nutthin' but praise for ya'll."

Uncle Snookey spoke for about twenty minutes more in his normal preachy fashion, then he received the "smack" from us and we got down to business. You see the twins and I knew that with Uncle Snookey's widespread connections with key underworld figures and our knowledge of South Peola's drug markets we could make enough scrilla to last us a life time and retire from this bullshit altogether. Uncle Snookey was more than a little impressed by our ingenuity, teamwork and business savvy for kids our age.

By September '88 our little drug operation was running smoothly with only two incidents I can recall. On the 8th of September Domino was arrested for assault and battery after he flipped out and beat Chauncey to within and inch of his life. Domino pleaded "no contest" at his arraignment hearing and was therefore given six months in jail due to other run-ins with the law on his rap sheet. Although Domino claimed that Chauncey came on to him sexually, we knew better. Chauncey although openly gay was quite discreet in his actions and besides he found Domino to be highly unattractive and disgusting in his mannerisms. Chauncey was hospitalized for several weeks after the brutal attack, suffering three broken ribs, a broken jaw and a number of other minor bumps and bruises received from being literally stomped into the ground. We were pissed, especially Dawn. Chauncey's place was our receiving and distribution location and we were earning anywhere from

$1,200 to $1,500 per week at that apartment. Now it seemed as though it would go up in smoke. Uncle Snookey came through for us just in time. Hemlock Hills housing projects was co-owned by one of my uncle's most trusted cocaine clients. Help was but a cellular phone call away.

Within three short days from the Domino/Chauncey incident we were presented the keys to building 6606, Apartment #313 and our business was again up and running. Dope fiends were elated to see us back and we made up double for the three day lay-off. Still, Dawn was so angry she wanted to have Domino killed inside the joint.

"Dat's one stupid son-of-a-bitch, dat fuckin' Domino. What the fuck was he thinkin'?" Dawn announced in anger one night, as we counted the day's earnings. "Cause of his dumbass we coulda lost out on everything we worked so hard to get! Yeah, but dat's okay doe, I gots me some niggas up in Akron Corrections dat will twist his shit up propa like fa me, ya heard?"

I was one to spare a nigga's life if I could and although it took me sometime to talk her out of it, I eventually changed my cousin's mind. Domino never really knew how close he came to getting murdered inside the joint.

The other little incident to occur that September involved Dawn, once again. Dawn and Shawn had gotten their ferocity from both their mother and father and they didn't believe in turning the other cheek. Their philosophy in life was to react violently to any real or imagined slight directed toward them, as Sharon Slarb found out the hard way.

Dawn had been dating Malik Hornesby ever since we'd arrived in Peola and she was greatly admired by Malik's mother, Mrs. Mavis, who considered Dawn her daughter-in-law. Dawn usually showed up at the Hornesby residence sometimes when Malik wasn't home and just kick it with Mrs. Hornesby or take her out shopping at the mall. Sharon Slarb was a rival of Dawn's since high school and Malik's ex-girlfriend as well as mother of his four-year-old daughter, Javoney.

Dawn and I had been picking up some money from Whiskey and Lil' Shane when she received a page. "Hold up...737-651-5911, dat's Mama Hornesby's number. Come on Rae-Rae, let's bounce, Big Mama needs me!" Dawn said with urgency. We didn't even stop to call; we just hopped on the Madison Highway en route to the Hornesby household in West Peola. Even though I must have been driving about 90 or 95 miles per hour Dawn was continuing to press me to go faster.

"Look, I'm going about as fast as I can without getting pulled over. We got dope, lots o' money and two pistols in here with us. I don't know about you, but I ain't tryin' ta get locked up," I barked as I rounded the overpass leading me onto Century Boulevard West. Dawn jumped out of the car damn near before I could pull up in front of Mrs. Hornesby's house.

As we pulled up I could see that Mrs. Hornesby was engaged in a heated argument with Sharon Slarb and her cousin Naomi Benjamin, a.k.a. Nee-Nee. The three women were yelling at each other so loudly you could hear the ruckus half-way down the block. There was no time to restrain Dawn from taking action, she had bolted from the car and was sprinting across the lawn before I could do anything.

"What's goin' on Ma?" Dawn asked coming up on the porch in the midst of the drama. Before Mrs. Hornesby could say a word, Sharon immediately took the offensive, aggressively stepping to Dawn...wrong move.

"Bitch, if you don't get your ghetto ass away from here and mind your own fuckin' business, you gonna fuck around and get the shit beat outta you!" Sharon snarled, pointing a threatening finger at Dawn, with her hand on her hip and her head swaying from side to side.

With cat like reflexes, Dawn snatched Sharon by her long so-called hair and dragged her off the porch and roughly down the steps. Once she had Sharon down on the lawn Dawn began punching Sharon repeatedly in her face, each time pulling away a fist covered with Sharon's blood. Mrs. Hornesby rushed down the steps trying to pull the two apart as Sharon was being pummeled by sharp jabs, hooks, and a crushing overhand right that sent the former prom queen sprawling over lawn ornaments and finally lying as a crumbled mass on the sidewalk. Nee-Nee mumbled to herself as she loosened her hoop earrings and sped down the steps to engage Dawn in further combat, when she stopped dead in her tracks. Nee-Nee's initial fury quickly turned to fear as she stood at point blank range looking down the barrel of a nine-millimeter semi-automatic. Dawn shook her head as she held a startled Nee-Nee at gunpoint.

"Naw, baby girl, you don't wanna do dat dere….but I tell ya what…get yo punkass cousin up on her feet and roll da fuck out cause if Big Mama ever tells me either of ya'll little disrespectful ho's been fuckin' wit her again you's gonna both die, ya heard me?" Nee-Nee nervously nodded "yes" as a tear welled up in her left eye and cascaded down her cheek.

"Now, get dat bitch and get the fuck outta here!" Dawn yelled pretending to strike Nee-Nee across the face with the pistol. Nee-Nee recoiled in terror covering her face and letting out a scream in the process. By now Sharon had risen to her feet and was stumbling about groggily on the sidewalk as blood dripped from her face. Nee-Nee rushed quickly to her side, taking her by the hand, and whisking her away across the street and into a red Nissan Maxima. They sped away down Chelsea Road and disappeared onto Century Boulevard, running red lights and stop signs in their haste to vacate the area.

Dawn calmly embraced a badly shaken Mrs. Hornesby reassuring her that all was well. After quite some time Dawn emerged from the Hornesby home and plopped in the passenger's seat. I couldn't help but laugh, I thought that I was a thug…shit, my twin cousins were always getting into some shit, especially Dawn. By then half the neighborhood was outside pointing at Mrs. Hornesby's home and us as we sat in my Beamer outside.

"Yo', Dee-Dee, there's a whole lotta folks outside let's bounce," I said looking at all the onlookers whom had been gathering in droves.

"Man, fuck dem people! You got some o' dat 'funk' in here somewhere?" Dawn asked calmly fishing around in the glove compartment for marijuana. I produced a bag of potent sinsemillia I'd stashed under my seat for later when I'd plan on chilling with Donita.

"Yo' beggin' ass owe me a blunt, ya heard?" I said preparing to fill up a Phillie cigar husk with cannabis.

"Ya know I got you, cuz." Dawn placed the weapon in the glove compartment. We drove away as the crowd stood mumbling and pointing. That girl was crazy, a straight gansta bitch...my cousin Dawn. Even when you thought you'd seen her do the most outrageous thing you could imagine, she'd always pull off something much wilder. I was about to find out up close just how over the top Dawn could be.

VIII

The Domino Effect

By the time I turned eighteen in September 1988 and Donita and I had become the proud parents of twin boys, Rae Kwon Jr. and Davón Lake. I guess twins must run in my family. Everyone adored our twins and said that I must have spit those babies out cause they look so much like me, but I tend to think they favored my late mother Selena. Donita's father was overjoyed with the fact that he was a grandpa, but her mother, Mrs. Grimes, was always hasselin' us about college, career goals…you name it. She could be a real bitch. Our boys never wanted for anything; pampers, formula, clothes…nothing. I made sure that Donita received the best prenatal as well as postnatal care at Peola's Shelby Hospital for Women. At $500 per day, not to mention the little extras like food, television, phone service, etc. Donita's hospital stay was quite costly. Lucky for me, I didn't have financial limitations like other eighteen-year-olds. Although I had to have my uncle pay for all expenses on his Visa platinum, I reimbursed him in cash. For thoses three weeks I must have forked out well over $75,000. I paid my uncle back $10,000 a month for at least seven months because although at that time I made decent money on the strip I was a year or so away from being at big baller status like my Uncle Snookey, but my goal was to surpass even him.

Donita was head over heals in love with me. She had never known a family like ours. She herself had come from good stock and both of her parents were upper middle class professionals. Mr. Grimes was the superintendent of the Meridian construction company and his wife was the dean of Savannah State University and she made the 3 ?-hour commute daily, maybe that's why she was so uptight.

Donita revealed to me that she knew all along that we sold drugs even when we all attended high school together. Most of her friends either got high or knew someone who did and they all flocked to us. Dawn and Donita were closer than sisters, and soon they began hanging out together in South Peola. It wasn't long before Donita was helping us with our drug business.

She was scheduled to enroll in Savannah State in the fall. She planned to major in accounting. Her mathematical skills were invaluable to us in handling the bookkeeping duties. After the twins were born I had to spend more time with them and Donita and less time in the streets, so I had Lil' Shane and his cousin Frankie hustle for me. Hemlock Hills and the rest of South Peola had, by '88, reached its saturation level of drug trafficking.

The Wreckin' Crew, who was financed by my cousins and me, had The Hills on lock, while Badlands Manor was controlled by the hotheaded Lee Ambrosia a.k.a. Whiteboy (a nickname he acquired because he was biracial) and his Badboyz Drug Syndicate, also allies and business associates of ours. We supplied Whiteboy and his crew with weapons and cocaine while Lee in turn sold our Wreckin' Crew homies heroin and in later years, Ecstasy. Lee and his cronies also helped us in our turf wars with the Decatur Street Crew during the early 1990's when all of South Peola's drug gangs began to expand and intrude on each other's territories. Only Geneva remained free of our influence, for it was totally dominated by blood thirsty Jamaican posses such as the Kingston Crew, The Rude Boyz and of course our nemesis the Decatur Street Mob. All of the other drug gangs wanted Geneva's fertile drug business. Geneva was by far the largest of the three projects and being closest to Peola/Savannah borderline, it received many a customer from across the border, but the place was damn near impenetrable.

The Jamaicans had their shit together, I'll give 'em that. They had armed guards patrolling the borders day and night, while the citizens of both Badlands Manor and Hemlock Hills walked around freely and generally lived peacefully among the dealers, which mainly consisted of their relatives and friends. It was a whole different ball game in Geneva. From rumors circulating on the streets, those poor Geneva residents lived in terror everyday of their lives. It was nothing for them to have the doors kicked in and have a group of dreadlocked thugs take over their apartment. Very rarely did these cats receive any resistance. Those who were bold enough to even stand up to them usually got beaten into submission or murdered. Women and teenage girls were routinely harassed and/or sexually assaulted many times in plain view of their husbands, boyfriends, or brothers. It was real fucked up over there and that was during a time when Peola's police force was either too short staffed or just plain didn't give a fuck about the bullshit that occurred daily in South Peola's Geneva projects.

I had my two drug runners deliver goods to several clients whom I did business with in the West End where I lived. These were people with money, beachfront homes in the Caribbean, private jets, yachts, and business ventures in California's Silicon Valley. Even my cousins didn't know about my side contacts, only myself, my girl, and my dope boys, Lil' Shane and Frankie, knew. I'd met these high society dopers from my days of rolling with Uncle Snookey in New Orleans and had become reunited with a few of them here in Peola. Just dealing with them netted me a profit twice as large as what I received on the strip. In '88 I mostly chilled, from the streets for a minute, proud of being a father for the first time and wanting to gain the trust and admiration of Mrs. Grimes as well as her husband. I went into business with my cousin Shawn, we each put up $25,000 and opened up a small automotive shop. Our employees where three of Shawn's high school buddies, Carl, Simon, and Jerry, who detailed the cars. They also restored classic vehicles to mint condition. The auto shop was an excellent smoke screen for Shawn and me since we'd be able to sell drugs right out of the shop. We had a more discreet, higher income clientele than we had down in the projects and we didn't have to worry about sharing our profits with anyone else. Dawn—the consummate hood rat—enjoyed the rugged atmosphere of South Peola while her brother Shawn and I eventually out grew hanging around thugs all day.

All was gravy until May '88 when Domino and Dawn had it out one Saturday night. It was closing time at the shop and Carl and the other grease monkeys had clocked out. Old man Jeb Boozer, who basically hung around, worked the cash register, cleaned up and helped out with minor autowork informed us that Domino was outside. We let Jeb out after paying him his daily $100 and Domino entered reeking of malt liquor and marijuana smoke. We hadn't seen him since he'd been locked up so we greeted him and sat down in the back office joking around and getting our smoke on. That's when Dawn called the shop's phone.

During the course of our conversation she asked what Shawn and I were doing and I told her Domino had stopped past. "Keep that muthafucka there Ray, don't let 'em go before I get there. I'll be there in a half hour or less." As the line clicked over to a dial tone I hung up the phone confused by her need to see him. I peeked into the office to find Domino and Shawn laughing loudly as Domino discussed his humorous jailhouse experiences. Motioning for Shawn, I had Domino wait in the office.

"What the fuck's going on? Dawn said she's comin' over here in thirty minutes after she found out Domino was here. What's up with that?" I asked him concerned.

"I don't know cuz, but we'll find out in a minute."

As we turned to reenter the office Domino stood outside the door. "Awright my niggas, see ya'll cats later. I gots ta go gets me some ass right bout now, know what I'm sayin?" Domino said brushing past us with a half-empty bottle of Colt 45 in his hand.

I quickly blocked the doorway so that I could talk Domino

into staying a little while longer. After about fifteen minutes of convincing this cat to remain, I broke out with a bottle of rum and got some Coca Cola from the little fridge we kept in the office and got Domino drinking again. I knew that as long as you provided Domino with booze and chronic, he'd fuckin' hang out with you all night. After about 11:15, Dawn pulled up in the parking lot. After she turned off the ignition switch, she crept around the rear of the building. As we were inside talking, Dawn burst through the side door and pumped Domino full of hollow point slugs. Shawn and I jumped from off the couch in shock and horror.

"What the fuck is wrong with you girl...you fuckin' crazy!!" Shawn yelled as Domino's dying bullet-ridden body slid off the couch and onto the floor, convulsing with rapid little jerks as his lifeblood pooled out onto the carpet.

"Fuck 'im!! Don't nobody steal from me...bitchass nigga!! Betcha black ass won't fuckin' steal dope no mo', will ya...punk bitch!" Dawn kicked the corpse of the 19-year-old ex-con before being dragged away by Shawn.

While the twins bickered and argued heatedly among them-selves, I intervened and in my own anger and urgency insisted that the two siblings stop arguing and quickly aid me in clean-ing up the bloody mess within the office and disposing of the body. "Look ya'll two, we gotta get this fuckin' place cleaned up and we gotta fuckin' get rid of this body right now!!" I yelled.

My cousins quickly snapped back to reality realizing the sit-uation we were in. While Dawn and Shawn agreed to get rid of Domino's corpse, I took nearly three hours cleaning the uphol-stery and rug that was either soaked or splattered with blood. Luckily for us we kept a lot of cleaning supplies and equipment on site due to Jeb the cleaning/handy man/cashier. I couldn't help but cuss out loud as I got down on my hands and knees scrubbing the couch and rug. Our office smelled terrible, a sick-ening blend of alcohol, reefer, gun smoke, and death. I had to spray deodorizer, light incense, and open windows to try and get rid of it.

The next day, it was business as usual and the guys came to work as always and didn't seem to notice a thing. During the course of the day, I pulled Shawn to the side and questioned him about the disposal.

"What did y'all do with it?" I asked inquisitively.

Shawn looked around cautiously to see if anyone was near, then he guided me into the back office and shut the door behind him.

"Alright...check it out; we had no choice but to go to our father. You know he damn near shit a brick when he looked in the back of Dawn's truck, but what could he say? He puts cats ta sleep all da time. So anyway, he called up a nigga he knows in Savannah dat runs a crematorium, same one who had Gerald Huggins body burned two years ago. Dawn had ta pay dude though, Daddy said he wasn't payin' for shit."

That was some bullshit there. After that, I kind of kept clear of Dawn for a minute because she was always getting into some shit. On the flipside, Shawn and I were mostly about chasin' that dollar. Shit, I didn't even want Donita fuckin' with her like that anymore. She was constantly whipping out pistols or fightin' somebody, even dudes. One time we all got tossed out of a night club because of her attitude and rude language. She came back later that night and placed C4 inside the bouncer's truck...it killed him and two bystanders. Dawn's hair-trigger temper continued to cause problems in and around Peola, thus bringing unwanted attention to everyone concerned. However, I knew that sooner or later Dawn's foolishness had to cease.

IX

Don't Be Scurred

Once again Peola's small town media was all a buzz due to the latest act of violence in the town's chic West Side. Even though Uncle Snookey was in tight with a number of town big wigs including the mayor, this latest result of his daughter's explosive temper caused some heat to fall on him. Police Chief Mickey O'Malley, originally of the Baton Rouge Police Department, was a close friend and confidant of the now deceased New Orleans Police Chief, Leon Rossum, who had succumbed to a heart attack in 1986. Like many other law enforcement officials from Louisiana, he knew of Marion "Snookey" Lake's notoriety and shared the late Rossum's hatred for him. An investigation was launched and Uncle Snookey as well as several of his business associates was brought in for questioning. O'Malley couldn't find anything to link Uncle Snookey to the recent bouncer's murder so he had to release him, but not without a stern warning.

"Lake, you've been duckin' the law a long time you fuckin' cocksucker, but I swear on my mother's grave that I'm gonna nail you're ass to the wall! Ya got that? You worthless piece o' shit ya!!"

Uncle Snookey arose from his chair in the middle of the interrogation room, placed a black felt fedora upon his head, calmly looked the enraged Irishman in the eye and arrogantly said, "You know what playa, I've been checking' out that little phat ass daughter you got there, curves and all the right places, huh? I bet you that lil' hoe sucks a mean dick...just like ya boy Rossum's wife used to."

"You son-of-a-bitch!!" Mickey O'Malley screamed as he lunged across the interrogation table trying to strangle the object of his intense hatred, only to be restrained by two nearby homicide detectives.

"Get the fuck outta here you asshole!" rumbled one of the detectives to Snookey, while still struggling to hold the furious Police Chief. O'Malley broke free and hurled insults at Snookey until he left the premises.

Things started to unravel in the Lake household around December of '88. Tired of her husband's infidelities and now engaging in her own extra-marital trysts, Aunt Melissa separated from Uncle Snookey on December 17, 1988, shortly before the Christmas holidays. She stuck around long enough for us to enjoy the holidays as a family, but shortly after that she relocated to South Carolina's Hilton Head Island—a resort haven, a lovely vacation spot surrounded by sandy white beaches, lush green fairways, and wealthy retirees. After the divorce papers were signed, Aunt Melissa walked away with a victory in court and a huge alimony check awarded to her every month to the tune of $3,000. This was only the first of Uncle Snookey's legal woes.

Because of the car bombing, Uncle Snookey knew that Dawn, being the most reckless among the three of us, had to be responsible for it. And Dawn continued getting into trouble for utter stupidity. In January, she had a miscarriage because she got into a fistfight during her third month of pregnancy. On Valentine's Day, she and Malik got into a heated argument over Malik's baby's mama, Sharon Slarb and it turned physical. Malik ended up getting stabbed in his side. He spent nearly a month in the hospital because of it. The doctors said that if the blade were to have penetrated his side a little higher it would have collapsed his lung. Mrs. Hornesby nearly had a heart attack behind that one. Needless to say, she and Dawn never spoke to each other again afterwards.

Soon, Uncle Snookey, already on edge because of his recent divorce and building criminal speculation around town, grew tired of Dawn's wild, out-of-control antics and shipped her off to her mother in South Carolina. With Dawn gone, things slowly began to simmer down around Peola again. Shawn, although he missed his sister's presence, knew it was for the best and he and I begun hanging out down in Miami and Atlanta during the weekends, club hopping and checking out the scenery.

Donita was pregnant again and away at school. That made it even more easier for me to play the field. Peola was too small a town for me to play around and mack like I wanted and Savannah was only a few hours away. Plus, Dawn went to Savannah State and her mother worked there. Playing it safe, I frequented Florida or went upstate toward ATL. I usually went with Uncle Snookey, who turned both me and Shawn onto the various strip clubs, bars and celebrity hangouts in Miami, Atlanta, Charlotte, and even D.C. We'd blow thousands in a weekend on booze, women, and gambling. Uncle Snookey was known seemingly by everybody, everywhere, so it was no problem getting us into these illicit and highly discriminating establishments. Occasionally I'd land a few sexy beach bunnies down in Hilton Head or Myrtle Beach or go further north to Charlotte and lay up with some big booty hoes from the Tar Heel State.

There was this one broad Brandi Welch, a white girl from Miami by way of San Francisco. I met her lap dancing at one of Miami's exclusive strip clubs. Brandi fell in love with me saying that she never met anyone as nice as I was. She was fuckin' built like a goddess; 38DD-36-38, about 5'9 and 135lbs. She was a fantastic fuck, sometimes ridin' the dick all night if I'd let her. She had sandy blonde hair and green eyes that would make you melt like butter when she gazed upon you. She moved from Miami up to Peola when she turned 20. I set her up in a high-rise apartment on the north side of Peola in Sorrel Dunes, which was mostly rented out by military types and retired senior citizens.

I moved out of Uncle Snookey's house by February '89 and got Brandi to sign for an apartment in her name for me near the auto shop. Here I could handle my drug business, lay up with various hotties and generally do what the fuck I felt. It was only April when I found out Brandi was pregnant. Brandi was carrying my child and I wasn't too happy about knocking her up. I already had a set of twin boys and Donita was pregnant and showing with another of my offspring. Try as I might I couldn't talk Brandi into having an abortion. Every time I'd bring up the subject she'd go ballistic, so I eventually just said "fuck it" and gave up.

"You's a muthafuckin'sperm donor, my nigga," Shawn would laugh and say. But I definitely didn't think the shit was funny. He kept telling me, "Nigga why don't you just go up in dese bitches wit a rubber on yo shit, den you kin stop makin' all dese goddamn babies."

Shawn even gave me packs of condoms he had lying around his dad's house. Good as his advice was, I never did heed to it and ended up having two babies born exactly three months apart by both Donita and Brandi. Donita gave birth to Chantel Latisha Lake born August 8th 1989, 8 lbs 9oz. Brandi dropped her load on November 8th, a little girl who we named Selena French Lake after my late mom. She weighed a whopping 10 lbs. 3oz, the third largest baby born in Peola in the past twenty years. I was 19 years old and the father of four children. Back in September, I purchased a new Toyota 4Runner to celebrate my birthday. Brandi fell in love with the silver Beamer of mine and drove it often while Donita was away at college. But I couldn't give it to her though, Donita knew that car like the back of her hand. So I gave the Beamer to Donita so that she could ride around with our kids in luxury and finally trash that ugly ass '78 Chevy Catalina her dad gave her.

By November's end, Dawn was back in town. Gone for only about eight months, Dawn related how she was bored to death living down in Hilton Head. "Life's to slow for me down there. There's nuthin' ta do, no kinda excitement, action, or challenge," Dawn said dejectedly.

"That's the kinda life you need right now, Dawn. There's too much bullshit out here for you to get caught up in." Dawn smirked at my remark and asked me where her brother was. No sooner than she asked did Shawn pull up in the driveway of Lake's Auto Repair and Service Center. The two siblings embraced warmly, after rushing to meet each other. As usual Dawn desired to travel down to South Peola and visit the old projects of Hemlock Hills. Now Shawn and I hadn't been around Hemlock Hills or any other part of Southside Peola for sometime, but we were glad to see Dawn and didn't want to disappoint her. Upon arriving there Dawn quickly exited the 4Runner, running with jubilation over to the group of weeded-out drug dealers who in turn received her with equal joy. During Dawn's brief hiatus from The Hills the Wreckin' Crew had steadily increased in their size and influence on the streets. Even though Dawn had been M.I.A., she approached Man-Man, Half-Dead and some other members of the crew and demanded her usual cut.

"Come on wit it! Y'all niggas know da deal, just like Scarface said 'Who put dis shit together'…me that's who!" Dawn said in her best Cuban accent. The young thugs reluctantly, yet promptly removed thick rubber band bound wads of cash and one by one each youngster peeled off a few hundred-dollar bills and handed it over to an impatiently waiting Dawn. "Dats what the fuck I am talking bout, organization…bidness, one hand washes the other…ya know?" Dawn announced smiling proudly as she walked away with several hundred dollars in her possession. "Just yesterday a bitch was dead broke, but how ya lovin dis?" Dawn displayed the money in her hand for all to see, spreading it out like an oriental fan. "Come on let's go over to the apartment," Dawn said waltzing over to Shawn and me as we stood on the corner of 13th and Fenris drinkin' Hennesey and shooting dice with a few of the fellas.

"Awight, hold up baby girl, we tryin ta get dis money up off dese fake ass balla's first," Shawn quipped playfully as he shook the dice within his hand.

"Go ahead, I'll meet ya at the apartment," Dawn turned to

leave followed by a half-dozen rowdy Malt Liquor guzzling, gun-toting teens. Finishing about seven games of dice, I walked away with $800. Shawn cleared $200 and ended up with a .22-caliber Baretta handgun with a fully loaded magazine plus a bag of cocaine. We cleaned up, but those cats were our homies so we eventually ended up treatin' half of them to pizza and a movie. Afterwards, around 11:45pm, while the neighborhood dealers were still outside making sales, most of the other Hemlock Hills residents were in for the night. I pulled up to the curb, unloaded my inebriated runnin' buddies said, "Peace out!" then pulled my vehicle around to the back of the apartment.

Dawn didn't have wheels anymore since crashing her Ford Bronco down in Hilton Head a few months earlier, so she had to wait for us to return before she could leave. Dawn was waiting for us on the steps of 6606. She sat with several other girls and guys smoking PCP-laced joints. "Yo, what took y'all mutha-fuckers so long...shit I coulda got married and had a family by the time y'all got back...damn!!" Dawn announced sounding irritated and upset.

Looking at her under the street lights' glow, I could see that her normally elaborate hairdo was disheveled and she sported a fresh black eye that showed up distinctly against her complexion.

"Who was you rumbling wit this time, girl?" Shawn questioned his sister as he took her face into his hand, examining her thoroughly. Dawn pulled back abruptly and smacked Shawn's hand away from her face.

"Get off me boy, I'm awiight...you need ta check dat bitch I knocked out dat's da fuck who you needs ta check on!" Apartment #313 had been lost to us after Dawn was sent away to live in South Carolina. Mae Bell Lowery and her two hard drinking, constantly pregnant daughters, Samantha and Bridget were now the current tenants. From what everyone on the stoop was tellin' us, Dawn had approached the door as always— knocking on it, expecting Chauncey to open up. Samantha opened up and during the brief encounter hostile words were exchanged between the two. Soon arms were swinging, fists were flying and hair was being yanked out as the two locked horns at the top of the third floor stairwell.

"Samantha took ah ass-whippin dawg!" one young Dawn supporter spoke with zest. The little wiry teenager continued gleefully, "She caught that fat bitch with a nasty uppercut and knocked her ass slam da fuck out!!"

"So where's Samantha at now?" I asked knowing how reckless and non-thinking Dawn could be at times.

"When da bitch came to, about five minutes later, she took her big ass inside where she belongs."

No sooner than she said that did both Bridget and Mother Lowery cut the corner and stood in front of the stoop confronting Dawn. Bridget rushed the stoop initially, but was quickly collared by her moms.

"Yeah bitch, what's up?! Huh...what's up now?!" Bridget screamed at Dawn, straining to break away from her mother's grasp.

"What da fuck's up? I'll show you what da fuck's up bitch!!" Dawn replied, jumping from the stoop and throwing her fists up.

"Y'all chillen' needs ta just take y'alls ass somewhere else instead of sittin' round here causin' trouble," Mrs. Lowery said shaking with anger while holding her youngest daughter back.

"Fuck dat shit, I ain't movin' for no muthafuckin'body!!"

"Come the fuck on Dawn, damn!!" I said, physically removing her from the stoop and away from the Lowerys. As I took Dawn away, kicking and screaming, Bridget hawk spit a thick yellow glob of phlegm into Dawn's face.

"Oh naw bitch, you'se a dead muthafucka!" Dawn growled as she broke free from my grasp. I reached out to smack my cousin, but I was too late. In slow motion, or so it seemed, I watched Dawn remove a silver handgun from her Gucci hand-bag that hung loosely upon her shoulders. Mrs. Lowery had a wide-eyed look of terror on her face as she watched Dawn with-draw the chrome nine millimeter from her handbag. She turned only to receive the first blast. Mother Lowery's head snapped back as is if some unseen force had harshly yanked her by her hair. The small red wound in the middle of Mrs. Lowery's fore-head opened up the rear of her skull into a 10-inch gaping crater that spewed blood, brain matter, and bone shards all over the stoop. The lady was dead before she hit the pavement. Two more shots flew wide and high hitting the building, ricocheting off the pavement and shattering a parked trucks' windshield 20 yards away. The next blast caught Bridget in the midsection then another shattered her windpipe. She slumped over, collapsing to the pavement as she choked on her own blood. Everyone had to hit the pavement as Dawn continued to fire round after wild round at real and imaginary enemies. As the smoke settled, everyone slowly, yet cautiously, got up off the pavement. Bridget lay dead on the concrete, thick dark blood pooled about her head and snaked along the sidewalk, while her mother lay but a few feet away from her, frozen in a silent scream, while her dead eyes peered motionless into the inky blackness of the Georgia night. The once still surrounding buildings begun stirring with activity and lights were soon illuminating in a number of win-dows throughout the complex. The commotion had brought var-ious drug dealers to the scene.

"Let's get the fuck outta here!!" said one little youth after sur-veying the carnage around him.

Dawn snatched him up by the collar and pressed the still smoking pistol to his temple. "Shut the fuck up! We're not going anywhere until we get this shit cleaned up...got dat?!!!" The lit-tle punk shook with fear, however he agreed with Dawn.

Shawn emerged from Apt #313 with the little twenty-two clutched in one hand as he opened the door. He had just put two slugs into the back of Samantha Lowery's head. At this point I couldn't believe what I was witnessing and I couldn't believe that all of this bedlam happened so fast and over something so petty. It took all night to get rid of the bodies and clean things up. Dawn was fortunate that she had the juice she did with the Wreckin' Crew and the other gang members and hooligans within the projects. Dawn's constant drug supply and weapon deliveries kept the pushers well paid and armed in order to protect their business interests; so whatever Dawn wanted, Dawn got. Also nearly all of Hemlock Hills' residents were an impoverished lot consisting mostly of single welfare mothers, ex-cons, junkies, and foreign laborers working various menial jobs. Although curious, they posed not real threat. People got murdered all the time and cops never got anywhere questioning these folks. They had to live here and so of course they feared the retaliatory measures they'd face if they squealed.

After that fateful night in November '89, nobody ever mentioned the Lowerys again. The cops came and investigated the shootings for a week, taking in several hustlers off the street for questioning. As usual they got nowhere in their investigation and had to reluctantly release the petty criminals they had in their custody. Like so many Lake victims before them, the Lowerys ended up at Robbins Crematorium down in Savannah.

Lindsey Robbins was a 50-something distinguished looking gentleman with wavy salt-n-pepper hair and beard. Dawn had met him the year before when she and Shawn delivered the bullet-riddled body of Domino. She knew better than to ask me to transport a couple of stiffs in my whip so she asked her brother Shawn to drive his hooptie pick-up truck. I'd never been to the infamous crematorium before; I was surprised by the sanitary, antiseptic feel and smell of the place. Once inside, we had to perform the unpleasant task of removing the stiffened corpses of the three women, placing them into simple pine coffins and then finally tossing them into the incineration vault. I'm sure the Lowerys ended up in an urn on somebody's living room cabinet.

Dawn and Robbins seemed extra chummy with each other and it seemed kind of strange to me and Shawn. After hosing out the back of the pick-up, Shawn and I entered the building to find no one there. We called for Dawn, who after about five minutes turned the corner with Mr. Robbins in tow. She was adjusting her blouse and reattaching her diamond earrings as Mr. Robbins whispered something into her ear making her chuckle.

"You so crazy!" Dawn giggled, hitting Robbins playfully on his shoulder. Robbins attempted to slip Dawn some money on the sneak tip. He wasn't slick enough though; Shawn and I glanced at each other in puzzlement. As the three of us exited the building, Mr. Robbins called Dawn over him, stood close to her and started speaking in a low tone.

"What the fuck is this shit about?" Shawn asked as we climbed in the truck.

"I can't call it dawg," I said looking over at the two. "Anyway...blow da horn cuz, it's bout time ta bounce."

Shawn shook his head while beeping the horn twice, prompting Dawn to break up her little conversation. As the two ended their love talk, they departed with a torridly sensual kiss that caused Shawn to seethe with anger. Dawn waltzed away from the crematorium towards the truck, smiling from ear to ear as she entered. As soon as Dawn sat down, Shawn immediately began questioning his sister's lovey-dovey relationship with Mr. Robbins.

"So you fuckin'dis old ass nigga or what?" Shawn got right to the point.

"Dat's none of yo muthafuckin'bidness nigga! Who da fuck you be fuckin?!" Dawn snapped in return.

Shawn swerved off the main street onto the side of the desolate country road, turning off the ignition, and ripping into his sister. "Looka here, let me tell ya stinkin' ass something, ya betta be thankful that I even brought ya muthafuckin' ass round here so you can take care of dis here bidness, and you got da nerve to fuckin' cuss me out?! Fuckin' wit ah ole' ass man like dat. What da fuck is you thinking bout?"

Dawn's face contorted in anger at her brother's piercing remarks. "Ya see dat's da shit I'm talking bout. You still think I'm a baby, but guess what muthafucka, I ain't nobody's baby no mo, ya heard me? And you, Daddy, Mama…I don't give a damn who it is, can't tell me who da fuck I can be wit and who I can't be wit ya heard? And if you really wanna know if I'm fuckin' Robbins well peep dis here. While you and Rae-Rae wuz movin' dem bodies and cleanin out da back of da truck, where do you think I was at, huh? I'll tell ya where I was…I was laid up wit Lindsey back in his office throwin' dis hot young pussy on him, dat's what da fuck I was doin'. And befo' I left , I sucked his dick reaaal good, so good dat he skeeted all over my pretty red face! Now, how ya lovin' dat!!" By now, Dawn's face was inches from his.

I swear that I could see it coming and just because Dawn had too much mouth for her own good, I let the chips fall where they may. Shawn, raging, reached back and slapping his sister across the side of her face with so much force that it sent her flying back into the rear seat. Her face was visibly red and the left side displayed the outline of her brother's fingers.

"Bitch, don't you evah disrespect me again, ya heard? Cause of you I got fuckin' blood on my hands, cause of you even Rae done got caught up in some shit! You are such a fuck up sometimes, ya know dat? Always comin' out ya mouth wrong ta people, always jumpin' out dere like you'se hard, always straight fuckin' up…period. Dat's why daddy put you out…cause you straight trippin.' Last time I talked ta Mama, she said you was down in Hilton Head wild'n out fuckin'every Tom, Dick, Harry wit a pimped out ride and some cheddar in his pockets, robbin' tourists and old folks…now dat's some hot shit. Mama is actually glad dat you gone, she got tired of yo bullshit, Daddy don't want ya little trouble makin' ass back. Ya know what dat boils down to, you done burned all ya bridges everywhere else cept' wit me and Rae-Rae. Truthfully speakin' we da only ones you got left that'll put up witcha. Ya see Rae-Rae might wanna spare ya feelin's and not come off blunt like me but o' yeah it's time to come correct wit you and call it like I see it. I loves you to death, you know that. But if you don't slow ya roll ya gonna end up in somebody's morgue…no bullshit.

Dawn, usually boisterously loud and defensive in lieu of criticism, had no response to her brother's sharp commentary. Instead, she lay on the backseat curled up in the fetal position weeping softly at first, but within seconds Dawn's lamentations became louder and quite mournful. Staring blankly down the dimly lit stretch of road before him, Shawn gripped the steering wheel in frustration and sadness. His knuckles whitened through his fair complexioned skin as surging emotions caused him to tighten up on the steering wheel even more. Never had I witnessed such a heated exchange between the twins and I'm sure that the disagreement caught both brother and sister off guard as well. Unable to contain his sorrow, Shawn broke down in tears along with his sister. While the siblings cried their eyes out, I sat in silence contemplating the events that led up to this and other not-so pleasant situations we'd manage to get ourselves into and in pursuit of fast money and shot-caller status. Many times before I'd realized that I'd made a grievous error in choosing the drug game over a college education and a possible opportunity to attract NFL or NBA scouts. Only time would tell, besides I was far too deep into the pusher world to turn back now.

X

Fuck Da Police!

Uncle Snookey knew everything about everyone flippin' dollars. From the most powerful and feared drug traffickers in the deep south and southwestern U.S. to the lowliest bottom feeders running around barefoot, selling rocks on some rural dirt road, the man had eyes and ears everywhere. With his numerous connections throughout the South, there was little news that escaped him. At times his street sense bordered on uncanny with thanks to his years spent rising from the level of small time street hustler to notorious drug czar. Uncle Snookey's intuition about people and their actions were nearly always on point.

When he got the scoop on the Hemlock Hills situation he was furious that his daughter had, for a second time, acted on impulse and killed someone (in this case an entire family with the exception of Samantha and Bridget's small children who were with relatives at the time of the shootings). Snookey usually had associates murdered for the type of stupidity in which his young daughter had already displayed twice in Peola. But by being the child of trigger-happy Snookey, Dawn was exempt from the typically lethal form of street justice her father enforced so many times in the past to numerous non-kin business partners of his. However, Dawn was told that under no circumstances was she to came back to Peola unannounced except to briefly visit with family and leave town immediately afterwards.

All of Uncle Snookey's tough talk unfortunately fell on deaf ears and his unruly daughter begun frequenting the area once again, staying with Shawn on the weekends and leaving back out to Savannah for the week where she stayed in an apartment near Ogelthorpe Mall. Dawn's sugar daddy, Lindsey Robbins, rented out the small two-bedroom apartment which Dawn stayed at on weekdays, laid up with Robbins when he wasn't at work or at home with his wife and three kids. Two of Robbins' kids attended Savannah State College right along with my girl Donita, the youngest of Robbins' kids was only 10-years old. Dawn said that she saw Robbins' family many times, even hanging out with Donita and the two oldest girls, Selena and Alicia, at a Savannah State homecoming dance. Shawn truly hated the fact that his sister was laying up with a trifflin' old coot like Robbins. But what could he do? At 18 years of age, his twin sister was no longer an illegal minor. She was indeed a woman and there was nothing any of us could do about her love life. Dawn knew that her brother didn't approve of her relationship with Robbins so she never mentioned the man's name in his presence. She also was quite adamant in getting Shawn to agree not to let either of their parents know about the illicit affair with the older man, especially Uncle Snookey. She knew full well that if any information concerning her sleeping with Mr. Robbins, a long time client of her father's were to get around to him, Robbins would definitely be done away with. Our silence didn't come without a price though, due to her volatile nature and penchant for stirring up trouble, we made her promise us that she'd leave South Peola alone whenever she visited Peola. Making sure that she kept this promise was our Wreckin' Crew homies, who kept their eyes open for Dawn just in case she tried to pull a caper and show up in spite of our agreement. She'd committed two murders there and her brother had blood on his hands as well, and with me being in their presence at the time of the killings, I'd be charged as an accessory to the crimes. We could not afford to have Dawn bringing attention to herself by acting a fool out there on the streets.

Shawn also took over her drug operations in The Hills projects. He'd usually pick up the cargo from Dawn in Savannah off of a barge at the harbor, then he'd have his girl Kyla transport it via automobile directly to South Peola, where I'd pick it up and have Dawn's little dope boys prepare it for distribution. We usually gave her her scrilla when she came on the weekends, if not then, then whenever we passed through Savannah en route to Hilton Head, S.C. to visit Aunt Melissa.

The reminder of 1989 went by smoothly enough. Dawn kept her usual drama on the down low and Uncle Snookey relocated to Las Vegas where he could get away from the South all together and begin anew out West. Investing his monies in the casino industry, Uncle Snookey continued his narcotic business teaming up with Carlos "Loverboy" Cellini of the Cellini/Alberto crime family originally from Trenton, New Jersey now firmly settled in Sin City. Uncle Snookey became acquainted with Cellini way back in the early 70's when both he and Cellini's first cousin, James Alberto, played for the Virginia Squires. The three men remained close many years after the ABA folded. The trio reunited; however this time they were playing a different game. With both Cellini and Alberto operating as high ranking Lieutenants within the widely feared crime family and Uncle Snookey holding his own as a highly successful drug trafficker from the deep south, Snookey did brisk business with the New Jersey mobsters on several occasions. So, it was a no-brainer for Snookey to plan a merger with them. He purchased a 35-acre horse ranch on the outskirts of Vegas complete with about a dozen purebred pinto ponies, a 155-foot wide, 55-foot deep man-made lake, an 18-hole golf course, and a gymnasium with an NBA regulation sized basketball court.

Uncle Snookey loved Las Vegas so much and rarely came back to Peola except for the occasional visit. He rented out the house that he and Aunt Melissa owned in West Peola to Shawn and myself, charging us only $1500 per month.

As 1989 gave way to 1990, a number of trials and tribulations came with it. First of all in January, Brandi went back to stripping again, even though I'd told her that I didn't want the mother of my child dancing. I'd put her up in an apartment, I took care of her rent, her groceries, clothes, jewelry, and of course the baby was always well cared for. All Brandi had to do was fuck me and take care of our daughter. But Brandi was very independent and had been taking care of herself since the tender age of 15. Stripping came naturally to her, it was all she knew and she made damn good money off of it. She performed every night at the ritzy Sultan's Harem strip club on East Boniventure Avenue out in Sorrell Dunes.

The strip club's clientele—mostly middle-aged white men—were for the most part quite harmless. The owner, Pedro Moralis, a 22-year-old Panamanian entrepreneur, happened to be a slave driver of a boss, who not only subjected his dancers to humiliating treatment, but often sexually harassed the young uneducated girls who came from out of town to work for him. Moralis had been trying to have sex with Brandi ever since he hired her back in November of '89. The past two months of Moralis' increasingly aggressive advances had been a virtual hell on earth for Brandi. On January 5, 1990, things really got out of hand and Moralis tried to rape Brandi while she was alone in the dressing room changing her clothes. Fortunately for Brandi, she was able to escape with only a few minor scrapes and bruises. She left Moralis, a solid build ex-soccer player, lying on the floor of the dressing room crumpled over in pain from a swift kick in the groin. Brandi called me up hysterical. I calmed her down, met her at a nearby bus stop and drove her home after picking up our daughter from the sitter. After mother and daughter were safely at home, I called up Shawn who in turn phoned a few of our dawgs from the Wreckin' Crew and we all paid an unexpected visit to the strip club. It took only about twenty-five minutes to completely ransack the joint, terrifying customers and dancers alike, sending them pouring out of the club and into the streets in fear for their lives. With many of the dancers either nude or semi-nude at the time, I'm sure that the pedestrians and drivers traveling along East Boniventure Avenue got one hell of a treat. We beat Moralis' ass so badly that it took him two months to fully recuperate. Even though the cops investigated the incident neither Moralis nor any of his employees cooperated with them. We had given a grim warning to Moralis that if he or any of the bitches working for him told the cops anything he'd be killed immediately. Needless to say, no arrests or anything ever came about from the incident.

When Moralis was finally released from the hospital, we blackmailed him into paying us (me and Shawn) $1,000 every week just to keep our Wreckin' Crew homies from showing up at the club and scaring off his customers; many of whom were already pretty shaken up from the last unpleasant encounter with the rowdy thugs. I also demanded that my girl Brandi be compensated for the trauma he had put her through. Moralis, being the bitch ass punk he was, forked over yet another grand each week for Brandi, even though she had quit working for him ever since the attempted rape. A few months later Moralis went out of business due to a decline in customers, increasing overhead costs, and the blackmail money paid to Shawn and I as well as Brandi. That was the last time anyone ever saw Pedro Moralis in town again. Last I heard he'd moved to Van Nuys, California and was starring in porn flicks.

Later that month, Donita's big mouth cousin Tomika, who worked at Thornton's Luxury Euro Import Autos saw me with Brandi purchasing a new $58,500 1990 red C-Class convertible Mercedes Benz. I paid for the whip in cash as Tomika stood in the distance watching our every move. Brandi was overjoyed as she drove her new toy from the show room floor and onto the highway. I was shown the full scope of her appreciation when we arrived at her cozy little apartment. Brandi and I must have engaged in about an hour and a half's worth of raw, lust-filled sex. So intense was our steamy coupling, that as I was beating the pussy up (doggy style, of course) a framed picture came crashing down from the wall startling us and awaking our infant daughter, who had to be rocked back to sleep. During the intermission, I decided to check my messages from Brandi's place. While Brandi was busy fucking and sucking me dry, Donita had left over a dozen or more foul messages on my answering machine, demanding that I call her back at once.

"Rae!" her message began, "boy you'd betta answer this phone! My cousin done told me that ya ho'in ass been up at the dealership buyin' a Benz for some lil' ole white bitch! Well you'd betta not let me catch up wit her cuz I'm gonna fuck her shit up, and yours, you grimey ass punk!! Beep." I chuckled softly as I hung up the receiver, pondering the outrageous emotions of a scorned female.

Before I left, Brandi made us dinner. We ate and she gave me a nasty, saliva dripping blow job that ended with me shooting off across her milky white forehead and into her long blonde hair. Afterwards, I walked over to our daughter's crib and kissed her gently on one of her chubby little cheeks then bounced. I drove Brandi's new whip over to Donita's. Donita met me outside of her parent's house where she hopped into the Benz. We had a heated exchange all the way down Century Boulevard, which increased once we pulled up into Ferguson's Park.

"So you been fuckin' this lil' heifer all along, Rae! How the fuck could you do this to me? I'm your goddamned baby's mama! I bore three kids for your sorry black ass, nigga! And you gonna fuck around on me for some trailer park tramp?" she screamed. In all our years together I had never seen my sweet Donita so enraged.

"Girl, you straight trippin' ya heard! You betta calm down and shut da fuck up, or you gonna catch an issue. Fuckin' wit me you'll getcha ass whopped. You believe everything yo pent up, no-man-havin' cousin tells you!" I growled back at her before spitting out a number of nasty words at her for good measure.

Donita was spewing profanities at me as well as hitting me. I grabbed her hands in order to restrain her but at that point she tried to bite me and even spat in my face. Getting out of the car, I wiped my face. I needed some air cause I was about to kill her. I intended to just leave her monkey ass right there, ranting and raving in the park. She'd make it back safely; her parents didn't live to far. As I returned from my walk, I noticed she wasn't in the car. I wasn't stupid, I had taken the car keys with me and although I was pissed off, I was worried about where she was. But before I could panic, Donita charged toward me wielding a switchblade. Somehow, I disarmed her and smack the shit out of her.

"Bitch, if you ever even think bout cutting me your folks better prepare to bury you dumb ass!" I growled pressing the point of a snub-nosed twenty-five automatic up under her chin.

Donita cried and cussed at me as I hopped into the Benz and sped away leaving her in a cloud of dust. Donita and I broke up for a month behind the Mercedes incident.

After no communication or visits from me, Donita started blowing up my pager and leaving dozens of apologetic messages on my answering machine. Before long we were seeing each other again, taking the boys down to Disneyworld in Orlando, visiting my Aunt Melissa in Hilton Head and of course screwing like rabbits every chance we got. Tomika, who loathed me and the entire Lake clan, was furious that Donita and I had gotten back together. But she couldn't say or do nothing to turn her cousin against me. After all Donita and I had babies together and besides that the sex was too delicious for Donita to ever let me go. Luckily for me, Donita had no idea who Brandi was or where she lived, because when we reconciled later on she admitted that she would have slit Brandi's throat the first chance she had. However, my state of bliss was to be short-lived.

Like I said earlier, Shawn and I not only offered automotive services at a reasonable price at our shop, but we also sold weed, coke, heroin, and when available, guns. Norman Dobrowolski, a local construction foreman and union delegate, was one of our most frequent and loyal drug clients. Everyday at noon, he'd come and buy an ounce of coke. Through Mr. Dobrowolski's connections, our dope business expanded. Soon, the shop was pulling in more dollars from coke than it did from auto repair, about 85% more.

Life for me and my cousins was lovely. We spent money like it was growing on trees. We traveled to Atlantic City and Las Vegas, blowing thousands at the poker tables. Then we'd turn around, come home, flip some more dollars and hop a flight out west. During our first trip Los Angeles, we meet up with Uncle Snookey, had dinner at the Beverly Hills home of one of his Mafia associates, went sight seeing and shopped in Hollywood.

After a jammed packed day, we said good-bye to Uncle Snookey and boarding a private jet provided by Carlos Cellini which flew us back across the country to New York. Once on the east coast, we continued our weekend of big spending, dropping thousands on custom made jewelry, top of the line designer athletic wear and premium bottles of $1,000 bubbly. Manhattan showed us all of her delicacies and the three of us were more than willing to partake of her fruit. Before flying back home we painted the town red—club-hopping into the wee hours of the morning.

The next morning I was surprised to find six half-naked chicks sprawled out all over our hotel room, asleep. There were empty bottles of Cristal and Moet lying all around the room. Cum-stained sheets and used condoms littered the floor, partially smoked blunts and several hundred dollar bills were lying around. My head was still slightly spinning from the night of debauchery. The air was stuffy and reeked of booze, butt and bud. I awakened an equally hung over Shawn who groggily steadied himself as he arose from beneath the sheets. We showered, dressed, and left the hotel room with the girls (who were all phat to death, I might add) still fast asleep in the classy Manhattan hotel room. We didn't even bother picking up the loose bills that were scattered all over the soft Persian carpet. Dawn spent the early morning hours sober and shopping while we got sexed and sauced. As we were making our exit, Dawn paged Shawn letting us know that she was picking us up in a limo to go to JFK. Back in Peola, we realized, we must have spent over $170,000 during that Valentine's Day weekend getaway.

XI

I'm Locked Up...They Won't Let Me Out

Jason Dobrowolski went to Cayman High with me and the twins, graduating with the Class of 1986. He played along side me on the senior basketball team, and actually was one hell of a point guard with wicked ball handling skills accompanied by a deadly jump shot. Guys on the team nicknamed him "Swish" 'cause of all the three-pointers he'd knock down. He was also Norman Dobrowolski's nephew and by now, poor Jason, was on the stuff hard...so hard that he took to stealing and burglarizing homes, hocking his spoils at the several pawn shops around town to help support his crack habit.

Around 11 p.m. one Friday night, Jason, both drunk and high, decided to rob a house...with the family asleep inside. Unfortunately for young Jason, he picked the worst house to rob in West Peola—Police Chief Mickey O'Malley's. Ordinarily, Jason would have been successful, but his skills were gone and so was his coordination. While in the kitchen, Jason tripped over O'Malley's dog and fell to the floor, busting his lip. Following the trail of blood, O'Malley—a 57-year-old, hard-drinking, chain-smoking, fat bastard—chased the crackhead...and caught him!

O'Malley was no fool; he knew that Marion Lake somehow had something to do with Dobrowolski's troubles. After hours of hard-core interrogation, which was O'Malley's signature style, Jason Dobrowolski spilled the beans, including who and where he received his constant supply of narcotics. O'Malley promised the terrified teen that he'd pull some strings with the District Attorney's Office and get him a lighter court sentence, playing on the fact the he was a kid with no prior criminal record. Jason was tried and convicted on five counts of burglary and three counts of grand larceny.

"What you need is a rehab center kid, not a jail cell," O'Malley said to a relieved Jason Dobrowolski.

However Chief O'Malley let Dobrowolski know that one hand washes the other and that the price for Jason's short stay behind bars was the names of the real criminals, the dealers who supplied him with his addiction. Jason Dobrowolski didn't need to hear another word, he cold dropped dime on everybody, including his own Uncle Norman and other residents of the wealthy Canterbury Arms community. Although Uncle Snookey was away in Las Vegas, O'Malley still issued a warrant for his arrest. Shawn and I weren't so lucky.

On March 17, 1990, St. Patrick's Day, Peola County Police raided our auto shop. The only legit gig that we ever had was taken away from us. The cops turned the place upside down looking for dope. They did find a small amount of marijuana, about an ounce, but nothing else of significance. Luckily for us, we never had guns for sale that often, whenever we did have them, they sold out within hours. Cocaine was also a hot street commodity that sold like hotcakes. Whenever we received a shipment of powder in from our Miami contacts it was usually gone in a day or two. Most of the folks we sold to were either fun-loving yuppie types, who lived to party hearty on the weekends; the white collar professionals, who snorted several lines a day to alleviate the daily pressure of the corporate world; and the young, upstart drug dealer, who would purchase a quarter pound or key of coke. Business had a quick turnover. That saved our little black asses from doing some serious jail time, possibly even federal, who knows?

Still, that didn't stop O'Malley's goon squad from roughing us up and shipping us uptown to the Peola County Police Department where Shawn, myself, and all three of our mechanics were placed in a holding cell for two and a half hours. Later that evening the grease monkeys, Carl, Simon, Jerry and Phil Bruce were released, but Shawn and me were held overnight. Our bail was set at two grand apiece, especially after fat fuck O'Malley learned that the both of us were immediate family members of Marion Lake. Chief O'Malley never got around to questioning us; Shawn telephoned Dawn in Savannah and she sped the whole way to Peola and paid the bail bondsman the four grand to release us. No sooner had Dawn gotten us out did O'Malley have warrants for our arrest, again. We were apprehended on March 22, 1990 in Savannah about a week after our first arrest, only this time Mickey O'Malley was laughing his fat ass off at us as we stood staring at him, seethingly, from behind bars.

Phil, our newest mechanic, had been questioned by the police—as had the others—only thing was, this fool not only fuckin' ratted us out but was caught with a half pound of marijuana and two unregistered .44-caliber handguns days later. As usual, Chief Mickey O'Malley brought Phil in for questioning. After about an hour of hard-core interrogation, Phil confessed the intricate details of our undercover drug/arms operation. Shawn and I were each tried and convicted on two counts of possession with intent to distribute. The District Attorney convinced the jury that we were guilty of running an elaborate drug ring but couldn't convince them that we also bought and sold arms. There wasn't enough hard evidence, plus our attorney put up a marvelous defense. At the end of the four and a half hour trial we walked away with one-year sentences and a year's probation. Of course, Uncle Snookey set us up with one of his most loyal lawyers. Silvia A. Katz had been Uncle Snookey's first lawyer back in New Orleans and she also gambled often on his casino showboat "Big Baller" along with her husband, Mr. Henry Katz III, a former Louisiana State Senator with ties to the mob. Uncle Snookey could not attend the proceedings for obvious reasons, so instead he treated the Katzs to an all expense paid trip to Las Vegas for a weekend of gambling and horseback riding out on his ranch in exchange for representing Shawn and me.

Shipped to Ackron Correctional Facility, right outside Peola in early April '90, I served six months, however Shawn not only did the full year but had an extra year tacked on for shanking Phil Bruce in the shower. Phil had to be flown by helicopter to Peola General Hospital's Shock Trauma Unit, because the prison's infirmary didn't have the equipment, or staff, to deal with the severity of his injuries. He nearly died from his wounds and he took almost a year to fully recover. Prison officials at Ackron moved him to another facility in nearby Savannah because Shawn openly vowed that he'd kill him if he ever got another chance. Shawn was always getting into fights, or getting written up for cussing out the correctional officers.

Always tall and slender, Shawn added more than thirty-five pounds of muscle to his frame, spending most of his free time in the yard pumping iron with the old heads. By the time he came out of prison he was somewhere between 210 and 215 pounds...a big leap from his old walk around weight of 170. I was now 20 and stood six-foot three, 245 pounds; however I had always been genetically gifted with muscularity and height. Though sometimes I worked out with Shawn and the cats out in the yard, I mostly spent my recreational hours shooting hoops, or boxing. During my six-month stay I got pretty sharp with my hands too. As a matter of fact, I joined the Ackron facility boxing team and was the youngest member to ever fight for the prison in its 95-year history. I won several prison boxing titles for the "A-Team" as we were called and compiled a prison record of 22 KO's in 25 fights. I never lost or tied a single bout. All that was fun and everything but what I really enjoyed was hustling while I spent time in the joint. I was always about that paper so unlike lots of newbies in the joint I didn't have time to work odd jobs for menial pay within the facility. Immediately, I got with some of the prison's more seasoned inmates who were scoring a little bit and starting talking business. Already popular throughout Ackron for my boxing skills, it didn't take long before I was able to pull some strings of my own. Unlike my cousin, who was a constant nuisance to most of the prison's guard force, I was the exact opposite, winning over even the prison warden with my athleticism and sense of humor.

Correctional Officer Amber Washington was an unbelievably attractive sexpot who almost every man in the joint, inmate and officer alike, wanted a piece of. Amber possessed a pair of soft light gray doe eyes, dark chocolate skin, the texture of smooth satin when touched, and a voluptuous figure accented by a rotund ass, which jiggled with every step she took. Even though she was phat as duck butter, I never did sweat her like everybody else. Shawn tried every trick in his player's arsenal to try and break the ice with the super fine C.O. but always fell short.

"That bitch thinks her shit don't stink. I say fuck da bitch!" Shawn would say after his latest rejection.

"Naw brah, ya game is just too fuckin' weak baby boy," I'd reply jokingly, further fueling his anger.

"Nigga fuck you, let's see yo punk ass try ta pull dat hoe, how bout dat?!" Shawn snapped back while doing sit-ups on our cell floor.

"I ain't trippin' on dat broad like all y'all dick-beatin' niggas round here. Ya see I gets pussy each and every time Donita or Brandi comes up here ta see me which is about three to four times a month, how bout you?" After I said that Shawn flashed me an evil look that let me know that I'd struck a nerve.

"Nigga just grab my fuckin' ankles so I kin knock out dese here sit-ups...damn!"

I chuckled to myself, noticing my cousin's face flush red with anger. "Just fuckin' witcha dawg! ...So sensitive!" I teased using my best gay imitation.

"Shut da fuck up and keep holding my ankles!" Shawn barked, showing a slight smile as he continued sweating through his exercise routine. "And stop talking like a faggot...faggot."

"Takes one ta know one," I quipped. That's when Officer Washington came from around the corner, approaching our cell holding a flashlight. We shielded our eyes from the bright glare of the light flooding into our darkened jail cell.

"You boys getting ya sweat on this time of night?" The sexy C.O. stared at us, me in particular, with those alluring eyes of hers. I got up off the floor and approached the cell door, leaving Shawn to mumble a few words under his breath.

"Kill dat light Miss Lady and come here," I said softly reaching out between the bars for her hand. Amber slightly hesitated, then slowly took my hand into hers all the while smiling devilishly.

"So I'm supposed to stand here and let you two get away with waking the other inmates with your loud talk and late night workouts simply because you 'da man' huh?" Amber asked turning off the flashlight bringing darkness again to the inside of our cell.

I leaned in closer whispering to her all the smooth player talk I could throw at her. Once she begun squealing with laughter I knew I had her. All the girls I ever bedded down I had won over with my sense of humor. Well, maybe not Donita, she pursued me first and at the time I wasn't really interested in her. By the end of April, I was goin' up in April's guts on a regular basis. Everybody knew that I was fucking Amber, because nothing happens inside the joint without somebody getting wind of it. You just have to be down with the right folks to watch ya back and in return you'd watch theirs. My popularity in the joint, served me well. I had many allies both behind bars and on the guard force. Nobody ever said anything negative about Officer Washington's in-house liason and me. Amber knew every nook and cranny of Ackron, and we fucked all over the prison at night during her midnight shift. We screwed in storage rooms, old untraveled hallways and musty stairwells. And in May, when Amber was promoted to Lieutenant we pulled all-nighters as I long stroked her right in the warden's spacious three room office complete with full bathroom, shower, bathtub plus a small lounge area stocked with food and booze in the fridge. We'd stay up all night having ourselves a ball up in the Warden's quarters. Sometimes I'd feel sorry for my cousin Shawn who was straight up trippin' most of the time for one reason or another. If he wasn't fighting someone, or cussing somebody out, he was in solitary confinement. Being the mack that I am, I talked Amber into giving him some ass to relax him a little and help him blow off some steam. He hit the ass maybe three times, but Amber stopped fuckin' with him after that 'cause she claimed that he was far too rough during intercourse and would cum too quickly.

"That's the last time I ever give ya stupid ass cousin some pussy!" Amber said after her last session with Shawn. Seeing that Amber was not only frustrated and angry but still very much, hot and horny, I had no choice but to give her the satisfaction she so desired. I fucked her so well that night, the bitch didn't make rounds at all…she slept for the rest of her shift. Shawn always bragged to me and a few other prisoners how he'd turned Amber out and how she always begged him for more dick whenever she saw him. I'd sit back listening and laughing to myself knowing that he was so full of shit he could've been a dirty diaper. But hey, if it made him feel a little better, and kept him out of trouble then I was cool with that and I'd accomplished my goal.

By the middle of May, I'd hooked up with Lionel Kurtz a.k.a. "The Hawk" a 43-year-old former long shore-man and native Floridian who was currently working on the eighth year of a ten-year sentence for drug trafficking. At five-feet eight inches tall and weighing in at about 150 or 155, Kurtz was not a big guy; however, he was one of the most respected and feared inmates on the C-wing level of Ackron Correctional Facility. Kurtz possessed that keen Jewish eye for business because for the entire eight years he'd been locked up in Ackron every and anything illegal that Ackron's inmate population desired circulated through him—cigarettes, alcohol, drugs, even women. He would arrange for women to come up for an inmate's conjugal visit and perform sexual favors for cash and/or drugs. The Hawk, who got his nickname from the shape of his narrow face with its slightly hooked nose and piercing blue eyes, always got his percentage of the money. If any prisoner paid for his sexual services with dope, he had to first purchase the product from Kurtz before giving it to the trick of his choice. Out of the 1,000-inmate population, only Kurtz had the juice to pull off capers like prostitution, alcohol and drug distribution.

I wanted so bad to be down with Hawk that I spent several sleepless nights figuring out a way to break the ice and approach him about doing business. My chance came one breezy, slightly overcast morning as the majority of the C-Wing level inmates exercised and played ball out in the yard. I noticed Hawk sitting alone in his usual spot on the rickety old bleachers near the basketball court, smoking a Marlboro and taking down orders from customers. I quickly jogged across the yard to him, but he ordered me to stop before I got too close.

"Hey, hey!" he yelled. "Stop right there, and don't run up on me like that! I don't know who you the fuck you are!"

"My bad, my bad...wassup?" I said, trying to calm him down as I got closer to him. "I'm Rae Kwon, my niggas call me Rae-Rae. I seen you out here on the grind everyday, all day. I'm feelin' you dawg, but I got a method that'll make you some real paper man. All you got to do is put me on, we'll work out a percentage a future date." I was sure that Kurtz would take me up on his offer, but the old Jew just grinned at my overconfidence.

"Go fuck yourself," he said still smiling, then went back to his business.

In the past, several prisoners had tried to link up with Kurtz, but were immediately denied access into Lionel Kurtz's wonderful world of money and power. A few of my closer associates within the joint, including my own cousin, were convinced I'd get dissed by The Hawk just like the others before me. However, my optimism proved all the pessimists wrong. Although The Hawk was successful he was just another inmate to the guard force and had to create elaborate schemes and a pinpoint timing process that was both time consuming and exhaustive. Before I was released, Kurtz told me that his intricate criminal business took him two years to develop and three more years to perfect. No guards were aware of what was going on and the only reason no one ratted him out by now was because the vast majority of inmates needed his products, and sought him out on a daily basis. Any would-be snitches most likely would've risked life and limb doing so. It took me a day or two to convince The Hawk to let me come on board and help him make even more money. At first, he was very wary about bringing Amber or any other Correction Officer into his business, and nearly backed out until I assured him that Amber, was not only trustworthy but would benefit him more as an ally than as an enemy.

Shortly after the three of us got together, we started raking in more money than we even imagined. We received most of our narcotics from one of Kurtz's old dope connects from down in Key West, Florida. Although he never revealed the identity of his distributor, there was a rumor among the inmates that Kurtz's connect was a former lieutenant under Panamanian dictator, Manuel Noriega. As for the tricks, The Hawk had been a pimp by trade, so procuring choice prostitutes was simply a matter of placing a phone call or two. Alcohol was smuggled into the joint by two or three of Kurtz's bimbos via his cousin, Marty, who owned a liquor store chain in Savannah. The big bootie hoes posed as wives and girlfriends while on the usual conjugal visits. Every other week, it seemed as though Kurtz, Amber, and I had hired a dozen or more outside workers to assist us in our jailhouse crime ring.

I had both Donita and Brandi drop off packages to me containing pure cocaine, which Amber made sure passed security inspection because she inspected all incoming packages and mail. The warden was away most of the time anyway playing golf down on Hilton Head. No one was around to watch Amber. When summer came around we had to be pulling in anywhere from a $1,000 - $1,200 per week. Not bad considering the fact that most prisoners make only minimum wage with a few exceptions.

Brandi and Donita each came by about twice a month until

I got out in October. I had to be on point when it came to which baby mama was visiting and when so no drama would start. In order to keep the two from mistakenly crossing paths during my visits, I called them regularly to find out when they were coming and insisted that they didn't surprise me. Never once did either female know that the other was coming. Donita was pregnant again during my six months in Ackron. She still looked sexy as hell even with a big pregnant belly. I could see guys lusting after my caramel-complexioned cutie each time she came to visit me. That made me proud to flaunt her about. Brandi, one of the few white girls to ever visit the nearly all-black prison, received wolf-whistles and plenty of cat calls whenever she stepped out of the fresh new Benz I bought her. Usually she came wearing a hip hugging spandex ensemble or for the times she knew we would be fucking, a form fitting miniskirt which revealed her shapely legs and bodaciously plump ass that rivaled that of the thickest sista you could think of. After only two months in the joint I impregnated Brandi again, unfortunately she miscarried in June (around about the same time Lt. Washington found out that she, too, was pregnant with my child). Amber, whose husband was an army sergeant stationed in Fort Benning, had no choice but to have an abortion; she hadn't seen her husband in months, much less slept with him. Actually according to her, she was well taken care of by her top military brass hubby and didn't want anything to fuck that up. After the abortion, Amber never gave up the ass again however she substituted with mind-blowing oral sex, which satisfied me just the same. By the time my six-month sentence came to a close, Amber, Kurtz, and I had netted approximately $10,000 from the five-month drug trafficking enterprise. The monies were split three ways with an extra grand going to The Hawk since it was his business to begin with. I walked away with three grand and I was fairly satisfied with that. I knew that it was only a matter of time before I would be stacking up dollars once my black ass hit the streets.

XII

Treat Ya Nose, Playa

I got out of jail on October 28,1990. Brandi picked me up right outside the gates. Finally, I was able to breathe again as a free man. Brandi also brought me a fresh change of clothes, 'cause I couldn't wait to get out of those baggy bright orange prison jumpers I'd been wearing for six months. Before I went to jail I had both my women hold some cash for me while I was inside. Between the two, I had about eleven thousand put away for safe-keeping, so I spent the first part of the morning collecting my scrilla and visiting with my children. Donita had once again given birth to a son, Jafar Lake, on October 23, 1990, shortly before my release. Donita and I were now 20 and the parents of four children—two-year-old twin boys Rae Kwon, Jr. and Davon; Chantel Latisha Lake, one and a half; and our newborn Jafar. Mrs. Grimes didn't think that her daughter would have a very bright future after having so many children at such a young age especially when she was still with a no-good hoodlum like myself. Mr. Grimes, on the other hand, was his usual supportive, good-natured self and was overjoyed each time Donita present-ed him with a new grandchild. Everybody that I knew gave Donita her props though because while I was doing my dirt, she earned her Bachelor's degree from Savannah State and in the next couple of years her Master's Degree from Georgia Tech University.

Meanwhile, Brandi had completed her G.E.D. and had landed a full time job as a receptionist/rental consultant at Sorrell Dunes apartment complex. She had gotten the job through an old client of the Sultan's Harem Strip Club. This old dude just happened to be a major stockholder in Apex Reality, the realtors who owned the Northern Peola luxury high-rise complex. She told me that all she had to do was suck off the 74-year-old rich geezer a few times while I was inside. She got the position and signed paperwork for his 56% stock in the high-rise complex. Silas A. Minnifield was a long-time stockholder and Brandi made sure that she took immediate advantage of a prime opportunity. I wasn't mad at her for that; Brandi was a survivor capable of using what she had in order to get what she wanted. She may have been white, but after years of exposure to black urban culture, she'd grown just as street smart as the rest of us. Old man Minnifield was worth a little over twenty million dollars and lil' ole Brandi drained at least ten million of that over the last five years of his life. When it was all said and done Brandi had been given five million dollars and at least a portion of his modest estate, much to the chagrin of his surviving relatives.

As for Brandi and me, we still kicked it, even fucked occasionally; however Brandi started attending the Peola Southern Baptist Church located in North Peola near Sorrell Dunes. By the spring of 1991 she was a born again Christian and was moved to preach to me about the evils of drug-dealing each and every time I dropped by to visit with her and our two-year-old daughter, Selena. She had done dirt for so long that she had become a religious zealot who could be seen around town with her Bible and an encouraging word for anyone willing to listen. Brandi stopped dancing and threw out every stitch of 'hoochie mama' clothing that she owned. When she burned over two thousand dollars worth of clothing she claimed that she was, "casting the Devil's wardrobe back to hell from which it came." From that point on she dressed in much more modest attire befitting a devout church-going lady. Soon, she converted old man Minnifield over from Roman Catholic to Southern Baptist, becoming his personal caretaker as well.

Brandi also returned my '90 C-class Benz that I'd bought her saying that she would no longer have anything to do with my dirty money. Her constant preaching and amateur missionary work worked my nerves to no end, but at least she was grounded in her faith and she'd finally found peace with God. Other than our obvious moral differences we still loved each other and Brandi still allowed me to be instrumental in the life of our little Selena.

"I could never remove you from Selena's life…you're her daddy and you'll always be her daddy, it's just that fast, ungodly lifestyle you're livin'. I fear that if you don't change your ways and give your life over to Jesus you may not live to see Selena or any of your other young'uns grow up."

"You know what, Brandi," I replied. "I dunno what's up wit you and all of this brand new 'holier than thou' shit, but you got me fucked up, cuz I'm a true hustla, and I plays the game, the game don't play me. So you ain't gotta worry bout my wig getting' split out here. I ain't never gonna go out like that and leave my kids fatherless. I'm too damn street smart for that, baby girl." She just shook her head.

I needed some money so I immediately invested my money in cocaine hoping I could begin anew. Just when I was ready to rebuild my empire, I found out the DEA had arrested my old coke dealer, Mario Sanchez out of Miami. I had to call Uncle Snookey out west. Uncle Snookey hated talking business over the phone, so he booked me a flight out to Tucson, Arizona where he'd been staying with one of his many girlfriends around the country. I arrived at the airport around 11:35 pm. Uncle Snookey had a white stretch limo waiting to take me over to a sprawling Mexican inspired villa sitting atop a lush mountain range overlooking the twinkling city lights of Tucson. I had only been out of Ackron for two weeks, and my lungs welcomed the fresh mountain air.

As the chauffeur opened the rear door for me to exit I was approached by two heavily muscled bodyguards whom escorted me toward the entrance of the majestic residence. As we approached the ten-foot wrought iron gates, one of the hulking guards punched in a number code, which caused the gates to slowly slide open. Once we entered he again typed in some numbers on the gate's panel, which caused the heavy gates to come together with a loud clanking thud. As the two beefy guards walked with me in silence toward the entrance of the hacienda, I noticed that they were packing heat in the form of two small Uzi submachine guns. The dudes looked either Latino or Native American and walked on either side of me. They didn't speak to me, or each other, and appeared to be quite menacing in their dark clothing and black Fendi sunshades. When we finally got to the huge double doors of the place a gorgeous Latin beauty awaited us in the doorway.

Dressed in a slinky silk night gown which accentuated her sultry sex kitten figure she greeted me in both Spanish and English as she beckoned me to follow her down the hall and out onto the spacious patio where scores of nude and scantily clad beauties of every ethnicity splashed in the pool or lounged and walked around the patio giggling, conversing, and drinking from the bar on the opposite side of the pool. My sexy escort led me over to my Uncle Snookey who was seated near the pool's edge dressed in swim trunks and a Caribbean style straw hat with a big booty cutie sitting across his lap and a bevy of equally fine women surrounding him, giggling and jiggling.

"Come over here Ray-Ray," Uncle Snookey said with a smile, "Dese bunnies won't bite...lest you ask 'em too!" Uncle Snookey quipped amidst the laughter of his bikini clad admirers. "Awiight time fa Big Daddy ta talk bidness, ya'll lil' bitches go 'head and dip in da pool...go' on now!!" Uncle Snookey announced as he arose from his pool chair smacking a young chick on the ass as she hopped off his lap, diving into the pool. Uncle Snookey and I walked over to the bar where he ordered a drink from a tuxedoed bartender behind the counter.

"What would you like Master Lake, Sir?" asked the sharp dressed bartender with a heavy British accent.

"The usual, Stevens," Uncle Snookey said while lighting up a cigarette.

"Of course, Master Lake, one gin and tonic on the rocks coming up Sir...and will the young man be having anything to drink tonight, Sir?" questioned the bartender as he prepared my uncle's drink.

"Long Island Ice Tea for me," I answered quickly while salivating over the dozens of half-naked honeys passing to and fro, several of who gave me seductive looks.

"Right away my debonair young chap." The bartender laughed as he noticed my obvious interests.

"Forgive my nephew, Stevens," Uncle Snookey remarked playfully putting his muscular arm around my neck. "But at his age, he thinks wit his dick more den wit his head."

"Well, I can't say I blame the young man, now," laughed Stevens as he handed us our drinks. "There is temptation aplenty out here on the patio tonight."

"No doubt dawg, no doubt," I responded winking at an Asian beauty as she strode past us accompanied by an Ethiopian girl who looked equally as stunning.

Uncle Snookey smiled slightly as he watched me watching all the eye candy around us. He then snuffed out the butt of the smoldering cigarette into an ashtray at the bar, tipped Stevens and gave him some skin before directing his full attention to me.

"Looka here Ray, let's step inside so we can have some privacy and talk bidness, cause long as we out her on dis patio ya ain't gonna be thinkin' 'bout nuttin cept dese bitches out here, ya heard me?"

I nodded in agreement. "Without a doubt", I responded, following my uncle into the lavishly furnished home.

Once inside Uncle Snookey and I seated ourselves upon a plush leather sofa in the immense living room area. As soon as we sat down we were both waited on by the same lovely Latina who greeted me at the front door earlier that night. My uncle introduced me to his newest girlfriend, Veronica, who warmly welcomed me to their home then exited the room just as suddenly and silently as she came in.

I began telling Uncle Snookey about the difficulty I had trying to find a good cocaine dealer since Mario got busted.

"Mario's got a good head on his shoulders, he's street smart as well as educated, he'll beat dat fifteen year sentence...shit, I'll betcha he'll only do five tops," Uncle Snookey remarked with confidence.

Veronica walked back into the room and placed a small rectangular mirror with three long, thin powdery lines of high grade Columbian Cocaine before us.

"Dis powda right chere come from dis Big Indian outta Alberquerche, New Mexico named Seth Youngblood, big ass white mountain Apache, who used ta play college football at The University of New Mexico. I used ta fuck his sister back in the day when she and I both lived back East during my ABA days. Youngblood likes fuckin' wit planes an all dat shit like ya pops used ta. So he flies down to South America and Central America on a regular, know what I'm sayin? Places like Columbia, Mexico, Panama...shit all da good Coke producin' countries, ya heard me? So take ya self a hit of dis good shit right chere and you tells me what's up." Uncle Snookey smiled as his girl Veronica removed a hundred dollar bill from between her bulging cleavage and handed it to him. He quickly rolled it into a tight little make shift straw, passing it to me he nodded in anticipation of my sampling the coke. Even though I'd sold cocaine for as long as I could remember I'd never snorted it...at all. I was strictly a weed and alcohol man myself, but I figured that if I had to sample a product of mine for business...so be it. Taking the rolled up bill in my left hand I leaned down toward the coffee table and placed one end of the bill into my left nostril while the other end was directed toward the first line of coke.

"Snort a half line in one nostril den snort the rest in da other," Uncle Snookey instructed me obviously seeing my awkwardness. I listened to what my uncle said taking the first hit strong and fast up my left nostril. The potent sting of the cocaine seemed to singe my virgin nostril. As it brought a tear down my left eye, I violently threw my head back from the immediate rush. The coke induced just that fast. The remaining coke residue tickled the interior of my nostril such that I tweaked my nose several times in order to relieve the itching sensation.

"Oh yeah, dat was a damn good hit Rae-Rae. Go ahead and polish off the rest," Uncle Snookey grinned as I leaned in to snort the rest of the line. The second line I snorted produced the same head rush and itchy nostril as before, only now my entire nose felt numb and I was overcome with an exhilarating sense of pleasure and tremendous euphoria.

"Daaamn! I'm higher than a muthafucka!" I exclaimed glassy eyed and giddy, chuckling foolishly from the cocaine-induced dreaminess.

"Yeah dat's the shit I'm talking 'bout my nigga! Dis shit ain't no joke Rae! Cats be buyin' dis shit up out here Ray. Muthafuckas be on dis 'caine so hard you gotta beat dey ass off wit a bat ta keep dem up off you. Now when ya cook dis shit up, ya damn sho nuff gonna have niggas givin up dey whole pay-check, ya feel me?" Uncle Snookey snorted a line as he spoke and administered about four hits to his brickhouse girl Veronica from a small tin box filled to the rim with Coke. He'd had the box inside the drawer of the coffee table and also had a long slender spoon inside it, which he had Veronica snort small heaps of cocaine with.

After I finished up the last of the cocaine lying untouched on the little rectangular mirror, Uncle Snookey gave me a message and warning, "Rae-Rae, I know right now you ain't got no steady income comin' in. If you'se any way like I think ya are you had somthin' put away befo' you gots locked up. If so, good, if not dat's OK too. 'Cause you is my brother's child and I gotta take care of you. I'm gonna get Veronica's brothers Manuel and Filipo, the bodyguards that you met outside ta take a flight out there round two or three a.m. this morning and buy a kilo up off 'em. That'll getcha started. Don't worry 'bout payin' me back. That's my gift ta you, Ray. You can sell it as is or break it down and cook it up, and sell it as rocks. Whatever da fuck you feel, 'cause no matter how you sell it, it's gonna sell. Trust a nigga on dat one. Ya see niggas down dere in Peola ain't never had no shit like dis here, ya heard so when you get back home you gonna have muthafuckas flockin' ta you like flies on shit," Uncle Snookey paused to tongue kiss Veronica as she enticingly ran her fingers through his kinky chest hairs. "Go get us some champagne baby. I want dat 1933, vintage from down in the cellar," Uncle Snookey told Veronica, smacking her playfully on her ass as she rose to fetch the champagne from the cellar.

"Now back to you, son. I know that when you got locked up, you and Shawn was makin' a killin' off dem rich crackas down dere in lil' ole Peola, but getting' locked up is a part of the risk you gotta take in da game. I'll admit you'se a natural, hell ya took ta hustlin' like an otter takes to water. That's why I trusted you from the jump. Even way back then when you was just four-teen. Now you'se 'bout to turn 21…a grown ass man. I'm prou-da ya, but I can't always say the same thing 'bout my own chillen…the twins, I love'em ta death, dat's my seed right dere. But they both too damn old ta be carrying on like they do, and I'm fuckin' fed up wit da shit.

Shawn, for da most part, can handle his bidness without too much drama, but Dawn…her little ass is just straight off da chain ya heard! Ya see I know 'bout da arrest warrant and shit dat da Chief of Police Mickey O'Malley has out fa me. Ya see ya'll don't know how far me and dat fat nasty Irish punk go back," Uncle Snookey took another coke hit off the glass from a line he'd put down as we spoke. He put down a second line of powder and offered it to me. I obliged and snorted it down in one strong inhalation.

My uncle started telling me all about his youthful run-ins with the law back when he was a teenager and how he and my dad got busted early on in his criminal career by late police Chief Rossum, who was but a rookie cop at the time. Veronica came up from the basement with the champagne that Uncle

Snookey requested and placed the vintage bottle into a small pail of crushed ice. Uncle Snookey took out a cigarette, lighting up immediately. Putting his arm around me, he pulled me in close in order for me to hear just what was on his mind.

"Rae-Rae, you gotta leave dat fuckin' Peola alone dawg. Shit's too hot in dat little town, right now. Ya see dat was yo first time getting' locked up, but cha best believe if you hang around in dis dope game long enough, oh, you'll definitely see the po-po again! So whatcha gotta do is always change ya surroundings and be more careful of who ya fuck wit. Ya gots two types of muthafuckas out here: Fuck-Ups and Haters. The Fuck-Ups, ya see don't mean ya no harm per-se, but they can and will fuck up the most simple assignments at the most crucial times. And of course Haters, you gotta just straight bleed dem type niggas. Now my twins...I love em, hell yeah, like any good father should...but sometimes they just don't get it...they fuck up regularly, especially my little girl. 'Cause of her, I damn near went to jail a few years back. Shit, you remember her blowin' up some bouncer and his boys a couple years back, right?" Uncle Snookey asked.

I nodded, "Yeah, I remember," I said pouring myself a glass of bubbly still very much high from the cocaine I snorted earlier.

"Well, I'm tellin' ya ta go somewhere anywhere 'cept back down to Peola. Shit, I don't give a fuck if you go elsewhere in da state of Georgia; Atlanta, Augusta, Athens, anywhere but Peola and Savannah, which is like being in Peola still. I moved out here ta get away from O'Malley and all da other po-pos down dere who got dirt on me. Dem muthfuckas got enough shit in me ta turn me over to da Feds. Now if you or da twins get in ta any more shit down dere, it's gonna fall back on me, 'cause I'm da real nigga dem muthafuckas want, know what I'm sayin? Dey wants to bust you or my kids in order ta bring heat down on me. I been duckin' dem peoples fa a long time now and I know dat O'Malley. He ain't gonna quit till' he gets me behind bars...Fuck dat shit! I ain't goin' out like dat, ya heard me?!"

"Awiight...you got dat Uncle Snookey!" I said somewhat taken aback by Uncle Snookey's sudden mood swing.

Snookey poured himself a glass of champagne as his girl ran her fingers through his curly hair kissing him gently on his forehead trying to calm his nerves.

"I trust that you'll do the right thing nephew, 'cause I ain't goin' ta jail fa nobody...I don't give a fuck who it is, ya heard?" Uncle Snookey paused then afterwards gave me an icy look, a look I've seen only when he'd made his mind up about murdering someone. He'd never looked at me like that before and to tell you the truth, it scared the hell out of me. However, I didn't let my Uncle know that.

"Okay Rae, go outside and mingle with all the lil' honeys, I know dats whatcha wanna do anyhow," Uncle Snookey said, returning to his earlier relaxed attitude. "Oh yeah, here ya go. Take dis canister of coke outside. Once you get dem lil' bitches snortin' some of dis good shit, you'll be knee deep in pussy." Uncle Snookey smiled broadly, his gold-capped teeth glistening under the lights from the overhead chandelier. Once I heard that, I felt much better and quickly relieved him of the container. Once outside on the patio, I began interacting with the girls who were guests of Uncle Snookey and came over to his mountain top villa every other weekend to enjoy two days of wild revelry and decadence. Uncle Snookey's love interest Veronica De La Hoya, a distant relative of the famous L.A.-based middleweight champion, owned the largest escort service in the Southwest. "Veronica's Assorted Sweets" could be found throughout Arizona, New Mexico, Nevada, Arkansas, Missouri, and much of Texas. Most of the two dozen or more lovelies who attended these weekends spent hour after hour partying, and having sex...just think marathon sex with dozens of dimes. I don't know where they came from, but it seems that every hour several different dudes showed up. At the time, I assumed they were friends of my uncle, but he later told me those cats were customers who paid anywhere from $2,500 to $3,000 to spend a weekend at "Veronica's Villa" indulging in every erotic fantasy imaginable. After a weekend's worth of livin' la vida loca,

Uncle Snookey had Seth Youngblood, himself, fly me from Arizona back to Georgia. The flight itself was cool, except for the turbulence caused by a thunderstorm we encountered flying across Tennessee. Every few minutes, I couldn't help but reminisce about my dead parents and how weather just like this took their lives away in an airplane crash so many years ago. I wasn't afraid though, just uncomfortable with the constant shake, rattle, and roll of the small three passenger airplane. I had a long detailed conversation with Youngblood on our flight to Peola. By the time I was safely standing on red Georgia clay, he became another important contact.

Triple Crown Publications presents

XIII

Southern Style Bullet Wounds

For the remaining two months of 1990, I did as Snookey suggested and moved away from Peola, Georgia. Donita was not very happy about my decision to move, but I kept in contact with her often, so eventually, she got over it. On the weekends I returned to visit with her and the kids as well as Brandi and our daughter. I my absence, I'd send money to Donita for both her and the kids. Although I sent money to Selena, Brandi refused to accept it, preaching her usual anti-crime sentiments. It wasn't until Brandi and I sat down and had a long talk that she loosened up a little, allowing me to buy my baby girl clothing and toys.

In December, Brandi and Selena moved back to Miami, Florida, where Brandi lived in luxury off of the inheritance from old man Minnifield. Her brief religious leaning also went belly up as soon as she hit the bright lights and fast paced life of sunny Miami. She reverted right back to the stripper she had once been. Even though she was stripping, she was and damn good mother. She reminded me so much of my own damn mother who had been an adult film actress up until the day she died, but never did she neglect me once. Needless to say, I was happy that Brandi was no longer, "holier than thou." It didn't take long for me to get her back into bed...my beloved Brandi had returned to me.

103

When I moved out of Peola in December 1990, I went to Hilton Head Island to live with my Aunt Melissa. It was cool at first, because my aunt and I had always been close, but it was her punk ass new boyfriend that ruined things. Aunt Melissa lived out in a palatial condominium overlooking a vast 18-hole golf course in the front of the residence and a picturesque sandy white beach immediately to the rear of the condo.

Every Saturday night, Aunt Melissa, myself and several of her friends would go over to the Palmetto Dunes condominiums and read poetry, drink chardonnay, and play chess—real high-society shit. Adam Nolan was an ex-marine who liked bossing people around and enjoyed showing off in front of crowds, especially groups of attractive women. Boisterous and loud, he almost always came off as an overbearing, arrogant asshole. We never liked each other that much and from what Dawn told me he even approached her sexually two or three times during her brief stay with her moms. Dawn said that cussing him out and threatening him with bodily harm only seemed to arouse his passions even more. Finally, when she approached her mother about Adam's doggish behavior, Auntie lashed out at her, calling her a liar and a flirt which caused their already strained relationship to deteriorate even more.

One afternoon, after I'd gotten back from visiting Brandi and Selena down in Miami, Aunt Melissa had thrown a birthday party for his bitch ass. I went into the condo greeted all the guests there, including Adam and showered. When I was through I got dressed in my flyest Armani gear because I was scheduled to meet with my parole officer at 2:30 p.m. sharp and then I had a date with this fine ass ex-model to go to party for one of my homies, Ernest Bryan, of the powerfully notorious Fuskie Crew. I couldn't be late.

On my way out the door, I overheard a commotion out in the living room. When I went to investigate, Adam, who'd obviously had one shot of bourbon too many, was groping one of Aunt Melissa's best friends Tawanna Fife. Aunt Melissa and her sister, Daphne, had stepped out to the grocery store to purchase some food for the party. And now Adam was showing his true colors in front of her girlfriends who were standing around stunned and frightened. Adam was a big man standing 6'4" and tipping the scales at a hefty 245 pounds of rock hard muscle from his days as a marine drill sergeant. Ms. Fife, pleaded with him to unhand her. Her pleas went unanswered by the drunken Adam who was literally trying to rape the poor lady right in front of everyone there. Rushing into the living room I pushed the inebriated punk with all of my might in the back sending the big lush stumbling head first into the couch.

"You awiight?" I asked Ms. Fife who was obviously traumatized. I gently led the weeping lady into the reassuring arms of her girl friends as I got back to the business of kicking Adam's ass. It took only ten more minutes for me to completely hammer the 43-year-old ex-marine sergeant into submission. (A lot of my friends teased me later on saying that it wasn't a fair fight because dude was half way drunk.)

Dude never pressed any charges against me. His bruised ego wouldn't allow it. That was fortunate for me too because had he filed charges against me I would have been in some deep shit...probably would've ended up in jail again for breaking probation. Aunt Melissa was furious with the both of us when she learned what happened even though her girlfriends insisted that I was merely coming to Ms. Fife's aid in a terrible situation. Aunt Melissa didn't want to hear it. But unlike her daughter I didn't wait around for her to kick me out of her crib. By the end of the week I had packed my shit and had Donita pick me up at Aunt Melissa's. From there I had her drop me off at Dawn's apartment in Savannah, because I wasn't quite ready to buck Uncle Snookey's authority and show up in Peola just yet. I stayed with Dawn until March 1991.

It was convenient; I didn't have to pay rent. Dawn was also living rent-free thanks to her old ass sugar daddy, crematory owner Lindsey Robbins, who rented the shitty one bedroom apartment for her. The four months that I lived with Dawn was cool enough. It was always fun hanging out with the twins, because there was never a dull moment with those two around. Shawn was due to be released on April 17, 1991 and the both of us were anxiously awaiting the day. The only thing that I did-n't like about living with Dawn was her trifling housekeeping. I don't know maybe it's because I'm a Virgo or some shit but I've always been a neat freak and a hater of sloppiness and slovenly living conditions.

Living with Dawn was like living in a homeless shelter. Dirty dishes were stacked one on top of the other in the sink for days, maybe even weeks. Dirty laundry littered the floor and her bed-room. The bathroom had makeup items, perfume bottles, and feminine hygiene shit everywhere. Several times I even had to get at her about leaving used sanitary napkins lying around on the floor. Roaches crawled all over the joint and her furniture was in disrepair. There was no fuckin' way I was gonna sleep in that nasty motherfucker at all. So I fucked around and hired a maid service to come and clean the apartment, and I also hired an exterminator to come out and spray down the whole place. It took the maid service two days to clean Dawn's grimy apart-ment. Finally, the apartment was tidy, sanitary and free of pests. You see I couldn't understand how in the hell someone like Dawn kept a pickle jar filled with nothing less than fifty dollar bills, walked around with almost every type of credit card known to man, and got behind the wheel of a different sports car every other week could live so foul. I told her this too. She sim-ply shrugged it off or playfully gave me the finger.

I kept a kilo of cocaine at Dawn's and although my uncle had warned me about making drug sales in either city it was kind of difficult not to sell anything. While I was in South Carolina, during my brief stay with Aunt Melissa, I bought around a pound of sinsemillia from some cats I knew in the Spanish Wells section of Hilton Head Island. It helped me get by. But at 21, I needed to make at least three to five grand per day or else I felt like I was broke. Dawn was getting scrilla from her sugar daddy every week and double when his wife was out of town; plus, she was fucking with this heroin dealer out of Ridgeland, S.C. She helped deal 'smack' for him and also got in on a 'hit' or two down in S.C. Dawn introduced us to each other and we hit it off like we'd known each other for years. Tall and lanky, Cameron Jacobs, A.K.A. C.J., kind of resembled Snoop Dogg. C.J., or 'Skinny Pimp,' as he was known in his hometown of Ridgeland, S.C., came from a long line of pimps and pushers. He told us once that his father before him had been perhaps the South's most prominent pimp running prostitutes from Savannah, GA to Key West, FL. He had no reservations about mentioning that his own mother was one of his father's numerous hoes.

Instantly, I felt as though C.J. was a kindred spirit to me especially since my own late mother had been a hoe of sorts. C.J. may have been a dealer, but there was none more kind and loyal to friends and family then he. He had a habit of purchasing the latest sportswear and designer sneakers for the local and underprivileged youngsters of Savannah's high crime Hitch Village and Yamacraw projects. C.J. routinely played the dual role of good guy/bad guy; pleasant and saint-like on the one hand and on the other cold-hearted and demonic. However, in his chosen field of work at times 'nasty' was necessary. And to illustrate how nasty C.J. could be, in March '91, I believe it was a Saturday evening, we'd just finished eating dinner at a buffet-style restaurant inside Ogelthorpe Mall, when C.J. spotted some cat that owed him money. C.J. didn't say a word to me or to the squat, partially bald, forty-something shopper as he trailed him out of the mall into the parking lot and toward his car.

"What's up dawg? Why is you followin' dis dude like you bout ta fuck him up?

With a straight face and not even making eye contact with me, C.J. replied, "'Cause I'm gonna." As the unsuspecting man approached his beat up gray Honda Civic, he lowered his shopping bags to the ground and fished around in his pockets for his car keys. When he finally found them he turned to unlock the trunk but instead found himself staring down the nickel plated barrel on a nine millimeter Desert Eagle semi-automatic handgun. The startled man jumped back suddenly dropping his keys to the ground.

"C-C-C.J.!! What da fuck is you doin'?!" the frightened man asked nervously.

C.J. didn't say a word for at least twenty seconds as he kept the pistol leveled on the terrified shopper. "Ray-Ray, come pat dis boy's pockets down, cuz," C.J. said as he got closer to the man, grabbing him roughly by the collar until the menacing point of the Desert Eagle was pressed against his temple. After a brief shake down, I easily managed to come up with about seventy-five dollars in cash. C.J. frowned and became even angrier when he noticed that all his money was not available.

"Get in da car!" C.J. barked pushing dude into his Honda headfirst. "Looka here nigga. I'm 'bout tired of playin' wit yo stinkin' ass partna, so you'se best ta be comin' up wit my cash." C.J. seemed agitated as he looked around the parking lot surveying the immediate area for cops. C.J. motioned for me to hop into the vehicle. "Come on Rae! Hop in dawg. We 'bout to go for a little ride." C.J. grabbed the poor whimpering fool up by his collar, placing the point of the pistol against his blubbery right side.

"Awiight porkchop I'm gonna give yo' fat ass one mo chance to gimme ma paper...you kin borrow it, steal it, rob it, whateva you gotta do, I don't give a fuck but you betta be comin' up wit my shit by da time we git up outta dis dirty ass hooptie you got or else you gonna be catchin' some hotballs, you got dat fatboy?!"

"Y-y-yes sir!" he answered sheepishly.

From that point on C.J. forced "Porkchop" to drive to an ATM in an unfamiliar area. Once there, Porkchop was instructed to withdraw every penny from his savings account. Without hesitation Porkchop did what he was asked and handed over $1,600 in cash to an anxiously waiting C.J.

"Here's all the money and some extra...now please young brah let me go...please!!"

C.J. laughed at the amount of fear shown by the trembling old head behind the wheel. C. J. asked if I wanted to drive; I agreed and he demanded that Porkchop hop in the back.

Porkchop did so with no resistance whatsoever and even promised to give us the car if we'd simply allow him to go free unharmed. I didn't see a problem with that and seemingly neither did C.J. who was giving Porkchop a stern warning about prompt and complete reimbursement of any cash loan to which Porkchop agreed whole-heartedly. By the time we got to our destination, Yamacraw Village, two loud gun shots rung out from the passenger's side to my right startling me so much that I nearly ran slam off the side street and into the dumpsters beyond it.

"Nigga! What da fuck is wrong wit you!!" I yelled instantly turning around to witness the gory scene behind me. Porkchop was missing the entire rear of his head because it was all over the backseat and rear windows. The fat man's dead eyes stared ahead lifelessly as the two small bullet entrance wounds begun to trickle fresh blood down his face, while spongy yellowish chunks of brain matter stuck to the rear windows and ceiling like pieces of bloody cottage cheese. C.J. leaned back and placed the nine millimeter's barrel into the corpse's chest once again pulling the trigger. The force of the blast caused Porkchop's lifeless body to heave forward abruptly before slumping back into the seat and sliding over to the side.

"Ya see cuz," C.J. said, leaning to me. "Ya can't let a stupid muthafucka go on livin' cause it just ain't right, ya know what I'm sayin? Specially if dat stupid muthafucka done fucked around an borrowed a "grip" from you and tried to duck payin' ya back. Fuck dat shit dawg! I'll blow dis muthafucka's brains out and ten mo' dat look just like 'em, please believe dat! Now come on Rae, let's get rid of dis here whip along wit Porkchop's ole shot up ass."

I gripped the steering wheel and closed my eyes a second. Hell, I even chuckled to myself; here once again I had gotten myself into some bullshit not of my own doing. When C.J. said that he was gonna fuck dude up, I didn't know he was going to murder this cat, at least not while we were riding down the street and shit.

That shit right there fucked my whole day up; as a matter of fact for the rest of the week I couldn't quite sleep comfortably. Now I'd seen plenty of people get killed, especially back in the day when my Uncle Snookey first got me into the drug game. I even helped him dispose of several bodies in my early teens. So it didn't bother me that he peeled dude's wig back an all, like I said C.J. was a crazy outta control type individual, just like my cousin Dawn. Those two were a match made in hell. But I was still on probation and I just could not afford to have anything happening that could jeopardize me, I was determined to stay out of jail from now on, at all costs.

At the end of March '91 I bailed out of Dawn's apartment. Although I loved being around Dawn and C.J., the two of them would eventually end up in jail or dead in a back ally somewhere and I just wasn't going out like that.

"This is for you to go out and buy some new fuckin' furniture and keep dis raggedy apartment up," I said handing her about two grand for my time at her crib.

"Nigga, you know good damn well dat I'm gonna blow all dis cake on some Fendi or Gucci shit."

I shook my head laughing to myself as I left. "Tell dat nigga C.J. I'll be stayin' in Ridgeland for a while."

Dawn raced to the door and stood between the doorway and me. "Who is she? Come on, tell me what little hoochie mama is you layin' up wit now." Dawn stood in front of me with her arms folded, tapping her foot impatiently awaiting my response.

I sighed deeply then acted as though I'd give in to her prying. "Come here I'll tell you in your ear." I had my cousin leaning in close to get the scoop. "Deez Nuuutttsss!!" I whispered jokingly in Dawn's ear.

"Boy you play too damn much!" Dawn snapped, slapping me hard on my left shoulder blade. "Dat's why I'm gonna tell Donita you ain't nuttin but a hoe," Dawn yelled at me sarcastically as I descended the narrow winding stairs leading from her upper tier apartment.

Turning around I flipped my cousin the bird. "Takes one to know one."

Dawn ran from her front door to her bedroom window to get a glance of the female picking me up in the sleek black and gold Lexus LS coup. I was off and into the distance before Dawn rushed downstairs.

XIV

Pimp Juice Flowin'

Diamond was the ex-model I'd met a month earlier in Hilton Head. We'd had lunch a few times and talked regularly over the phone. She lived out in Ridgeland, another one of South Carolina's sleepy low country, down-home towns. Working as a dentist on the island, Diamond Harrison made over seventy-five grand a year, a hell of a salary, especially for the low-income area. The 24-year-old resided in a wonderfully furnished double wide mobile home situated on two and a half acres of land, nestled behind a thick grove of Spanish Moss laden Carolina Oak trees. Diamond's place was a baller's hideaway; a veritable safe haven surrounded by ten-foot tall iron wrought fencing and nearly a dozen huge free roaming rottweilers. The dogs were well trained by Diamond and would attack anyone who Diamond commanded them to. Other than that they were all just like playful puppies, only much bigger.

During the whole time I'd known Diamond, I wanted to get her in bed. Standing a svelte six-foot, with short cropped wavy hair, almond shaped, bedroom eyes and devilishly deep dimples which accented a beautiful smile, Diamond had it goin' on in the looks department. Her physique, though slender, was quite shapely and pleasing to the eye, especially her long beautiful legs and juicy round behind. But baby was a virgin. Something I didn't know until the very night we slept together. The pussy wasn't exceptionally tight and impenetrable as I'd thought it would be. It was very wet when I entered her and only her awkwardness and slight apprehension due to my penis size gave away her secret.

"Please be gentle with me Rae Kwon, cause this is my first time being with anyone ya know." Reassuring Diamond that I'd make sure that she'd never forget her first time, I smothered her with passionate kisses all over her mouth and neck. Diamond seemed to resist me slightly only to give way to her own mounting desire initiated by my sweet caresses which began at the nape of her slender neck trailing down toward her firm breasts. I listened intently as Diamond's breathing became increasingly heavy while I licked and sucked her erect nipples. Diamond began to perspire as I kneaded her tits within my huge palms, causing her to wiggle about the sleigh bed anxiously yearning for the raging fire between her thighs to be quenched.

"Ooohh...ooohh, please fuck me, please, ooohhh!!! Diamond pleaded as my hungry tongue worked it's way down her abdomen, across her belly button and into the pouting lips of her dripping vagina.

"Ohhh, fuck! Ooohhh shit!...Baby don't s...stop please!" I felt Diamond's slender fingers pressed tightly against my cornrows as she pushed my head down, placing the entirety of my face deep within her moist, pink crevice. Diamond let out a sharp shriek as she reached the point of no return, then while her tense muscles relaxed slightly, she seemed to whimper and moan with each subsiding spasm. "Ooohhh...my...God! Damn that was good!" Diamond moaned practically out of breath and dripping sweat. I hadn't cum yet and I was merely priming her to take the dick, so as Diamond lay nude upon the moistened satin sheets of the king sized sleigh bed looking incredibly sexy, I took my dick into my hand while stroking it several times bringing it to a completely rigid state of erection, then I dangled my member near her face.

At first she seemed unsure about what to do, that's when I began my smooth talk, coaxing her to take me into her mouth. Soon Diamond was licking the head of my dick so good I nearly shot off right in her mouth. But I wanted to stand up in that pussy so I let her lick and suck on my dick for a minute so that she could get used to the process, because fucking with me she had to learn how to give good brain. Diamond wasn't the best dick sucker in the world, not like Brandi, or even Donita for that matter. But she sure as hell was nasty with her oral service. Lots of saliva and slurping sounds went along with her brain clinics. When I finally deflowered her, I had her give it to me doggy style. I might have started off slow and easy but about fifteen minutes into our love making I was slamming my 9 1/2 inch rod into her virgin pussy with the energy and force of a jack hammer, and Diamond was loving every minute of my thug passion.

"Fuck me baby oohhh...shit...fuck meee!! Diamond squealed out loud.

"Ya want dis dick...huh? Ya want dis dick bitch?" I moaned to her, a phrase that seemed to incite more lust in Diamond instead of anger at me for calling her out her name. With each and every punishing thrust Diamond buried her face deeper and deeper into the mauve colored pillows. My thick fingers sunk into the baby soft flesh of her full hips as I pulled her back toward me, each time I thrusted forward. Diamond's pump ass cheeks rippled like Jell-O. Finally, I couldn't take it anymore and I exploded deep within the walls of Diamond's sweet pussy. Diamond and I collapsed in exhaustion, sweaty in a post-sex embrace accompanied by the sexually charged ballads of R. Kelly. The next morning I awoke to find that Diamond had left for work about an hour earlier. It was 9:30 a.m. and she had a note attached to the refrigerator's door.

Rae Kwon,

You may drive my Bronco to take care of any errands you might have. You'll find breakfast in the microwave and I've left $20 and my Visa Card on the bedroom dresser so that you can gas up the truck and shop or something while you're out.

Luv Ya!

Diamond

P.S. I get off today at 5:30p.m.be prepared for round 2!

XOXOXO

Smiling to myself I crumpled the little handwritten note toss-ing it into a wastebasket in the corner. After eating breakfast I rounded up the rotties outside and fed all of them, then dipped after locking the door and activating the alarm. Diamond was a health nut who didn't drink, get high, or smoke cigarettes. She didn't mind if I did those things around her as long as I didn't smoke weed in her crib because any type of smoke caused her asthma to act up.

I kept my kilo of coke at her home with the promise that there'd be no transactions at her home whatsoever. Though her demands caused me to put in a little more work getting the coke around to buyers, it was okay. I knew that I was living rent free and was getting my brains fucked out two, sometimes three, times a day as well as being served hearty meals regularly. A nigga couldn't really complain all that much, for real. Plus, I mostly hung out at C.J.'s crib, which was only about fifteen min-utes away by car. It was at C.J.'s that most customers dropped by to pick up packages of dope. Business was strong but not near-ly as bountiful as I'd hoped it to be. Sitting in the crib one day I was watching the news on channel 11 when the anchors announced that a Cameron Jacobs of Ridgeland, S.C. was taken into custody for the murder of Edward C. Hilliard of the Hitch Village Projects on Savannah's East side. Apparently, Chatham County police discovered Porkchop's decomposing corpse par-tially buried in a shallow grave next to a marshy wooded area about fifteen miles outside of Peola.

I was both livid and nervous all at the same time. Would C.J. snitch? Would any witnesses appear? Did they trace the slugs found inside Porkchop's cadaver with the Desert Eagle handgun used by C.J. to commit the murder? What happened to Porkchop's Honda Civic? Man, I fucking going crazy with worry over that shit. I didn't even bother telling Diamond what it was that was troubling my mind. I'd just disappear and go to an area bar and get drunk or ride around town to any of the local playgrounds with the rock looking for some cats to hoop with. But after getting into two fistfights (both of which I won easily), Diamond pleaded for me to cut back on my drinking and to stay out of the bars.

"Rae Kwon if you want to relieve some stress then you can do it here at home baby, I don't want you going out here getting into trouble or worse." Diamond pleaded.

I'd laugh reassuring her that I could more than adequately take care of myself out on the streets. "Listen here babygirl, you ain't gotta worry bout nothin' happenin to me down here in dis lil' ole' backwater town. I'm from New Orleans...murder capitol of the whole fuckin' nation. Dese country ass nigga don't wanna see me. On top of that I'm straight vicious wit da hands boo!" I joked throwing playful punches at Diamond before finally grabbing her and hoisting her into my arms lovingly.

"Quit! boy you play too much!!" Diamond giggled kicking and squirming trying to break free from my grasp. We both fell onto the living room sofa, wrestling and tussling like first-graders. One thing led to another and soon we were making passionate love right there on the living room couch as Oprah talked to guest who wanted to reveal a secret.

If only she knew who she was fucking with, I thought to myself as I looked into Diamond's unknowing eyes.

XV

X Marks the Spot

April 5, 1991. Diamond called to say that she wouldn't be home until around 8:00 or 8:30 p.m. That gave me some time to start separating the kilo of coke I had out back in the tool shed. The dogs, though used to me by now, would on occasion act crazy if I attempted to venture too far out back when Diamond wasn't there. A while ago, I almost put some bullets in Diva, the oldest of the purebred German Rottweilers and matriarch of the group, for charging at me. Trial and error taught me that if I fed the dogs well before I made a trip outside they usually just laid around the yard sleeping or maybe gnawing on one of the many plastic chew toys littering the yard, but they didn't pay any attention to me at all not even old Diva herself. Even still, I always packed my trusty tech-nine whenever I went out into the yard while Diamond was out.

I fed the mutts and then went out into the shed and took out the powder. I'd been sitting on this white goldmine for damn near two months now. I didn't want to sell it in Savannah because of Uncle Snookey's warning and also because my cousin Dawn means well but she's damn greedy when it comes to cash. I didn't see a need to share my profits with her since she was already getting money from Lindsey Robbins in exchange for sex, she also was getting money and drugs from C.J. Thankfully, she has a stash saved to get C.J.'s skinny ass outta trouble. Main man only did a week in a Chatham County jail.

Dawn got him out on a $2,200 bail. When his case finally went to court in mid April, the district attorney didn't have enough hard evidence to convict him of murder; he was acquitted. The two lawyers that C.J. had representing him were as sharp as they come according to my cousin Dawn, the news reporter of the projects.

Since March, Diamond had been supporting me. I didn't have to buy anything; she bought me an entirely new wardrobe. I was always treated to full course meals, plus I got to push either the Lex or the Bronco whenever I needed to with the exception of weekdays when she drove her Lexus to work. It was like being married without having papers on you. But I soon grew bored with the monotonous routine of being a live-in-lover because I knew that sooner or later Diamond was going to hint around at tying the knot and a nigga just wasn't ready for all that yet. So finally I cooked up some rocks; enough to get me started on my way. By the time Diamond came home from the office I'd completely broken down the kilo and had it divided into one part crack and one part powder. Hilton Head's, population of affluent residents, would serve me quite well in getting back on my feet financially.

I contacted my good friend Ernest Bryan whom I knew from the short stay with Aunt Melissa on the island. Ernest knew anybody who was important on Hilton Head and was the former head honcho of the Fuskie Krew, a large and extremely violent loose-knit group of drug trafficking youth originating from Daufuskie Island, a small island next door to Hilton Head. Paralyzed due to injuries resulting from a failed gangland hit, Mr. Bryan, who at one time masterminded the criminal organization which had the entire Beaufort County region on lock down, now invested his time in providing adequate low income housing to the needy residents of Hilton Head and Bluffton. He also helped to restore Singleton Beach, a summer hangout for most of the island's black youth as well as a favorite haunt of several figures of criminal notoriety, including Lamont 'Big Gabby' Cantrell, a colossal man weighing damn near three hundred pounds, who insisted on being chauffeured everywhere by limo. He owned several popular nightclubs around the region including the trendy Sand Dollar Lounge located right on the beach itself. Gabby had many of the same connections as did Ernest with the exception being that Ernest was no longer actively involved in drug trafficking or any other criminal activity while Big Gabby had his huge hands involved in business interests both legal and illegal. There were also other assorted thugs and underworld types whom vacationed at Singleton Beach, however I didn't know them all by name.

April in South Carolina's coastal regions felt like summer time, as far as the heat and humidity were concerned. It was nothing to take to the beach on an early April day and discover it was crowded. Once I arrived at the beach, Ernest, or Ernie as he was more commonly known by associates, was patiently awaiting me, sitting behind the wheel of a pimped out burgundy and gold Lincoln Town Car casually puffing on a thick blunt while paying close attention to the activities of the beachgoers. Ernie greeted me as I approached the drivers' side window.

"Sup playa, whey you been?" Ernie asked pulling down his gold rimmed personality glasses a bit across the bridge of his nose in order to glance at an attractive group of thong-wearing beach bunnies passing just ahead of us.

"Ain't been doin' too much a nuttin', lately cept chillin wit my girl in Ridgeland," I answered taking the blunt Ernie passed to me.

"Come on and git in da whip…it's hotter den a bitch out there." Without hesitation I quickly made my way into the air-conditioned haven of the Lincoln. Once seated, I questioned Ernie about possible clients to sell coke to.

"You know I don't fuck around like dat no mo' playa…but Big Gabby should be ya man. Dawg he still wit all dat shot-callin' big-ballin' shit."

"Awiight den hook a nigga up, shit!" I quipped taking in a lung-filling inhalation of hydro smoke. Ernie casually reached down pulling a cell phone from his waist belt, dialing numbers quickly as he took the blunt from my hand smoking the rest of it down to an insignificant roach. While Ernie began speaking with who I assumed was none other than Big Gabby I began toying with his JVC stereo system and fishing through his vast collection of cassettes. Finally settling on an N.W.A. tape, I reclined my seat. While enjoying my cannabis-induced buzz and taking in the beauty of the beach with it's gorgeous white sand, laden with driftwood, as the incessant call of seagulls above, intermingling with the laughter of vacationers completed the perfect pre-summer scenario to which I was drawn into a day dream that temporarily separated reality from my state of euphoria.

"Rae Kwon! ...Rae Kwon!" Ernie's booming voice and his consistent shaking of my shoulder abruptly snapped me out of my brief nirvana like high. "Damn dawg, you was gone...dats some good green ain't it?" Ernie leaned over and smiled broadly with the pleasure of knowing how potent his product was. I yawned and stretched out my stiff limbs acknowledging the potency of the hydro's THC content. "You in luck my nigga, just got off da line wit Big Gabby an he's tryin ta meet up wit you like ASAP, know what I'm sayin? But he had to take care of some kinda situation right now so he said to tell you to hook up wit him later on tonight around 8:00 p.m. He'll meet you at Osaka's Japanese Steakhouse out in Harbourtown. You don't know da island like dat, so I'll show you how ta git there," Ernie smiled. I was elated knowing that I'd finally meet with somebody other than my Uncle who could pull the kind of strings that could put me on the map for good. I made a helluva lot a money in the six year span of my hustlin' life, but I had little to really show for it except a closet full of designer clothing, costly name brand sneakers, custom made jewelry, and several top-of-the line vehicles in which I either totaled, sold, traded in or ended up losing altogether to the cops when I got locked up back '89. This time it would be different, because I wanted to live life on a millionaire type status, never looking back again. Little did I know that on April 26, 1991, I'd make an association that would change my life forever.

Ernie and I arrived a little early for our meeting at Osaka's, after enjoying most of the day on Singleton Beach at the Sand Dollar Lounge. We wanted to arrive early, because everyone knew how much of a stickler for time Big Gabby was. He'd been known to turn down major business deals, drug related or otherwise, if the other party showed up even a few minutes late. Just to be safe we got to the restaurant at approximately 7:45 p.m., ordered some rice wine and bullshitted around until Gabby came through the doors escorted by his three bodyguards and his wife, Suzette. Big Gabby was a grossly obese man who lumbered mightily as he made his way over to our dining area. I didn't have a clue as to why he'd pick a Japanese joint to dine at since there was no way his big ass was gonna sit down at the squat little tables prepared for most patrons. But the fat man had plenty cash and money talks, so unlike every other customers eating at Osaka's, our party of seven was given special treatment and seated outside on the patio overlooking the lovely Cooper's River and the pleasant ambiance of Hilton Head's Harbourtown at night. Of course, Big Gabby required a specially made chair in order to accommodate his gargantuan frame. Osaka's was one of his favorite eateries and the friendly Japanese staff knew him well and took every provision possible to provide him with the best service; he was their best customer.

Big Gabby was huge but still dapper looking in his custom-tailored silk suit. His three muscle-bound guards helped Gabby down into the extra wide chair. Gabby wasn't a bad looking dude, just fat as all outdoors. Sporting a black silk derby to match his ensemble, Gabby's thick Fu-Manchu mustache and pigtailed goatee gave him a somewhat intimidating appearance. His thick bone-straight hair was pulled back into a ponytail, which flowed down his back. When he removed his dark Ray Ban glasses his slanted eyes gave testimony of his part Asian ethnicity. Big Gabby greeted Ernie and me warmly and the three of us shared a few light minutes of laughter and jokes before ordering. The whole time we were joking around I noticed Gabby's wife Suzette a comely, twenty-something, sex kitten, undressing me with her eyes from the far left corner of the table. With skin the color of buttermilk and seemingly just as smooth, this pretty young thang had a pair of deeply set pale green eyes. They were penetratingly alluring despite the innocent schoolgirl appearance that her cute freckled face possessed. Even though her husband sat right beside her the whole time she was giving me all these seductive looks as she ate her meal. At one time I wondered to myself whether Gabby or anyone else caught on to Suzette's preoccupation with me at the meeting, but that's when I observed that Gabby was either too busy talking or eating to notice his spouse flirting right beside him. Two bodyguards stood on either side of our table while the third one guarded the door allowing only the Kimono clad waitresses to come and go freely. Just as I was about to excuse myself from the table for a bathroom break, Suzette arose.

"Honey, I'm gonna excuse myself for a minute, I gotta go pee." Gabby nodded, barely looking Suzette's way as he gorged himself with Teriyaki chicken and Sapporo beer. From where I was seated I could plainly see that the man's wife was a definite dime piece, but it was only after the broad rose up outta the chair that I damn near passed out behind her physical voluptuousness. Wearing a sheer white Christian Dior dress which left little to the imagination Suzette's hourglass shape left me mind boggled as to why she would give a fat pig like Gabby the time of day, much less pussy even if he was perhaps the wealthiest black man around these parts. Suzette stood and turned around slowly walking toward the double doors leading to the inside of the restaurant showing off her long, suntanned legs and juicy, round ass, which grabbed the attention of several men awaiting seats outside in the lobby area as she bypassed them in route to the ladies' room. I knew that she wanted me to get at her...and I would, in time.

Our meeting took about an hour and a half with Gabby wolfing down nearly five hearty plates of Japanese food, while washing all of it down with imported beer. Not one for common table manners or etiquette we had to endure a number of booming belches as well as the occasional chair rattling fart or two from Gabby's trifling ass before the fat bastard requested the check. When the bill arrived it easily totaled over four hundred dollars, an amount in which Big Gabby paid via credit card. The plastic that Gabby paid the bill with was a Black Visa Card which was even more prestigious than the Platinum Visa Cards I'd seen Uncle Snookey purchase items with back in the day. Very few cats could afford the excessive cost of owning a piece of plastic like that shit there, I'll admit I was impressed by Big Gabby's and big balla status. Yet still, I'd made up in my mind that I was gonna long stroke his bitch. And damned if I wasn't right. At the end of the meeting when Big Gabby and his hood-rich entourage entered the glistening, black limo, awaiting them in the dimly lit back lot, his wife lagged behind just enough for her to turn around suddenly, gently gripping my balls as she stood within inches of my face, her perky breasts gently grazing the hair on my chest.

She whispered quickly into my ear, "I wanna fuck you…call me." With those words she enticingly ran her wet tongue along my ear. *Shit!* …I thought to myself feeling that familiar bulge stiffening inside my boxers. As Suzette briskly walked away from me, her ass, shaking like Jell-O, almost made me forget about the little business card she left in my hand as she bolted. Pre-cum soaked the insides of my boxers as my rigid member emerged outside the left leg of the underwear, pressing warmly against my inner thigh. Taking the business card into my right hand I placed it into my pocket, adjusted my dick and made my way back into the restaurant where I strolled Ernie back to the big Lincoln parked right outside the restaurant. From there I got Ernie to drop me off back at the beach, so that I could pick up the Bronco.

Driving home I remembered saying to myself how lucky I was to be in this position. Big Gabby had agreed to buy the entire kilo of coke from me and invited me to visit one of his clubs in Atlanta in the beginning of May. There he said I'd meet some friends of his whom he felt could be of service to me. By the latter part of April '91, I'd fucked Big Gabby's wife on several different occasions, the sex was good and everything except that the bitch was crazy. She acted as though I was her man or something, constantly blowing up my pager buying me expensive gold necklaces and shit. One Saturday, after we got through fucking, she asked me to close my eyes. I refused at first demanding to know why, as well as letting her know that I wasn't in the mood for child's play. But she continually begged me until finally I gave in to her pressure. As I sat up right in the sweat soaked sheets I heard Suzette's rapid footfalls exit then returned to the room just as quickly. When Suzette excitedly requested that I open my eyes, she presented me with a dazzling, diamond-encrusted Rolex masterpiece watch costing—I'm certain—about eighty grand or better. Suzette was always buying costly little trinkets at her hubby's expense. She sure as hell didn't have to do anything except look pretty and give her portly partner an occasional blowjob. Suzette made it quite clear that she had no romantic feelings for her lard-assed husband whatsoever and that she married him strictly for material comfort and stability.

"Gabby thinks I'm all in love with him. I do admit I do a helluva acting job," Suzette revealed adding how disgusting it was to suck her husband's dick, which was the only sexual encounter that they could have, since Gabby was so obese. Only married for two and a half years Suzette said she'd had two affairs during her marriage. The bitch had some good pussy and her blowjobs were the bomb, cause unlike a lot of broads Suzette loved to swallow cum. And I'd shower her pretty little face with gobs of the thick white stuff. But she also had a dark side; she was extremely clingy and unwilling to realize that although she was a dream fuck in many respects, that all she'd ever be to me was a piece of ass. She wasn't comfortable at all with being my part-time lover and wanted more from me. Once she tried hiding my car keys so that I couldn't leave the Knight's Inn where we laid up from the night before. After threatening to leave her alone altogether she quickly produced the car keys while tearfully begging for my forgiveness. On another occasion I met her at a Sea Pines Resort where she claimed Big Gabby went to get away from the stress and strain of public life. It was here at this exquisite resort and country club that I nearly killed that bitch.

I was never one to hit a woman or threaten them with violence; however, there were exceptions to the rules at times. The incident began simply as a perfectly planned morning rendezvous. With Gabby and Diamond either out of town or swamped with work, we had plenty of time to enjoy each other. That morning, Suzette and I played a few sets of tennis then we went horseback riding until noon. After that we ate lunch at the country club before retreating to our suite. We ended up screwing for at least an hour, before I showered, dressed, and got set to dip.

"Ohhh, I get it, so you're gonna visit, fuck me and step, huh?" Suzette asked me, her pretty little face reddening with anger.

"Girl you know I got things ta do, besides we had lots of time together and we did plenty of things today, so don't even come wit dat bullshit!"

Suzette sat up on the bed, her naked body wet from the steamy sex we'd only concluded minutes earlier. "Do I look like some two dollar trick to you Rae Kwon?" Suzette asked again, locking that steely gaze upon me impatiently awaiting a response that never came. "I said do I look like a fuckin' two dollar trick bitch!!" Suzette snarled, hurling a ceramic vase at my head, which she snatched off the nightstand beside the bed. As it shattered against the wall behind me, I knew that it was time to leave.

"You trippin'." I scooped up my car keys on the way toward the door. It was then that I felt a piercing pain on my right side, which caused me to buckle over in agony. I grabbed hold of my right side, brought my hand up to my face from my side, and my hand dripped crimson. Like an enraged animal I turned to face my attacker, Suzette was rushing toward me, wildly swinging a box cutter whose wicked blade was stained red with my blood. I reached out and firmly caught one of Suzette's slender arms at the wrist. I could've snapped her fuckin' arm like a twig, but instead, before she could take another possibly fatal slash at my face or neck, I reached back and let fly with a punishing blow, sending her crashing up against the far end of the wall. Suzette layed upon the floor of the spacious suite groaning. I came over and knelt beside her still suffering from the deep cut in my side, which continued to bleed heavily. I grabbed Suzette roughly by the hair with one hand pulling out a small glock with the other. I forced the muzzle of the handgun into the bitch's mouth. "I should blow yo muthafuckin' brains all over this room," I screamed. "Now git yo ho'en ass up and git me to the fuckin' hospital ya stinkin' ass bitch!!"

Suzette stared wide-eyed with terror down the barrel of the glock as it remained nestled in between her teeth. As tears streamed down her now black and blue bruised face, she pleaded for her life. I removed the weapon from her mouth, yet I still kept it leveled on her as I backed away. I had Suzette rip up the bed sheet with her blade making a makeshift bandage for me while I washed the wound with water. Though the blood had soaked through my shirt, it looked worse than it actually was. The blade merely sliced through skin and muscle and fortunately no deeper. I had Suzette wrap the cloth strips around my abdomen as tight as possible in order to stop the bleeding. When she was done she had to pay one of the housekeeper's to get the blood up off of the room's carpet before we left. A couple hours later, both of us emerged from the Hilton Head Island Medical Center. I'd received ten stitches to close the wound. Suzette told the doctor that it was an accident. After we stepped, Suzette tried everything she could to make up with me, but to no avail.

"I can't fuck wit you," I said flatly to Suzette as she sat staring at me teary eyed in the back of the stretch limo while we cruised through the Island's brilliant landscape.

Suzette took my hand into her own, sliding next to me. "P-please...Rae Kwon gimme another chance, please baby...I...I love you!" Suzette sobbed leaning her head against my shoulder.

"Naw, you much too possessive for me, baby girl. Plus you gonna fuck around an git a nigga kilt out here wit dat hot shit you doin'," I replied calmly lighting up a joint which I'd been saving since earlier in the day. Suzette lifted up those magnetic green eyes, gazing at me sadly as she ran her fingers across my chest.

"Please Rae Kwon, don't do this to me," whispered Suzette choking back tears. For a second I almost broke down. True, I didn't want to hurt her, but shit, she was a married woman. Didn't matter if she was happily married or not, I needed her husband's clout to get me to where I wanted to be. I told Suzette that we'd need some time apart for a while, and maybe just maybe, I'd think about getting back together with her. I got out of the limo and winked back at Suzette who smiled weakly as she observed me walking over to my ride. As the darkly tinted back window of the limo slowly rose upward, I could see Suzette wiping the tears streaming from her now reddened eyes, heartsick because she knew full well that she'd fucked up. I never did deal with her sexually anymore afterwards and as a matter of fact, I didn't really see her too much after that day, maybe a total of two or three times. Eventually she just disappeared altogether. Sources close to Big Gabby claimed that he divorced her on suspicion of adultery, while others professed that Big Gabby had his unfaithful wife murdered along with one of her handsome young lovers, Charlie Red, who just happened to be one of his Savannah-based nightclub managers, after catching the two leaving out of a Beaufort area Marriott. Word on the street was that several other cats that had slept with the fat man's wife also met similar fates to that of Charlie Red.

"Yeah Gabby had Suzette and all dem niggas dat she was fuckin' chopped up and buried out on Skidaway Island," one of Gabby's drug runners told me during a weekly pick up. "Dat's a cryin' shame, Suzette was some kinda fine, I'da fucked her...then again maybe not, huh?" The coke dealer grinned as he puffed on a thick cigar stump. "Wouldn't you fuck her too, youngsta?" The old head questioned as I sat in the back of the Sand Dollar Lounge.

"Yeah, I guess so," I replied, double counting the briefcase filled with hundred dollar stacks neatly lined up one on top of the other. The man laughed out loud, his laughter soon giving way to a harsh wracking smoker's cough.

"You guess so? Boy I'm damn near sixty years old and when I was your age I used ta put a mile of dick up in bitches like Suzette. Har! Har! Har! Har!"

I quickly gathered up my briefcase and rolled out. I wasn't trying to hear that bullshit, plus the conversation was hitting too close to home. Once inside the crushed velvet confines of my new lovely pearl white '62 Impala, I peeled out from the Sand Dollar Lounge leaving a thick cloud of exhaust smoke and beach sand. The gray-haired dopeman stood out on the steps of the Sand Dollar Lounge grinning to himself, still chewing on the cigar stump as the dust and smoke begun to settle around him.

"Dat fucka dere done gone fool," I thought to myself as the powerful six-cylinder engine of the classic muscle car whisked me away, thundering along full tilt off into the humid South Carolina night.

XVI

Dopeman, Dopeman

May 3, 1991, my cousin Shawn had been out of jail now for a few weeks and been blowing up my pager and leaving plenty of messages at the house. Diamond suggested that I invite the twins over for dinner so that she could meet them but I made it clear that those two, though I loved them dearly, were by no means genteel company. That was the end of that idea, which freed me up to swing past Dawn's crib out in Savannah. Diamond wanted to travel with me but once more I shut her down knowing how unpredictable and rowdy the twins could be. I didn't want Diamond around that type of atmosphere. At Dawn's apartment, I must admit, I was impressed that the place was actually clean, well furnished and kept up pretty good since I had left nearly two months earlier. Dawn embraced me, smelling of designer perfume and marijuana.

"Ya want something to eat?" Dawn asked going back into the kitchen.

"Yeah. I'm hungrier den a muthafucka."

Dawn placed a few large slices of pepperoni pizza into the microwave and plopped down on the living room sofa where she'd been counting a large amount of money at the coffee table just before I'd arrived. "Have a seat nigga, and stop actin' like you'se a guest," Dawn remarked patting a spot on the large leather sofa beside her. As I walked toward her, on the coffee table, I saw what seemed like no less than $30,000, vials of crack cocaine, and a large clear plastic bag filled with aspirin-like tablets bearing Mercedes-Benz logos, amongst several assault weapons, a huge machete and a modest quantity of marijuana, which I'm sure Dawn was using to smoke for herself.

"I see you been getting' ya hustle on since I been gone, huh?" I said coming from the kitchen, munching on a pizza slice.

"Ya damn skippy," Dawn answered hardly looking up from her counting.

Sitting down next to my cousin, I toyed with one of the unloaded handguns lying in front of me, a blue chrome .44 magnum, to which I took an immediate liking. Dawn quickly glanced up from her focused calculations to observe my admiration of the weapon.

"Ya want dat 4-4?" Dawn asked packing a nearby bong with marijuana buds.

"How much you want for it?" I asked while inspecting the barrel.

Dawn shot me a look of mock anger. "Come on now, how you gonna ask me a question like dat? Ya family, ain't ya? It's yours fa free, nigga!"

"Thanks beeattch!" I laughed. While we smoked and choked off the bong hits, I inquired about the strange bag of pills lying on the corner of the table.

"Oh dat shit, some shit called 'Ecstasy.' C.J. and Shawn caught some wannabe ballas nappin' out on Bull Street late one Saturday night, straight took dem boys fa all dey cash, guns and dope. Dis here green we smokin' and all dis here crack and shit belonged ta dem niggas. Now it belongs ta us," Dawn said proudly, choking off the potent marijuana. I asked about the result of possible retaliation from the robbery victims. Dawn exhaled a lungful of smoke which billowed out from her mouth and nostrils in thick whitish gray clouds adding to the haziness of the smoked-filled living room, my cousin stared at me with slightly bloodshot, glazed over eyes giggling stupidly as she attempted to answer my question.

"Don't worry bout dat cuz, C.J. and Shawn done already bust dem nigga's heads, ya heard me."

I couldn't believe what I was hearing. Here it was only weeks since this fool got out of a two year bid and already he'd committed murder. "So what'd them fools do wit da bodies?" I asked picking up the bag of Ecstasy off the table. Dawn took yet another bong hit before answering my question.

"You knew we be takin' bodies to my nigga Lindsey," Dawn said, referring to her sugar daddy.

"Do your thang," I said as I opened the bag of tiny tablets. The front door handle turned as a key from the opposite side entered the keyhole. Shawn, C.J. and Lee Ambrosia entered the living room, with loud profane talk and laughter, sweaty and smelling foul from hours of playing pick-up basketball.

"Damn ya'll stink!! Get ya'll asses in the shower befo ya'll sit down on my shit!" Dawn spat, putting the bong down and racing to the door to prevent the three guys from coming any further. As Dawn argued in the doorway with her twin brother and boyfriend I got up and walked over to the door myself, greeting them and especially giving some love to Lee Ambrosia.

"Sup, white boy?! What da fuck you doin' hanging out round here?" I asked warmly embracing the Badlands Manor big baller.

"Nuttin but fuckin' wit dese cats out on da court, an takin' muthafuckas money an shit dats all. You tryin' ta come hoop wit us? We only need two mo heads and we gonna make a killin' in about an hour," Ambrosia replied, smiling through gold capped teeth while showing off a thick wad of cash, which the trio had won over the past few hours out on the blacktop.

Lee didn't have to say anything more, I immediately agreed to go, first stating that I needed some basketball gear and would meet up with them at the Savannah State College Gymnasium. As the three thugs left, Shawn and Dawn exchanged playful wisecracks at each other's expense causing us all to roll with laughter as they descended the stairs. Afterwards, Dawn and I finished up a final bong hit and thanking Dawn for the .44 revolver and the bag of Ecstasy that she, nor C.J., could flip.

After walking down the long winding stairwell leading from Dawn's apartment, I was approached by a well dressed white boy who'd just gotten out of a candy apple red Ferrari. He cautiously approached me asking if I knew where he and his girl could purchase some weed. I had a little bit of bud left on me, so I walked over to the whip and brought out an ounce of my most potent stash. I sold it to him for $450. Just like that, four-fifty without even trying. I now had extra cash on me to go shopping with instead of charging anything on Diamond's Visa Gold Card. I felt like a king as I cruised through the streets of Savannah with the top down off the six-deuce Impala, the breeze kissed my face and the warm summer sunlight danced upon the metallic pearl sheen of the powerful Chevy and glistened upon the sparkling gold Dayton rims, which highlighted the white-walled firestones.

I stopped into Riverfront Plaza, picked up a pair of Michael Jordan sneakers, a #23 Chicago Bulls jersey and matching shorts, socks and a new basketball. From there I headed toward Savannah State College. Once there, I noticed Ambrosia's charcoal gray Bentley parked just outside the gate leading toward the gym. I quickly suited up and removed the rock from the cardboard box in which it came in and dribbled it down the long hall toward the gym. Going over to where my peeps were sitting on the bleachers preparing themselves for the next game, I saw that Ambrosia had brought some big tall cat, maybe six-foot-five or better and sturdy as well. We introduced ourselves and heard a whistle sounding the end of the game just before us.

The rules were simple, 33 wins, five-on-five, $200 per player. After about 25 or 30 minutes our squad walked off the court victorious having won 33-20. We collected our winnings from a dude who sat on the bleachers keeping score, refereeing and holding the pot. Asking only for $50 per game for his services, he'd been at the gym since morning refereeing as least a dozen pick-up basketball games. I know he had to come outta that gym with at least a grip. The other squad wasn't so pleased to give up that paper and insisted that we played them again. So persistent was the captain that Shawn and he nearly went to blows. Finally, we accepted. I wouldn't have normally given a rematch, but Shawn and me were killing them with the jump shot while C.J. and Lee punished them off the dribble and with assists. All of us played defense well against the Savannah State alum and the big youngster whom the fellas called "Lurch" dominated in the paint, on the boards and above the rim. Those college punks could do little to stop us from simply toying with them, and to make matters worse, their very own supporters began to taunt and ridicule them.

They played much more physical with us the second time around. As a matter of fact down right dirty at times, drawing not only fouls, but stern warnings from each one of us during the course of the second game. As the game got further and further from their grasp the Savannah State dudes got more and more nasty—swinging elbows, delivering flagrant fouls, you name it, and those cats did it. Soon after one elbow too many, Shawn who'd been exchanging heated words with their captain since the first game, caught one right upside his temple opening up a nasty gash near his left eye. He responded in kind by catching dude with a lightning quick right hook followed up by an equally devastating left. The stocky bare-chested guy fell to the floor with a thud, which is where he laid unconscious as our teammates engaged in a rollicking free-for-all, which lasted for several minutes before campus security arrived on the scene. My mob and I were able to disappear among the sea of on-lookers who'd taken the opportunity to start acting rowdy themselves by storming the court, tossing chairs, climbing up the basketball hoops, and just acting stupid. It was however a blessing for all of us because campus cops would've locked us up for sure that day. Even though the fight was a savage one, most of us escaped with only a few bumps and bruises. I had a black eye and a busted lip, Shawn had a lacerated brow which required a few stitches to close, while C.J., Lee, and Lurch came away with a few facial cuts and some slight swelling. Once we were back at Dawn's we lamented over how much money we'd lost until Lee laughingly pulled out the two grand from his shorts.

"How in da fuck did you happen ta get da money?" C.J. asked puzzled.

"Oh you think cause we fightin' some niggas I'm gonna leave da scrilla layin' dere? Shheeettt! Nigga dat was da first muthafuckin' thing I snatched up," Lee said calmly leaning back on the couch checking the messages on his pager. Shawn glanced over at Lee, wincing from the throbbing pain of the butterfly stitches in his swollen brow.

"Yeah an dat's when dem muthafuckas snatched yo bitch ass up huh?" Shawn grinned playfully causing us to respond with much needed laughter. Lee Ambrosia looked over toward Shawn flipping him the middle finger.

"Come eat dis dick," Lee retorted drawing yet more foolishness among us. Pretty soon everybody ended up clowning on each other, as was our routine whenever we got together. It was always however done in the spirit of fun and togetherness.

Later that night while C.J., Shawn, and 'Lurch' occupied themselves by playing Nintendo. Lee and myself discussed the business of dope and moving drugs back to Peola. Peola was now almost fully controlled by the Decatur Street Crew, the Rude Boyz and the Kingston Krew; all violent Jamaican posses, who extended their power beyond the projects of their original Geneva, and currently held both Badland Manor projects with most of Lee's Bad Boyz syndicate either imprisoned or killed by the invading Jamaican hordes. Lee had no choice but to leave Peola altogether and relocate to Atlanta where he was now sponsoring "raves," rock concerts held either in open air venues or sports facilities such as gymnasiums etc. That's when I asked the million-dollar question...did he make any real money in it.

Lee admitted that the job itself paid pretty well about two grand for every concert with about a thousand of that going to his uncle, who was his manager. I didn't think that a grand a show was anything much to talk about but according to Lee, he and his uncle did raves just about every weekend.

"A grip fa every show, huh? I still don't see where you makin' enough paper ta live," I said nonchalantly.

Lee smiled at my ignorance of his front, and what really went down at these raves of his. Pausing to pour himself a glass of Remy Martin, Lee extended his hand offering me the remainder of the robust cognac. "See you don't quite understand, playa," Lee answered slightly shaking the glass of cognac on ice in his left hand. "Ya see, I don't do this shit fah a flat pay dat I gets legally, oh naw! I do these raves strictly fah da bitches and cuz I kin sell dat X all night long and walk away wit no less than three grand after a weekend of clubbin' and it all goes in my pocket!"

Knowing that he had my undivided attention, Lee slowly sipped on his Remy awaiting a response. From there, I was all ears as Lee Ambrosia summed up in detail the workings of the Ecstasy market and the lucrative nature of the trade.

"Dis shit is probably the hottest thing goin' right now dawg, maybe even hotta than coke right now!" Ambrosia said with increasing excitement. By the end of the night the both of us had orchestrated what would become perhaps the largest Ecstasy smuggling ring the South had ever seen.

I left Dawn's around 2:00 a.m.; everybody except Ambrosia and myself was fast asleep from an entire night of boozing, drugging, and later gorging themselves on Chinese carryout. Before we both left Savannah, Lee and I exchanged pager numbers promising to hook up on the 4th of July. It was already well into May when we spoke about our caper, so I anxiously awaited the day which I hated since childhood, because aside from it being a holiday it was also the anniversary of my parents death.

By June '91, everybody was hip to the game. Ambrosia and

I managed the entire criminal operation. We had Shawn, Dawn, and her boyfriend C.J. selling the stuff at wholesale prices to other smugglers across South Carolina and Georgia. The hot-headed trio also acted as the enforcers of our crew whom we dubbed "The Dirty South." Quick to maim or even murder rivals unfortunate enough to incur our wrath, we really had no competitors, in fact, most of the other MDMA smugglers worked well with us and mostly everyone shared in the wealth.

By July 4, 1991, we'd persuaded Big Gabby to invest in an Atlanta area rave in East Marietta Township that was located in Cobb County, one of Atlanta's wealthiest suburban communities. With Ambrosia's vast rave knowledge and my street smarts when it came to drug trafficking; we profited so handsomely that Big Gabby began sponsoring huge Atlanta area raves every single weekend. By years end the fat man was sponsoring raves exclusively, having sold all six of his Savannah and South Carolina area dance and strip clubs. At first these huge, densely packed dance marathons were usually held in local high school or college gymnasiums and football fields. But then, as the demand for Ecstasy and other street drugs increased, so did the lewdness and rowdiness of the mostly white college-age party-goers. We didn't want to blow our cover, so Ambrosia, Gabby and I decided that it made more sense to host our parties in warehouses, old barns or nightclubs located in out of the way rural spots. Big Gabby would pay off the owners and provide actual charter buses to transport many of the young revelers to the raves and back home, for free.

By August, Big Gabby had us meet with some students who attended Clemson University where we set up a back-to-school rave off campus. The one-time event was so successful that it soon carried on through the Christmas season of '91. We were moving something like 425,000 hits every month or so by September '91. I could smell millionaire status at last! All of us were livin' large by 1992, C.J. "Skinny Pimp" bought Dawn an awe-inspiring, split-level colonial style home housed within a well-to-do gated community in Marietta, Ga. Its beautifully manicured two-acre sculptured lawn, complete with a ten-foot, limestone Poseidon shaped water fountain, made C.J. and Dawn's crib reign supreme among their neighbor's homes. Meanwhile Shawn, always the car buff, seemed to live to collect classic automobiles. He still lived in Peola, purchasing his parent's old mansion out in West Peola. Once when Donita and I and the kids visited him during the New Year's Holiday, the boy had at least two-dozen classic cars from the fifties, sixties and seventies parked side-by-side in the driveway.

Lee Ambrosia loved gambling and on the weekends he'd invite Donita or Diamond and me (whichever one I'd choose to bring with me) to hang out with him in Las Vegas for a weekend of lavish living. One Saturday night he spent $10,000 on Diamond and me at the MGM Grand Casino, drinking Cristal and Moët like it was Pepsi or Sprite at the high rollers tables across from famous entertainers and athletes. While out in Vegas, I couldn't leave without introducing Lee to my Uncle Snookey who was almost as impressed by Ambrosia as he was of him. From that meeting an important business merger was solidified causing Uncle Snookey and his underworld colleague Carlos Cellini to purchase a couple thousand hits.

After about a month, in February '92, Uncle Snookey phoned me in Ridgeland asking for more of the "Club Drug" tablets. By the end of February we were shipping over five thousand hits to the desert alone. By March '92, we had begun to branch out to other southern cities such as Miami, Tampa, Charlotte, Charleston, Columbia, Richmond, Memphis and my old hometown-New Orleans. By April '92, Lee had recruited enough streetwise thugs to resurrect his old Bad Boyz Syndicate. It was these twenty-something toughs who made frequent trips to Detroit, Michigan, the heralded rave capitol of the world. Once there, Ambrosia's flunkies would purchase a large shipment of Ecstasy from Jeremy "Acid" Fawcett, a former heavy metal guitarist who now specialized in smuggling MDMA into the U.S. from Europe and Mexico. Money was flowing in like water, and everybody affiliated with The Dirty South seemed to be getting rich. Even the little dope boys who ran minor errands for us were sittin' pretty on rims, and flossin' ice at the most chic nightclubs down in Miami, Atlanta and Charlotte. However, the stylin' and profilin' didn't come without its lows.

A rash of undercover busts beginning in the Motor City with the arrest of Jeremy Fawcett set off a major panic attack within the ranks of our Ecstasy ring. Atlanta's finest out at Dekalb Peachtree airport nabbed three of Lee Ambrosia's Bad Boyz drug runners in May. Chino, Marlo and Fife got nailed with a dub apiece for possession of eight kilograms of MDMA concealed within fruit crates. Although Fife and Chino remained silent, Marlo snitched on everybody down with us. The po-po's in Hotlanta didn't move quick enough to prevent the savage killing of the three criminals—straight orders from Big Gabby from his tropical bungalow down in Montego Bay, Jamaica. Lee didn't appreciate Big Gabby interfering with his crew, though he too would have gotten someone to off the trio himself.

"Dat fat fuck!! Don't nobody need him to mind my goddamn bidness!" Ambrosia vented the night of the hit. Then, Ambrosia, in a fit of rage, called the fat man on his cell phone spewing a torrent of obscenities over the line that was met with equal hostility from the vacationing kingpin. To make matters even worse C.J. and my cousins Shawn and Dawn all felt as though it was Ambrosia's responsibility to have picked up on the police surveillance sooner than he did, thus preventing the subsequent arrests of his careless trio of smugglers. Even though all of us could breathe again after Gabby dispatched his gunmen to murder the three young criminals, it was still not enough in my cousins' eyes, or that of C.J. who at least three times spoke candidly about getting ridding of Lee Ambrosia himself.

"We wouldn't have even been in dis bullshit, if Lee woulda played his fuckin' cards right!" C.J. growled late one Friday night while having a few drinks at a local pub.

"I say we have him come over to Dawn's get his ass drunk and let Dawn take a straight razor to his goddamn throat, half breed muthafucka!"

I couldn't believe what I was hearing, but I heard right.

Knowing C.J., he and my cousins were probably plotting ways to get rid of Ambrosia without me knowing. They knew that I was the peacemaker and also a good friend of his. So I went through the weekend persuading the three not to bump off Lee. Finally, after I pressed the issue for so long they reluctantly agreed to forgo their deadly plans. Yet still, I know how my cousins could be. They were rowdy since childhood and had gotten much worse as they matured. Dawn had murdered at least a dozen folks since moving to Savannah, with at least four of those killings being conducted along with her boyfriend C.J., who boasted a track record of 25 murders since the age of fifteen. Shawn had only one murder on his hands, but had staid clear of the sprees that followed his sister and her boy. He had, however, the quickest temper of the trio and was always spoiling for a fight. It was only a matter of time before his total began to rise too. I stressed to them that if we kept a low profile from now until the situation subsided we'd all be fine. Then, we could start flossin' again. Ironically, as soon as I'd finished speaking there was a knock at the door. And speak of the devil, Lee Ambrosia, fully clad in a dashing blue Armani Suit, complete with matching snakeskin loafers came through the door accompanied by two stunningly attractive raven-haired cuties each sporting a pair of black form-fitting evening gowns accented all over with one-carat diamond sequins. As Lee and his two lovely dates entered the living room, Dawn flashed a nasty look toward Ambrosia and his female companions. I was at least pleased with C.J. and Shawn, who welcomed Ambrosia as usual, even engaging him in small talk. Before he left he dropped four V.I.P. passes onto the coffee table.

"Check it out I just opened up a new spot out in West Peola, it's called 95 South. It's a smooth club, dawg, you gotta check it out. It has three different levels where da DJs spin Hip Hop, R&B and House/Reggae. Grand opening is on Saturday night. Oh yeah, proper attire is required, no athletic wear or sneakers. Wish I could stay and talk shit wit cha, but I gots ta go and get my fuck on!" Ambrosia winked as he turned toward Dawn's front door.

"I know dat's right playa, handle yo bidness boy!" I responded, lusting over Ambrosia's women as they exited the apartment. Even though C.J. and Shawn greeted Ambrosia earlier, I knew that deep down the two, along with Dawn were plotting something wicked inside those warped minds of theirs.

April 7, 1992, began the first of a series of police questionings by Cobb County's finest. The interrogations were about the murders of Chino Hawkins, Phil (Fife) Marley, and Marlo Reece. C.J. and Dawn were the first two to be snatched off the street by the po-pos, and it didn't take long for the authorities to go round up Lee Ambrosia, Shawn and myself. That wasn't a good time for anybody. Thankfully, the Cobb County Police couldn't piece together any more info than they already had concerning the murders and therefore they had no choice but to let us go. Though I'm certain that the presence of the two high-profile attorneys sitting in the lobby as we filed past had a lot to do with our short-lived stay within the County Slammer. Big Gabby obviously had an informant at the precinct because he just knew about too many things before hand, including our arrest. No sooner had we been taken into custody we found ourselves back out on the street.

XVII

Da Dirty, Dirty

On April 12th, I was phoned by Big Gabby and instructed to meet with him in Hilton Head that evening. I was told to come alone. Later that evening I showed up at Big Gabby's Sea Pines estate and from there we traveled by limo over to Harbor Town where he'd already reserved seating for us in advance at Osaka's Japanese Steak House. Once there, as usual we were seated out on the spacious patio, which was decorated beautifully with 18th century Japanese Sculptures and paintings along with the serenity of a gently cascading miniature waterfall within an enclosed oriental rock garden. Though the night itself was one of a gentle breeze and cloudless sky, allowing the soft glow of the full moon to bath the distant Cooper's River in its magical radiance, there was an uneasy feel to the meeting from the start. I was curious as to why Gabby needed me to travel all the way from Atlanta down to Hilton Head so urgently. After about an hour into his boring vacation story, I wanted to tell him to shut the fuck up and get to the point. Finally, he asked one of his burly, bodyguards to give him "the shit." With my eyes locked on the exchange between the two men, I had my trigger finger at the ready to draw my deuce-deuce and start blasting my way outta there if Gabby or either of his two henchmen tried any kind of slick shit. Gabby took a small tin box the size of a Cracker Jacks box from his bodyguard and laid it on the table in front of me.

"Go ahead and open it up Rae, you actin' like it's goin' bite you or somthin'," the fat man said, grinning. Slowly, I looked around me observing the three hulking bodyguards surrounding us as we sat at the table. Gabby pushed back slightly from the table and began to chuckle to himself as he noticed my apprehensiveness. "Open the mutherfuckin' box!" Big Gabby rumbled, still laughing. The bodyguards began to move in closer, with the one nearest me cracking his knuckles. I stood up and quickly backed away from the table.

"Fuck dis shit nigga! I ain't openin' no mutherfukin' box. If y'all niggas tryin' ta wreck lets do dis, bitch ass niggas! I spat taking off my gold herringbone chain in anticipation of a fistfight. As the bodyguard closest to me begun to approach, Big Gabby placed a fat hand on his waist.

"Hold up Jimmy. No need for all that, specially not in here," Gabby said restraining his protector. "Whether you like it or not, lil' nigga, you gonna see what da fuck's in dis box right chere," Gabby said opening the little tin box with a quick twist of the wrist. Inside was a bloody severed penis. As I recoiled from the sight of the grisly item displayed before me, Gabby nodded his head prompting two of his goons to lock hold of both my arms forcing my head forward in the direction of the chopped off dick.

"Listen up you wannabe-hard-nigga, do you know who's dick this is?" I gritted my teeth in anger as I made direct eye contact with a menacing Big Gabby. "Answer me you little bitch!!" Gabby snarled as he dangled the tin box in front of my eyes.

"Fuck you, you fat ass punk!" I snapped back spitting in Gabby's wide face. Suddenly, I was struck hard on the left side of my face by the open palm of the bodyguards to my left, which was followed by a solid punch from another on the right of me that sent me reeling backwards only to be jerked right back up again and steadied up on my feet.

"Ya boy Lee Ambrosia fucked up dawg. Yeah he fucked up real bad a few weeks back, you do remember dat don't cha?

Well anyway you see, I can't have no fuck-ups like dat, know what I'm sayin'? Cause dat stupid lil' half-cracka fucked me I made sure he don't fuck nobody no mo ya heard?" Gabby had his guards threw me back down into my seat. Being that the seats at the Japanese restaurant were already very low to the ground, I ended up rolling off the seat onto the patio's floor, hitting my head. I stared upward groggily catching sight of the laughing men standing me. All I could think about was killing every one of them.

"Get him on his fuckin' feet and take his ass out to the limo," I overheard Gabby order his bodyguards amidst their taunting laughter. Slowly, I began to come around. By that time we'd left the steakhouse and I was in the back of the limo in between two of Gabby's bodyguards while Gabby sat up in the middle portion of the luxury vehicle talking business over the phone. The whole time as we rode along the moonlit, lonely roads leading toward Ridgeland all I think about was revenge for both myself as well as for my fallen friend. Gabby and company dropped me off at a spot near my girl Diamond's house, warning me that nobody in the Dirty South Syndicate would be spared if there were any more fuck-ups.

"So you go and tell all ya lil' family and friends dat if dey wanna keep makin' money we kin do dat dere, but if dey put me in a bad position like dat fuckin' Lee Ambrosia, who had da balls ta call and talk shit too, they gonna fuckin' die! You got that boy?" Big Gabby spoke through the window. "Oh yeah here's ya pea-shooter back. Be careful wit dat thing ya might hurt yaself!!"

With that said, I stood helplessly watching as the big limousine pulled off slowly becoming but an ink spot in the distance along the winding country road. "Dat's why I fucked your bitch, you fat fucka!!" I screamed shattering the silence of the lonely country road. As I slowly walked under the large Spanish moss laden oak tree, I began to plot my revenge. At the beginning of May I'd moved out of Diamond's house in Ridgeland and lived on Daufuskie for two months, renting a small beachfront two-bedroom apartment on Bloody Point Beach. I figured that my involvement with Big Gabby and the Dirty South Syndicate had gotten far too dangerous to remain with Diamond out in Ridgeland. Diamond was my heart and I didn't want to get her killed behind my drug-dealing bullshit. Lee Ambrosia had already ended up on a casualty list that would only grow as the months passed.

On May 17, 1992, the mutilated decomposing bodies of Lee Ambrosia and his two female companions were discovered inside the trunk and backseat of Ambrosia's 1990 Bentley that had resurfaced in the murky waters of a small, marshy region just outside Bluffton. All three victims had been shot twice each in the back of the head, an obvious professional hit. Ambrosia was only 22. During that same month, five other dealers loosely associated with Big Gabby and Dirty South's Ecstasy distribution ring ended up murdered in a similar fashion.

Soon there was talk on the streets and back roads of the low country that the execution-style hits were the handywork of none other than Hilton Head's own homicidal beauties, Naomi and Candice Forrester. The lovely, but deadly Forrester girls, owners of two beauty salons on Hilton Head and a ritzy health spa on Daufuskie, began their criminal careers early on as adolescent call girls while living in their native Atlanta. As they entered their early twenties, the sexy fair-skinned cuties began pulling off armed robberies of Atlanta's area retailers, some surprisingly in broad daylight. Relocating to South Carolina's low country region, they now operated exclusively as independent business owners and killers for hire. Both women had been seen during the months prior to the murders, dining with Gabby at Osaka's Japanese Steakhouse and hanging out with the rotund crime boss at his old Singleton Beach nightclub, the Sand Dollar Lounge. No one had to tell me that the recent body count was due to Big Gabby's contract with the Forrester girls. As for me I'd gotten rid of the last little bit of Ecstasy tabs that I had at a small nightclub on Daufuskie, and was happy to be rid of it at last.

During the remainder of May on into June, I traveled several times between Peola and Miami spending time with my kids and their mothers Brandi and Donita. By then my children were all growing rapidly and I began to see life from a totally different perspective while taking the time to actually bond with my kids for a change. Even Brandi and Donita had changed for the better since I'd been away wildin' out. There was no longer casual sex between the mothers of my kids and myself since both now had boyfriends. Donita was dating a Georgia Tech quarterback and Brandi was currently engaged to be married in July to a successful Miami-based sports agent. I couldn't be mad at them, in fact I was quite happy that both women were finally loving life within mature, fulfilling relationships. I could never really provide either of them with that and because of my lifestyle would've more than likely caused more harm than good to them and our kids. However, from then on I made it a priority to not only provide for but spend quality time with my children. This created an amiable relationship with both mothers, which remains until this day. I had to use Diamond as a co-signer in order to rent the apartment because the property manager demanded to see proof of earned income, residence for the last ten years, and credit information. All this red tape caught me off guard, because the few places that I rented before never turned me down after I produced a wad of cash, taking care of the security deposit as well as first month's rent. But with the Pelican Point Apartments catering to an older, upscale clientele; I knew that my youth and race definitely caused a red flag to go up at the rental office. Diamond used her home on the application as my residence for the last decade, she had false work information printed up at her dental office that portrayed me as a currently employed a dental tech for the last five years. Diamond somehow got around to getting me an acceptable credit rating. Had it not been for Diamond I probably wouldn't have gotten the apartment. During that time my introspection led me to appreciate her all the more. I'd been a dog the whole time we'd been together. While she was the consummate loyal lover, though niggas were in her face twenty-four seven, she was always true to me, and I loved her for that.

Daufuskie, though somewhat like a miniature version of Hilton Head was more of an environment for older people than those my age, and after two months in exile from city life and running the streets I got bored to death with sitting around doing nothing but spending money. Every one of my little children loved the little isolated island, where they could romp and play for hours at a time throughout the woodlands, beaches and streams of Fuskie's untamed wilderness. I'd take my little ones camping and hiking often entertaining them with ghost stories by the campfire as we toasted marshmallows. I taught them to swim and fish during the morning hours. Although their mothers hated the idea of roughing it out in the woods, Diamond loved adventure and became a sort of surrogate mother to my little tribe with both parties becoming immediately and strongly attached to each other. I've got to admit although the place got to be rather dull for me personally; it was a lot of fun to watch my kids and Diamond enjoy themselves so much.

While I spent May and June of '92 getting to know my off-spring better and building a stronger union with Diamond; C.J. and my twin cousins were in Savannah going hardcore gangsta. I talked to the twins nearly every other day, if not every day during the week, Shawn or Dawn would boast about how much easy money they'd gotten during the week through random acts of armed robberies, with the local Savannah dope hot spots as the target areas of their nightly hits.

"Dis shit here betta den hustlin' Dawg!" Shawn would brag over the phone.

"You need to bring your monkey ass out here and git some of dis money, ya heard me," Dawn said once during a three-way call between her, Shawn and me.

I'd always flatly refused to live that way, preferring to stick with good old fashion hustlin.' That attitude of mine always caused my cousins and sometimes C.J. to rag on me, questioning my heart and courage. I'd hear shit like, "Oh nigga you done lost it uh? Ya used ta be bout it now ya just soft, cause ya bitch gots ya pussy whipped," or "Nigga wuz up witcha? Don't tell me you got bitch in you," and all types of other playful put-downs at my expense. Ribbings to which I'd usually respond with a simple and resounding, "Muthafuck all y'all!" That reply usually ended the jokes with a round of hearty laughter from all of us.

However, I was truly concerned with the path my cousins were taking, 'cause I knew that it was but a matter of time before something tragic would befall all of them.

By the end of May, C.J. and Dawn were expecting. I was happy about Dawn's pregnancy because I thought that by being knocked up she would chill with all that thuggin' shit, but it seemed like she just got worse. On June 5, 1992 both Dawn and C.J. robbed Savannah's First Union Bank located on Abercorn Street in Savannah's historic district. The Bonnie and Clyde like duo got away with over thirty grand early that morning wounding a security guard in the process. Shawn who was always tagging along with his twin sister and her lover drove the getaway car, which was later found abandoned and ablaze in a trash littered alley in the Hitch Village projects by Chatham County Police. The critically wounded security guard, Vincent C. Foster III, later died of his wounds, which caused Savannah's Mayor and Chief of Police to step up the investigation of the crime as well as issuing a $12,000 reward for any information leading to their arrest.

Somehow Uncle Snookey had heard about the robbery and was understandably furious; nevertheless even the anger and tongue lashing by their father didn't halt the twins' devil-may-care attitude. I remember warning the twins repeatedly about wildin' out especially with cops all over the city looking for them. I even suggested that they move down to Daufuskie or Hilton Head in order to lay low for a while, at least until Dawn had her baby. But they didn't seem to want to listen. For me, the final straw came when C.J. and the twins begged me to go with them to Detroit in order to purchase a fresh shipment of European Ecstasy. Even though I refused to take the trip up north several times, Shawn and Dawn wouldn't take no for an answer and finally after several blunts and about two hours later I agreed to travel with them. I'd contacted Seth Youngblood shortly after agreeing to travel and we flew by private plane to Motown from Savannah. Youngblood charged us a thousand dollars for the round trip flight to Michigan and back. We flew up there I'd say around 2 a.m. on June 28, 1992. This time around

149

the flight was much smoother than the first time I flew with Seth, though the combination of morning sickness and some slight turbulence made the initial flight to Detroit somewhat uncomfortable for Dawn.

Once we touched downed on Michigan soil, Jeremy "Acid" Fawcett had two of his long haired, tattooed ex-rockers led us through Detroit's highways out into the suburban area of Auburn Hills where Fawcett's mobile home stood starkly against the ornate greenery of the Michigan forest. We drove up into the driveway, which was nothing more than a pebble covered dirt path, muddied by a recent shower. The two leather vest-wearing bikers rode their Harleys into a shed by the rear of the large trailer before hopping off and leading us inside, where their boss awaited us.

Once we were inside Fawcett's home I was amazed at the vast amount of drugs, firearms and heavy metal instruments lying around. On the walls of the untidy trailer were posters of rock groups like Metallica along with pictures of Fawcett and Ted Nugent together in concert. The place reeked of cheap liquor, cigarette smoke and cat piss. The mixture of offensive odors made Dawn nauseous forcing her to return to the car. I'd never met Fawcett before and he'd never met us either. He was understandably uneasy with strangers coming to him seeking to make a drug buy, especially one of the fifty grand variety, which is what C.J., Dawn, and Shawn were after. Knowing only the now deceased Lee Ambrosia from The Dirty South drug syndicate, Fawcett didn't buy the story of Ambrosia's murder nor wanted to sell us the Ecstasy at all. Before we knew it, things begun to turn ugly real quick.

"You fucks come in here with some chicken shit story bout Lee getting' whacked and then y'all want me to just accept that and sell you a shit load of X? Well, guess what, Buckwheat…go fuck yourself!" With that said, Fawcett demanded that we leave or get shot for trespassing, which naturally caused Shawn to welcome the challenge by rushing toward the middle aged ex-musician in a blind fit of rage. Acting quickly, I grabbed up my cousin in a bear hug, while literally throwing him down hard unto a nearby couch, causing two large-breasted blondes to bolt out of our way. Shawn didn't take kindly to me roughing him up like that and he let me know about it by letting go with a steady stream of profanities as we struggled on the couch for a few seconds.

"Nigga you gots ta chill wit dat shit today!!" I snapped at Shawn.

Shawn who had grown even stronger since he'd gotten out of the joint, finally after a brief, but intense tussle broke free of my grasp. "Bitch don't you ever put yo muthfuckin' hands on me like dat again. Do dat shit one more time and I'll break your fuckin' jaw, cousin or no cousin!" Shawn was visibly fuming with anger, but I didn't give a fuck, I wasn't about to allow his impulsive actions to be the cause of us all getting killed, and I told him that to his face.

By that time, all those white boys from the trailer park were up in the joint with guns drawn. C.J. and I quickly threw our arms up into the air, realizing in no uncertain terms we were in a hell of a dilemma, which could easily and instantly turn deadly if handled the wrong way. C.J., Shawn, and myself were ordered to have a seat on the large leather sofa sitting in the middle of the cluttered living room. Before sitting, they took our guns. Luckily for us Acid Fawcett was older, wiser and a lot less gung-ho about killing than his much younger, trigger happy partners. Being the most even-tempered member of the Dirty South Crew, I didn't hesitate in catching Acid's attention by loudly mentioning certain things about Ambrosia's past purchases.

A lean wiry cat with some of the most bizarre body piercings I'd ever seen began to approach me, ready to strike me with the stock of his submachine gun, when Fawcett commanded him to stop and return to his position which was no more than five feet away from me. It took less than fifteen minutes for me to talk Acid out of killing us and selling to us instead, for he was finally convinced that we indeed did know Lee Ambrosia, were members of Dirty South and that Ambrosia was indeed dead. We walked out of what could've been a death trap unscathed and with over seventy kilos of Ecstasy. Dawn slept through the entire ordeal outside in the rental car. Jeremy Fawcett pulled me to the side to apologize for the misunderstanding.

"Hey sorry bro, but ya know ya can't be too careful nowadays. Hey, I'll tell ya what, if you guys stay for the night, I'll treat y'all to some drinks."

I refused, knowing good and damn well that neither my peeps nor me were trying to hang out at some heavy metal club. But Fawcett assured me that he'd give us the hook up.

We cruised through some of Motown's top hip hop night clubs, drinking Cristal, getting our swerve on up in the V.I.P. rooms. We even mingled with Detroit's black socialites and professional athletes. We partied at, at least seven different clubs in the city going from one throbbing dance floor to another. While Dawn, for obvious reasons didn't drink; Shawn, C.J., and I ran up the liquor bill up into the thousands. All we did that whole night was party, drink, smoke, snort coke, and party some more. It was also the first time that I or any of us began experimenting with Ecstasy ourselves. The high was kind of weird. It stretched out the buzz you'd get from alcohol and made me feel really horny. That night, before we left, Shawn and me ended up having sex with two blonde chicks on Fawcett's couch.

Two weeks later, on July 10, 1992, Federal agents, who'd been tipped off by an informant, arrested Jeremy Fawcett. Fawcett had about eight kilos of Ecstasy in his possession at the time of his capture. Feds nabbed about a dozen of Acid's biker buddies out in Lansing with about two million Ecstasy tablets stashed away inside of a U-Haul truck. This is when everything came crashing down.

XVIII

Everybody Gotta Die

After the Feds shut down Jeremy Fawcett and his crew during the summer months of 1992, it just seemed like things started moving at break-neck speed. Everybody who did business with the white boys outta Detroit started getting harassed by the FBI. Federal agents even took Uncle Snooky and his mobster homie Alberto Cellini into custody by the end of August. Both men were released from jail on September 13th; however, the stage was already set for disaster. The once lucrative South, Midwest, and Southwest Ecstasy ring began to unravel almost immediately. The constant police harassment, drug busts and arrests destroyed what was for a time a smooth sailing operation and gave way to accusations and finger pointing from one drug crew to the other.

By mid-October the bad blood and foul-mouthed threats turned deadly. Enraged over an Ecstasy deal gone sour, both Alberto Cellini and Uncle Snooky phoned Lemont "Big Gabby" Cantrell demanding an explanation for the mismanaged drug deal which cost two Cellini mob members their lives. According to my uncle and sources close to Gabby, the phone conversation between the two underworld figures was full of harsh words, profanity laced threats and yelling. Soon bullet-riddled corpses were popping up all over Hilton Head and Savannah. Gabby went into hiding for the remainder of the year to avoid death or kidnapping. I remember Ernest and other cats I hung out with on the island claimed that Gabby had fled the country taking refuge out in the Caribbean, possibly in the Cayman Islands or Montego Bay, Jamaica.

While Gabby was enjoying comfort and peace of mind in a tropical paradise, his organization was dwindling. Defecting members took the opportunity during Gabby's hiatus to either join up with rival crews or start their own group. Gabby had finally bitten off a little more than even he could chew, attempting to strike back at the Las Vegas-based Sicilian crime family. On two separate occasions, his hired killers were discovered by Cellini's quick thinking wise guys and were promptly killed. A short time after these murders were carried out, Big Gabby showed up in South Peola. Rumor had it that during the three-month sojourn in the Caribbean, Big Gabby had become fast friends with a swift talking Jamaican Ganja farmer named Willis Holden a.k.a. "King Tinny." Holden acquired this odd name during the mid-sixties as lead vocalist of the greatly popular but short lived musical group Judah.

King Tinny had grown up in impoverished conditions in Kingston's Trenchtown. He often boasted of the fact that he'd been one of Bob Marley's childhood playmates. King Tinny was a humorous, but dangerous man. Owning over one hundred acres of marijuana-laden farmland, located in the mountainous Warika Hills; Tinny's heavily armed militiamen patrolled the perimeter of the precious ganja fields 24/7. With Jamaica's economic woes and America's demand for cannabis, King Tinny literally made a fortune farming and shipping marijuana to The States. Tinny organized a drug dealing posse, made up of an assorted group of his rowdy sons, nephews and Kingston Street toughs. They were then flown from Kingston to Miami. From Miami, dozens of dred-1ocked drug dealers made their way to Georgia settling in Peola. Once ruled by three separate gang crews-Hemlock Hills, Wrecking Crew, and Badlands Manor Bad Boyz, formerly led by the late Lee Ambrosia and Amherst Rude Boys-and other loosely knit Jamaican posses, South Peola's crime infested projects were now totally controlled by ruthless Jamaican drug gangs who struck terror in the unfortunate through strong-arm tactics and death threats.

Ironically, Big Gabby relocated to Peola in 1993, moving into an enormous chateau right in the same wealthy gated community that the Lake family had lived in years earlier. Having already unified himself with King Tinny, Gabby acted as a kind of stand in for the old ganja farmer here in the States. Big Gabby soon had a bustling drug market going again with the Jamaicans importing their much sought after home grown bud, in addition to selling crack cocaine and heroin. Big Gabby was now Police Chief O'Malley's newest headache.

On February 22, 1993, Dawn gave birth to a nine pound, three ounce baby boy named Marion, after her father. Little Marion was born at Savannah's Candler Hospital at 12:37 p.m. He kind of resembled both C.J. and Dawn. Dawn's mom came up from Hilton Head and her father flew in from Las Vegas to lay eyes on their first grandchild. It was indeed a momentous occasion for the entire Lake family. It did my heart good to see us all together again in such a loving, warm atmosphere. It reminded me of the holidays we'd shared together back in New Orleans and Peola. For the three days that Dawn rested in Candler's after giving birth to her son, she was visited almost nonstop by a slew of relatives, friends, and hospital staff who knew of Dawn's parents. Dawn's hospital room was full of gifts and cards, even more than she'd gotten at her baby shower weeks before. But the celebration was to be short lived.

An odd-looking package addressed to the Lake family arrived on the February 26th—the very day Dawn and her newborn prepared to go home. The box was somewhat bulky and was written in rather sloppy handwriting. On the back of the box was a rubber stamped emblem of Ethiopian's Lion of Judah in green, red and gold. Dawn had spent most of her time in the maternity ward opening cards, gift wrapped boxes and the like so quite naturally she reached out for this final piece of mail. To this day I still blame myself for the horrific events that unfolded right after my cousin took hold of that package. I remember as a child my grandmother always telling me to go with your first instinct, well my instinct was screaming at the top of it's lungs that something was very wrong. The last thing I remember was

Dawn struggling to tear open the box and C.J. assisting her. Then a deafening explosion, a bright, hot yellowish orange flash of flame and then darkness...total darkness. When I awoke in the emergency room, I'd received third degree burns over sixty percent of my body especially my upper torso, arms and a small portion of my face. C.J., Dawn and the baby were dead. I was told later that they were all killed instantly by the powerful blast of the mail bomb. I wept for weeks after coming out of my two-day coma. The shrapnel disfigured Shawn so badly that he had to undergo several months of plastic surgery and skin grafting in order to repair his terribly scarred face. The blast also left Shawn partially blind, his left cornea was destroyed.

Our surviving family members were devastated by the loss of Dawn, C.J. and their newborn son. But no one hurt more deeply than my Aunt Melissa and Uncle Snookey. I couldn't attend any of the funerals, because I was still recovering. The Savannah police launched an investigation and failed to come up with any leads. I had a hunch that Big Gabby was involved. Laid up in the hospital I had no way of finding out the truth, but thanks to an old friend, I'd have some answer and quick. One evening, Lionel "Hawk" Kurtz surprised me when he showed up unannounced at my room. Brandi and our little daughter Selena had left only minutes earlier and I was sitting upright in my bed watching Sunday football. The diminutive Kurtz entered my room, dressed to kill in a sharp executive suit that made him look much different from the Akron inmate I remembered. Kurtz strolled over to my hospital bed and gazed at all the tubes and light blinking gadgetry that was attached to me. He shook his head slightly then took a seat beside me on the chair next to the bed.

"Man, somebody really tried to get your attention," Kurtz said finally making eye contact with me. I didn't comment, just smiled weakly while nodding my head. "You got any idea who did this to you?" Kurtz asked leaning in a little closer to me.

"Fuck naw...if I knew that, muthafucka wouldn't be livin' right now," I growled staring out the window.

Kurtz smiled as he reclined in the soft cushioned chair. "Well ya know I have my sources back in Peola and there's a guy out in the hood...South Peola to be exact...and he's pretty much controlling everything illegal from drug trafficking to gun smuggling. Some fat fuck who goes by the name "Big Gabby," does that name ring a bell? Well it should cause he sure been talking a lot about how he and his Jamaican cronies fucked up your whole family and get this...he's so brazen he's vowed to finish off the surviving Lake family members. Says that your uncle tried to kill him a little while back. Now I don't know how true all of that shit about his beef with your uncle is but what I do know is that he's the asshole that killed your loved ones and nearly killed you.

"Usually when it comes ta shit like this black on black crime bullshit, I really don't care cause it doesn't effect me one way or the other. I've got a good thing goin on back home in West Peola with a couple of dagos and I ain't gonna fuck that up or go back to the joint for nobody. But you're a good kid...a damn good kid...and it pissed me off to hear about something like this happening to you and your family, because it coulda just as easily had been me in your shoes right now. So, I tell you what. I don't like this cocksucker any more than you do. I don't like him competing with me in my neck of the woods. I don't like the way he operates, killin' women and babies. There's no honor in that, it's cowardly, crudball chicken shit! That's what it is. So I'll be keeping in touch with you kiddo, here take my numbers. I'll be out of town for the remainder of February on business, but I'll be back in Peola next month and by then hopefully you'll be outta the hospital and we can make plans to dispose of some garbage. Got it?"

With that said, The Hawk gently placed his left hand upon my forehead in a gesture of affection and departed my room, leaving a small white and red business card attached to a get well greeting card with a thousand dollars inside. My hunch was right and it felt bittersweet as I lay there plotting vengeance against Big Gabby, while my cousin, her baby and C.J. lay dead in their graves. It burned me up so much that I could do little but cry out in anger and frustration shattering the silence of the quiet little hospital room. When the nurses arrived from the hallway, I was sobbing heavily as I buried my face in my bed sheets. The senior nurse, Mrs. Gloria Santos, who spent anywhere from fifteen to thirty minutes a day just keeping my spirits up by laughing and joking around with me, ordered all the other nurses out of the room and shut the door gently behind her. She then came over to me and warmly embraced me as I wept freely against her bosom as if I was a child and she my mother. And like a mother, she comforted me with soothing words, prayer and song, at last helping me find solitude and peace.

To this day I occasionally visit with old lady Santos, helping her with miscellaneous household chores and things, never forgetting the kindness and caring she showed me during those dreary days of my life back in '93. I didn't get out of the hospital until April 30th, but even after my release from Candler's I had to visit with a physician twice a week for the next four months to undergo a tedious and highly expensive series of skin grafting and plastic surgery. Dr. Samuaadi was a good friend of Diamond. Both of them had attended medical school together during the mid-80s. It was she who recommended that I see him for all of my continued medical appointments. By summer, I looked like my old self again and not the Freddy Krueger looking burn patient that I was after the blast. During the months in between, I'd put on a whole lot of weight and by summer I was a little on the chunky side do to the lack of activity and the constant pampering I received from my fiancée (Diamond and I got engaged on March 23rd) and the nurse staff at Chandlers. I was stuffing myself every hour on the hour with hearty helpings of Diamond's home cooked meals as well as the steady diet of pepperoni pizza delivered to my room every other day. It was still all gravy, because not only did I get myself healed up properly, but I also hit the weight room with a vengeance slowly sculpting my body back into the chiseled work of art that it was before the incident. Although the two and a half months that I spent in the hospital were indeed long and many times boring as hell, I had lots of time to do some soul searching and plotting. I didn't want to leave the game just yet, because I wasn't where I wanted to be financially before I gave it up for good. Diamond pleaded with me to stop "that hustling bull shit," as did both my baby mamas.

As I sat on the living room couch watching TV, Diamond let me have it. "How many more gotta die Ray, before you finally get it through your thick skull that this is some garbage. You don't need this shit in your life anymore. All you gotta do is make up your mind and leave this shit alone. I'll support nearly anything you wanna do but I can no longer support you selling drugs in our communities just so that you can enjoy the little extras that fast money can bring at the expense of your life and those of others, as well. I love you so much…hell too much really, because before you, I'd never allow any guns in my house, ever. But then you came along with your hard edge, street-style charm and charisma and God knows you da bomb in bed, no wonder you got all dem babies. If you gotta sell drugs and get yourself caught up in all this nonsense, then go right ahead. I'll just step back out of your life until you get all of this dope dealin' madness out of ya system." Diamond was right for sure, but still there was no way that I could give it up just yet. I decided that what she didn't know wouldn't hurt her.

Triple Crown Publications presents

XIX

Even Kinfolk Can Go Straight Gutter

Kurtz would drop by to see me once a week usually on Sundays. We'd laugh and joke about our Akron days and watch NFL games, or sometimes play chess or a card game or two. One Sunday, The Hawk came over bearing gifts—photographs of Big Gabby seated among a multitude of his smiling dreadlock wearing Jamaican thugs drinking and carousing at the Lion's Den, one of Gabby's' newest night clubs that catered to a Carribean crowd. In the seven or so photos, I noticed that the person whose face had been circled with a red marker was none other than Lindsey Robbins, owner of Robbins Crematorium, and ex-lover of my cousin Dawn. But sure as shit, there he was skinnin' 'n' grinnin with Big Gabby and his Jamaican homies up in the club. At first I thought, *so what,* until Kurtz hipped me to the fact that, not only was Robbins a fast friend of Gabby's but he also was a co-conspirator in the parcel bombing which took the lives of Dawn, C.J., and their child.

During the short time that I'd known Kurtz, I never once heard the man tell a lie...not once. Kurtz was one of the most outspoken, candidly truthful individuals I knew. Although I knew that his info always came with a price. He wanted total control of Peola's illegal drug market, but Big Gabby stood in his way. Gabby was creeping into Western Peola, traditionally

Lional Kurtz's territory. Though the old Jewish drug dealer wasn't above resorting to violence to solve certain situations, he was from the old school where there was honor among thieves. In Kurtz's younger days, mobsters, bootleggers, and criminals of all sorts followed certain unspoken rules of the game, which usually weren't broken very often and when there was a disagreement between certain individuals or crews, diplomacy was the rule and not the exception before parties resorted to solving their grievances with gunplay. But today's criminals were cut from a different cloth according to old man Kurtz, who simply couldn't stand the brash manners and brazen disrespect of the modern dope man whom he called "punk kids." Kurtz told me that there were two reasons for him telling me all of this information; first, he wanted Peola's fertile drug market all to himself, especially West Peola (that's were all the real money was). Second, he said that his respect and admiration for me, coupled with his extreme loathing for Big Gabby and his Jamaican posses made this an easy choice. When asked why he didn't just off Gabby himself or pay a professional to do it for him, Kurtz smiled.

"Well ya know what kid, that's the easiest way to do it. But first of all, there's no way in hell you'd catch me, a little ol' Jewish guy, smack dead in the middle of the projects tryin to kill somebody. Picture that! The next reason is, as amazing as it may seem, I don't hang out with mob guys like say...Gotti, Giancana or Traficante. I sell to a whole bunch o' Italian guys, whether they're tied up with the mob or not I don't know, and don't really care. As long as I get my money and they get their product everyone's happy. Sure I know some guys that I did time with in the joint that'll bump off a guy or two for ya if the price is right. But most of those guys are beer-drinkin ex-truckers or bikers whose brains are so fried from booze and dope that I'd as soon hire Tom & Jerry to whack Gabby. And professional hit men...huummm let's see, last time I actually knew a professional hit man was back in '77, in Pensacola, Florida. Eugene Jeffries, called him "E.J." He claimed to have done some hits for Tampa's Don, Santo Traficante, during the early and mid-sixties. E.J. got busted on drug charges in '79 and did a dime down in Miami, when he got out in the summer of '89, he left for Quebec with some French-Canadian broad he'd met while he was in. That's the last time me or anybody I knew who knew E.J. ever heard from him again. So there ya have it young man. My dilemma. Ya satisfied now?"

I shrugged my shoulders nonchalantly. "I guess so, dog. Come on let's go get something ta eat cause I know a nigga like you'll talk me to death," I responded with a chuckle

Kurtz drove us to West Peola where we dined at Big Mama's Kitchen, a fabulous five-star restaurant specializing in Southern Cuisine, the place was a local favorite of West Peolites both white and black. It was there that I learned through Lionel Kurtz of his relationship with Mr. Robbins.

"Yeah, I sold that guy kilos of cocaine for years, and then he started buying semiautomatic weapons from me while I was locked away in Akron. My nephews Edward and Kent handled all my shipping and receiving duties while I did time. They'd tell me how Robbie would make the long ride from Savannah upstate to Atlanta where he'd make the pick up from them. He'd conceal dozens of cocaine bricks or cases of guns and ammo inside the coffins he conveniently brought along with him in one of his many hearses. After one particularly close call he had with a Georgia State Trooper check point, he decided to add more space beneath the coffins in order to store the coke or guns, making sure to leave a stiff in the caskets at all times. At times I'd talk to the man nearly twice a week while I was on the inside. He'd buy just that much product from me."

Robbie was also a chronic blabbermouth who gossiped even more when he had a drink or two in him. He bragged constantly about his big yacht down in Florida, his two or three houses and all his secret mistresses. Either his wife didn't care about Robbie's extra long work hours or was just too stupid to realize what was going on right under her nose. He'd brag about bedding numerous women right in his home when his wife went out to the store or over to a neighbors. He even once bragged that he fucked his wife's best friend while she prepared Sunday dinner down stairs, oblivious to the adultery going on upstairs in her bedroom. He loved getting over on people; it was so much fun for him to say that he got away with murder. Kurtz was hesitant to explain how Robbins boasted that he'd been fucking the young daughter of the infamous drug kingpin Marion "Smookey" Lake. "Robbie would literally talk a hole into our heads about all the kinky things he'd do to his 'lil gangsta bitch' as he called her. When my nephews, who like myself were skeptical of Robbins's tale, called his bluff he promised to bring back proof of his affair."

My eyes grew wide with disbelief as I went through the envelope of photos that The Hawk slid across the cherry wood dining table to me. One by one I viewed the colorful glossies within my hands. All of the pictures were of my late cousin Dawn, completely nude and engaging in an array of erotic poses. The final three pictures were all of Dawn engaged in both oral and anal sex with Robbins and some other dred-locked dude. "Who the fuck is this nigga," I questioned Kurtz.

"Some guy who calls himself Rawbone, a crazy Jamaican immigrant by way of Los Angeles. Did a little time out on the West Coast during the early eighties. He was part of L.A.'s infamous Scorpio Cartel scandal."

I took the pictures and placed them back into the envelope. "Look Hawk, we've got all the proof we need ta bleed dese fuckas ya heard me? So lets just give my uncle Snookey a call an let him do what he does best. He's gonna straight punish dese cats once he gets dese pictures here." The Hawk paused to allow an attractive young waitress to clear our table and bring us back two pitchers of imported draft beer. Once the waitress was off to assist other patrons Kurtz leaned in close while pouring himself and me two tall mugs.

"Listen up kid…Let me tell ya something. I know that Marion Lake is a real badass, big time money-maker with all the high priced lawyers, V.I.P. status, and super stud notoriety with the women and I'm nuthin more than a lil old bald stumpy white guy. Of course I don't make nowhere near the kind of money your uncle does. I'm nobody real important. But what I can tell ya about the difference between your uncle and me is that I'll never, ever, turn my back on a friend. Snookey Lake can and will fuck you over if you let him…and he's not above hangin' ya out ta dry if it'll save his skin." I didn't know if I show shed a tear or shoot Hawk for talking crazy. It showed on my face. "I know, I know you're probably wondering how in the hell do I know all this shit. Good question…I used to work with Snookey after his pro-basketball career came to an end."

At the end of the day we'd polished off four more pitchers of brew, traded street stories and begun painting a picture of my uncle that was even more sinister and disturbing than I could've ever imagined. Over the three and a half hours that we sat there eating and drinking, Lionel Kurtz unfolded a startling tale of my uncle's steady rise from hotheaded dock worker down in mid-seventies Florida, to cocky drug dealer and hit man in Atlanta during the late seventies, and finally to egocentric millionaire in his native New Orleans during the early eighties to the present. All of the various details of my paternal family were just too accurate to disclaim as rumors or outright lies.

"Snookey was the man who landed me in the slammer," Kurtz whispered solemnly between drinking a mug of beer and taking deep drags off of his Salem cigarette. He must have polished off a half a pack of smokes during the time we sat talking. "Yeah he ratted on me and several other guys from Jackson's Wharf down in the Florida Keys where we worked loading and unloading shrimp boats. When he first come down to Florida looking for work, he claimed he'd gotten booted outta his older brother's house in New Orleans because he'd made a move on his old lady. From there he ended up in Baton Rogue with his mother, helping with the family farm once his father died. Marion told us that after working a few low paying odd jobs around town, he again tried his hand at the only thing he excelled at—basketball. So he spent his free time training and shooting hoops with local yokels around the neighborhood. He then tried out with the newly formed NBA franchise New Orleans Jazz but as fate would have it the team moved out west to Utah before he could be signed to a contract.

"Spurned, he turned to alcohol and marijuana to drown his sorrows. By this time, hummm...I'd say around 1971 or so, yeah, '71, I was visiting with Earl Strong, my former dock foreman turned Pentecostal minister. Earl spoke on Mother Lake's behalf asking me to hire Marion and take him to back to Florida in order to give him a fresh start since things weren't exactly going so good for him in Baton Rogue. I knew I owed Earl, 'cause he did a hell of a lot for me over the years so I couldn't say no. The following week, Marion was working our nerves...or should I say arguing every other day with the longshoremen or the occasional shrimp boat crewmen. Not wanting to simply fire him like so many of my fellow shift foremen and dockhands suggested, I had a better idea or so I thought at the time. Seeing how much of a street wise tough Marion was, I decided that he'd be a perfect fit to be my cocaine courier. Night shift foreman Dean Kimmel and I had quite a lucrative venture going with Jesus Escobar, Miami's top cocaine smuggler. Jesus also owned Escobar Shrimping, a fleet of over three dozen shrimp boats.

"At night at lease three times a week Jesus dispatched two of his shrimping vessels to the wharf with several thousand dollars worth of packaged cocaine hidden inside sealed crates of shrimp. Once the crates were stored in the wharf's freezer room, myself or Dean would go in after the dockworkers, pry open the crates and remove the powder. It was fool proof until Coast Guardsmen took down another coke smuggler's boat. Although the huge bust (nearly twenty-five million dollars worth of coke) was unrelated to Escobar or us, the Coast Guard began patrolling the Keys with a vengeance, boarding everything from private yachts to luxury cruise liners. So Marion began making personal drug runs to Miami and back for Dean and me. It worked out well with Marion taking to the business like a duck to water. But very often, both me and Dean would have to have a sit down with him, because his increasingly flamboyant lifestyle was being carried over to the job, bringing with it suspicion and angry complaints from jealous dock workers, most of them had it in for him from the start. Marion would never listen.

"Two incidents occurred that forced us to finally get rid of

Marion. During the early spring of 1980, Marion arrived early one morning at the wharf after an unauthorized two-week absence. He drove up to the job in a brand-spanking new Lincoln town car, wearing a snazzy pin-striped suit with two well-stacked broads on each arm. Dean went ballistic, I remember him slamming the office door shut behind him and letting me have it, 'Lionel, I just can't fuckin' take it any more! I want that goddamned uppity nigger outta here!' It took me nearly an hour to calm Dean down after that little stunt Marion pulled off...but what could we do? He had us by the balls and he knew it, as he sat on the hood of that Lincoln smiling at me through the window. I knew that he enjoyed irritating us as well as everyone else on the wharf. Marion did pretty much what ever he wanted to during the day, including clocking out early, showing up for work late or many times not at all. And when he was at work, he didn't once lift a finger to do anything except lounge around the office, talking on the phone and raid our fridge. But even though he's one arrogant son-of-a-bitch, he was still bringing us home thousands in cocaine sales. Eventually, he made several more drug contacts in Tampa, Orlando, and Jacksonville. Marion might have been one sorry ass long shore man but he sure was proficient at drug dealing.

"However, the final straw came around Christmas of that same year. Each year, Dean and I would throw a Christmas party for the two-dozen or some guys who worked the dock. There was always plenty of food, booze and music, the workers could bring their wives, girlfriends and kids along if they chose to and there'd be raffles, and cash prizes of all kinds. Marion arrived as usual in a big fancy car, this time a Cadillac, dressed to the teeth in expensive custom-tailored threads with two good-lookin women in tow. The party went well for the most part with Marion actually carrying on courteously with several of the workers and their guests. But as the night wore on and alcohol flowed, things turned ugly. Billy Joe Hatchett, one of our most reliable and skilled laborers, was a good ole' boy from Talbert, Florida, a small farming community just outside of Pensacola, hardly visible on a map. But anyway, Billy Joe didn't hide his dislike of blacks and barely tolerated his black co-corkers. But his hatred for Marion ran deeper than what he held for the average black and it reached the boiling point at the holiday festivities when Billy Joe noticed that one of Marion's female companions was a blonde-haired, blue-eyed beauty. Stinking drunk, Billy Joe approached Marion. The two men took their grievances outside and into the street where they both engaged in one hell of a row. Both young men were pretty sizable guys so it took several workers to break up the fight as they locked horns out on the lawn. Afterwards Marion laughed and joked about the fight as his lady friends tended to his minor bruises. Dean talked Billy Joe into turning in for the night even driving him to his apartment, but that wasn't the end.

"As everyone finally begun to file out of the party, to everyone's amazement we found Marion's once beautiful Caddy a total wreck. The windows were all bashed in; the fine exterior paint was scratched with the words 'Die Nigger Die.' Marion laughed when he saw the damaging work. Everybody just stood around looking puzzled at one another. Marion, quick to blow a fuse, just seemed to chock it up as a loss and simply phoned another of his pretty young things to pick him and the other two girls up. Marion had a tow truck crew come pick up the car and returned to work the following week with over $13,000 worth of cocaine in the trunk of his car. When I questioned him about it he flat out told me that it was a gift for several 'favors' he'd done for the Escobar family.

"Dean and I were not only curious as to what type of 'favors' Marion had been doing for the Escobars, but also both of us were really pissed off that he had the audacity to do personal business with our supplier behind our backs. During that same week, Billy Joe Hatchett who hadn't missed a single day of work for the last three years wound up being a no-call/no show for three days before we started calling his home, looking for him. There was no answer except the same old, drawn out, monotonous message on his answering machine. After two full days of leaving messages on Billy Joe's answering machine, Dean and I took a trip down to Billy Joe's apartment complex where we convinced his landlord to open up his apartment after explaining our concern over the young man's sudden disappearance. Once inside Hatchett's place, every thing looked as though the man had been gone for a long while. The television blared loudly from the rear bedroom, a newspaper from the week before Christmas lay sprawled out upon the living room table. Stale doughnuts lay hardened on a glass plate by the microwave oven in the kitchen, while a week-old pot of venison sat spoiled on top of the electric stove beside an unopened case of Budweiser. Several neighbors of Billy Joe have claimed not to have seen the strapping young man since Christmas night when Dean drove the drunken redneck home. We didn't waste anytime contacting the cops who quickly began investigating Billy's disappearance. Our fears were at last confirmed when dental records came back from the Miami police laboratory revealing that the skeletal remains of a "John Doe" recovered from a wooded area near the everglades were indeed that of Billy Joe Hatchett. An autopsy of the weather beaten remains revealed that two .38 caliber slugs had penetrated Billy Joe's skull from the rear at close range.

"A short time later two other bodies were also discovered on February 7, 1980 at a landfill site just outside of Gainesville, Florida. Those two were recognized as Donald Stripe and his brother Wade Stripe, first cousins of the deceased Billy Joe Hatchett and like their unfortunate cousin they too were killed execution style. Dean paid for all expenses covering their memorial services. The cops never did solve those three murders, but Dean told me that he just knew that Marion had something to do with it.

"One day during one of Dean and Marion's many arguments, Marion boasted about the killings, admitting that he had murdered the trio himself and that there wasn't a damn thing that Dean, myself or anybody else was gonna do about it. After a few more minutes of cussing, yelling and a near scuffle, Dean fired Marion on the spot, promising to file an order with the police banning him from Jackson's Wharf.

'You're one low-down, dirty piece of shit ya know that Lake I hate the fuckin'ground you walk on ya arrogant son-of-a-bitch!' Dean cursed at Marion that day. Marion flipped us both the bird as he exited the office."

"So Snookey basically disrespected just about everybody at the wharf," I asked. "Then what?"

"Nearly everybody on the dock stood watching as Marion squealed out of the parking lot, speeding along the gravel road leading toward the freeway," Kurtz continued.

"I know Uncle Snookey's attitude, it's fucked up," I interrupted, "but it seems to me that Dean's wasn't too much better. How did he regroup after all that?"

"Dean just ordered the laborers to return to work which the guys responded to reluctantly. Though abrasive with everyone at Jackson's Wharf, Marion's constant clashes with Dean, myself and others gave a bit of liveliness and spice to a rather dull work routine and his outrageous behavior made for some juicy lunch time discussions among the dock hands.

"With Marion gone once and for all, we had to renew our personal relationship with Escobar to ensure ourselves a steady flow of cocaine as we had before Marion came into the picture. By then the Coast Guard had disappeared from the Florida Keys and drugs were once again being smuggled regularly by sea. By the spring of 1980, we had ourselves quite an operation going again until April 22nd. Dean, me, and two other associates of ours were in the office weighing and preparing the newly bought coke for distribution when Federal agents surrounded the wharf, I mean the boys in blue were everywhere. They came off of speedboats onto the docks surrounding our wharf. They lit up the entire dockyard from above with search lights from a circling helicopter, drug sniffing dogs were turned loose all over the compound and in less than an hour the media had gotten wind of the drug bust. Me, Dean, Troy Bookman and Martinez Arguello were immediately arrested on federal drug charges and the feds officially took control of Jackson's Wharf while they combed the entire premises for further incriminating evidence of drug trafficking. And sure enough they found enough kilograms of coke to convict each of us with enough felonies as to put us underneath the state penitentiary and throw away the keys.

"On May 14th, all of us were sentenced to 25 years in the Florida State penitentiary. Dean Kimmel, however, would never live long enough to see the inside of a jail cell. He died of a heart attack two days after the sentencing. Martinez Arguello who was discovered not only to be an illegal alien from Mexico, but was also wanted by Mexican police for several drug-related killings in Tijuana, was promptly turned over to Mexican authorities. Troy Bookman as far as I know is still serving time down in Florida for instigating a prison riot in '88. As for me I did my time quietly.

"Even though I was originally sentenced to a quarter, I ended up only doing a dime after doing two years in a maximum-security facility down in South Florida. I got in good with prison authorities who vouched for my relocation to a more lenient minimum-security prison. Florida had left a bad taste in my mouth, too many bad memories were there, so I opted to finish out my eight years outside the sunshine state, and that's how I ended up in Georgia at Akron Correctional facility where I met you. I remember while still serving time in Florida I was visited one day by Marion. As we sat opposite each other I felt nothing but contempt for the man as he mocked me from across the glass divider. At first I just stared at him for a while wondering what in the hell was he doing there. Marion kept motioning for me to pick up the phone, I did.

'Lionel, Lionel, Lionel, TSK, TSK,' he said. 'Look at you man. You done gone and got yaself busted. Dats fucked up boy, all I can say is please watch ya ass, cause you niggas like to buttfuck round here. But anyway, I just came ta see how ya lovin' dis here lil' vacation, ya know, courtesy of yours truly. Oh what? You didn't know? Yeah, I da one gots yo Hebrew ass up in here. See you and dat fat, nasty redneck Dean, y'all muthafuckas tried ta play me, didn't y'all? Yeah well guess what, y'all white muthafuckas picked da wrong nigga ta fuck wit, but I ain't mad at cha though, I guess if I was you I'd do da same thing. Lets get da lil' young black buck, he don't know no betta let em slang dese drugs, dis weed, dis coke...yeah he'll be happy wit da crumbs we feed him? Is dat what y'all thought? Well y'all crackas thought wrong ya heard me? Cause Big Snook want it all baby, and I don't give

171

a fuck if I gotta go though my own mama ta gets mine. See I ain't like dem dumbass niggas and stupid Spanish cats y'all got workin' da docks fa ole bullshit pay. And fa what, ta go home to ya bitch smellin' like saltwater and fish? Oh naw, not da kid baby cause I'm a player nigga and I always will be. You just like my dumbass older brother, nigga used ta get hoes cause a me back in high school, we used ta run trains on bitches when we were teenagers. Then this stupid little black fucka gonna kick me outta da house cause I was tryin' to cap a little piece from Selena.

'Shit da bitch wasn't nuttin but a porno hoe ta begin wit she's gonna get fucked anyhow why not keep it in da family? But anyhow I had ta teach dat ungrateful nigga a lesson. And I taught his ass good too...don't nobody cross "Snookey" and live ta tell bout it. I don't give a fuck who you is."

I could believe it. "All this time I was helping my biggest enemy," I thought helplessly.

Kurtz continued, determined to get everything out. "After Marion's tirade on the other line, he warned me to stay away from Florida and Louisiana telling me he'd have me killed in prison if he so chose to but said that he was satisfied that I was doing time for now. Through the years Marion's notoriety grew and the hatred for him not only from myself but also from inmates who Marion had crossed evolved as well. By the time I arrived at Akron, Marion was living in Peola and I always got the inside, latest scoop on his exploits from prison sources. I know that your uncle set both you and his own son Shawn up when you all got busted at the auto chop. He feared that you two would bring unwanted exposure to him and his mafia friends if you weren't somehow taken off the streets."

The more Kurtz spoke the more I seethed with anger at his revelations. Kurtz finished up by telling me that uncle Snookey wanted Shawn, Dawn and I out of Peola because he secretly wanted control of Peola's drug market even though he'd relocated to Las Vegas. Everything that The Hawk told me cut me like a knife. I hadn't been this hurt since my parents died and it seems as though everything I believed in was a lie.

XX

A Time to Kill

During the beginning of September, I made sure that Shawn was okay, he'd moved in with his mom out in Hilton Head and though my man was now blind, he was still the same old foulmouthed thug. Aunt Melissa patiently put up with Shawn's bad attitude with other people because he was now her only child left. I'd visit Dawn's grave at Hilton Head's National Cemetery and place fresh flowers on her grave and that of her infant son Marion every month. Sometimes at night I'd come to the cemetery, park the whip and go over to Dawn's grave, with blunt in hand and talk with her, promising her that I'd avenge her and her child's deaths. C.J.'s family buried him somewhere in Ridgeland, I never did find out where. I'd see teens throughout various parts of Savannah, Peola and Hilton Head wearing Dawn's photo on tee shirts and get choked up.

I was 100% when October came around. On a mission, I'd been spying on Robbins since early September-watching him go back and forth between his house, work, and the homes of his various mistresses. After six weeks of surveilence, I was ready to handle my business. I followed Robbins as he and one of his bitches checked into a Knight's Inn Hotel. I rolled up into the parking lot as Robbins escorted his tipsy date giggling and slightly staggering into the hotel's front entrance. It was around 9:45pm and the autumn darkness covered the land like a dark blanket. The night was crisp and slightly cool so I reclined the driver's seat of the old Ford Taurus I'd borrowed from Kurtz and got comfortable in the car's toasty heat, patiently awaiting my opportunity to strike. Within the glove compartment I had the big blue .44 that Dawn had given to me as a gift. I decided against using it because I had no silencer on me at the time. Instead I slipped on a pair of rubber gloves that I'd got from Diamond's dental office and took from the glove compartment a medium sized roll of twine that I found in the back of Kurtz's trunk. Slicing the tough rope with a box cutter I measured the length, and exited the car. Fortunately for me, they parked at the rear of the vastly crowded parking lot. With a homemade crowbar I broke into Robbins' Pathfinder and settled in his backseat. After nearly two hours, Robbins and his floozy came walking out toward the parking lot. I glanced over the front seat to see Robbins who was standing about thirty yards away holding hands and sweet-talking with his girlfriend.

"Yeah muthafucka...go right ahead and mack, cause dat'll be da last piece o' ass you'll ever get." I tightened the rope around my hands. After a lengthy session of fondling and kissing Robbins bid his chick good night and began making his way toward the truck. I lay perfectly still along the back seat as I heard his approaching footfalls coupled with the sound of car keys. Robbins entered the truck and shut the driver's door with a loud slam. I felt the driver's seat sink slightly beneath Robbins' weight, and smelled the crisp, lather of the soap he'd just washed up with. Before I could spring up from the backseat, I recognized the digital beeping of a cell phone. I remained calm. Robbins made two calls, one to his wife whom he told he'd be home in thirty minutes and the second call, I assumed, to one of his buddies boasting about his latest sexual conquest. No sooner did he end the conversation did I take the opportunity to pop up from the backseat violently wrapping the twine around Robbins throat and pulling the rope as tightly as I could. Though Robbins was a pretty good-sized dude, I was bigger, younger and a whole lot stronger then he. There was no way in hell that he could free himself from the deadly vice grip. Robbins gagged, hacked, and chocked up bloody foam like saliva from his mouth, as he fought to free the chords of rope from around his neck.

"This one's fa Dawn, bitch!! Ya heard me?!" I snarled into the dying man's ear. Robbins fought wildly to free himself from the noose that was digging into the flesh of his neck blooding his pale blue oxford shirt around the collar. At one point his wildly kicking feet slammed into the horn on the steering wheel honking it loudly once or twice. I had to finish the job fast. In the rearview mirror, I saw his lifeless eyes rolled back into their sockets leaving only the whites visible. His tongue rolled out on the left side of his mouth and I could see multiple bloodied teeth impressions, where he'd damn near bitten his tongue off during the struggle. Thick, yellow snot was smeared from both of his nostrils across his wide moon pie like face and the entire cabin of the truck stank, due to Robbins defecating on himself as I literally choked the shit out of him. The front of his khaki-colored Dockers pants was soaked with urine as well.

Slowly, I slipped out of the driver's side door and walked briskly back to the car on the opposite end of the parking lot. A security guard driving a small car with blinking police lights drove right passed me as I entered the Ford Taurus. The security guard waved at me and continued circling the parking lot area. Once he was some distance away, I hauled ass as quick as I could go. Once I got home I burned the bloody rubber gloves and rope. I spent the remainder of the month spending quality time with Diamond and taking my kids to Six Flags Atlanta for Halloween. In November, I made two trips up to Peola to buy some coke from Kurtz. He was pleased to learn about Robbins. That's when he told me that one of his prostitutes was dating Rawbone, a member of the violent Jamaican posse Rude Boyz and fellow plotter against my cousin, Dawn.

"This one's on me. Here's the address to the apartment where he'll be laid up with Bunny. She already knows what's going to happen when you get there so arrive at approximately 12:15 a.m." Kurtz placed a business card with the address of Byrd View apartments. One the back was the apartment number #121. Although I didn't have reason to believe that this "Jake" Rawbone had anything to do with Dawn's murder, I just couldn't get the image of him and Robbins out of my mind engaged in a threesome with my cousin. Sure Dawn was pretty promiscuous during her short time here on earth, but anybody who dealt with Robbins and Gabby deserved to die.

I went home and spent some time with Diamond, who was excited about planning our wedding. The next day I arrived in Peola at 10:52 p.m. I phoned Kurtz letting him know I made it. Then I drove to his West Peola townhouse to drop off a shipment. Inside his cozy little den was something like a dozen chicks—all of them were prostitutes who lived with Kurtz. He introduced me to them one at a time, pulling Bunny, a gorgeous light skinned sista to the kitchen to discuss the night's procedures.

"Now sweetheart after you sleep with this guy, my pal Rae Kwon is gonna make a house call. He'll get there exactly at 12:15. I know that I told you about this earlier, but I thought that I'd refresh your memory." The cute redbone smiled and acknowledged her duties. Kurtz dismissed her back into the den with the others. She walked away slowly looking back at me several times, tempting me with her enticing hazel eyes and hour glass shaped body as she strolled out into the den, her juicy round ass wiggling beneath the sheer satin panties she wore with every step. Kurtz folded his arms and chuckled to himself as he watched me watching Bunny. "She's quite a looker isn't she? Just turned 21 last weekend. She's an ex-model from Seattle. She's one of my best earners too. Want to test drive her?"

At first I decided against it in my mind. For one, as a rule I usually didn't have sex with prostitutes and two, I'd spent lots of time thinking about truly committing to my fiancée. But this chick was just too damn fine not to hit. So Kurtz, without even hearing an answer from me, went over to the doorway and motioned for Bunny to come over. She returned and Kurtz simply glanced over at me and walked out of the kitchen. Bunny dropped to her knees, as if instinctively, unzipping my jeans and freeing my penis from my boxer shorts. Slowly, the attractive girl, with the alluring eyes and centerfold body was deep-throating my thick shaft, bringing me to the brink of climaxing in her mouth. Grabbing the back of her head I began thrusting myself forcibly within her warm, moist mouth. Bunny moaned lustfully as she slurped down the length of my erection.

"Alright baby girl...here comes the load!" I exclaimed withdrawing myself from her saliva-laden mouth.

"Come on baby give it to me, shower my pretty lil' face with your hot cum!" Bunny remained still upon the kitchen floor on her hands and knees, her mouth agape ready to receive my sperm shower.

"Ooohhh!! Fuucckk!!" I grunted as a thick, white, stream of semen surged out of my throbbing member, splashing into her curly, amber-colored hair, and leaving thick, white globs of cum dripping off her pretty freckled face.

"Ummm, that was sooo good baby. Your cum tastes sweet too." Bunny squealed as she cupped my testicles, the remaining semen from my dick shuddered with pleasure as Bunny slurped the last drops of cum as it billowed out of the end of my shaft.

Afterwords, Kurtz had Bunny tidy herself up, preparing to visit with Rawbone. During which time I left out to go get some money that was owed to me from one of my coke clients about a half of mile away. When I returned to the neighborhood, Kurtz informed me of Bunny's departure, so I left right behind her. Rawbone was pushing a champagne colored Lexus LS, which was one of only three vehicles parked outside his building. I waited patiently once more in what I begun calling my "murder mobile," the old Ford Taurus.

Twelve o'clock came around rather quickly, so I roused myself from a rainfall induced nap and slowly begun slipping on my disposable gloves. With that complete, I opened up the glove compartment removing from it the .44, a case of rounds and a silencer. Dressed in all black, I glided ghostlike through the shadows of the trees lining the apartment's walkway. The rain began falling much heavier as I made it to Rawbone's apartment. Once inside the apartment's entrance I began climbing the long stairwell hearing a variety of sounds coming from the apartments around me as I ascended—muffled conversations, television chatter, a baby crying. At 12:15 a.m., I stood at apartment #121 clutching the cold steel within my right hand concealed under the cloak of my rain soaked trench coat. I could see the tiny circular peephole darken as Bunny peered through. Slowly the door opened and Bunny stood nervously on the opposite side waving me into the apartment.

"C'mon, C'mon! He's in the bathroom!" The prostitute whispered frantically stepping aside. I immediately made my way across the living room, toward the bathroom situated down the hallway. The bathroom door was somewhat ajar allowing a small amount of light to illuminate the darkened hallway. As I approached closer, I realized from the unpleasant sounds and smell issuing from within, that I'd come upon Rawbone just as he was relieving himself.

"Go get me some toilet paper," Rawbone said thinking that it was Bunny who was approaching the doorway.

I abruptly kicked in the door, simultaneously drawing the .44 from inside my trench coat. Rawbone sprung for a sawed off shotgun that he had propped up against the bathtub next to the commode, but just as his fingers touched the stock of the stubby weapon, two shots ripped into his shoulder, spraying streaks of blood across the gleaming white tile of the bathroom. I squeezed off yet another shot which caught the muscular Jamaican in the upper left chest, splattering the wall with more crimson. The fourth and final blast blew out blood and chunks of brain tissue as I placed the end of the silencer against the middle of Rawbone's forehead. Rawbone's lifeless body slumped over, partially lying in the bathtub. Blood and gore was everywhere as I observed the aftermath of my first and final meeting with Rawbone. Bunny took a few extra minutes to steal whatever valuables she could find within the joint. The broad left up outta there with over twenty-five grand in cash, an armful of diamond jewelry, and several credit cards. I could have cared less about taking anything, I was satisfied that one more piece of shit nigga was gone.

The only thing that pissed me off that night was when we got ready to leave the apartment, Bunny wanted to take a Heroin fix, since the hunger for the drug began to overtake her shortly before we were out the door. Even though I adamantly refused her shooting up right there at the murder scene, she insisted. At first, I took it for a joke but then as I made it outside the door, I realized that Bunny was indeed serious. Turing around, I threw open the unlocked front door and found her prepping herself to administer an injection. I dragged her ass outta there kicking, cussing, and clawing. By the time she and I had made it down the stairs I had no choice but to smack the shit outta her in order to stop her hysterics.

"Listen up Bitch, I ain't gonna go ta jail behind some dumb shit you doing, ya heard me, so calm your monkey ass tha fuck down!!" I snarled at Bunny.

"Fuck dat!!" Bunny retorted. "I need a goddamn fix. I don't give a fuck about you or the fuckin' poe-lice!"

I'd reached my boiling point with that hoe, so I grabbed her by her curly hair and pressed the muzzle of the big blue handgun upside her pretty lil' face. "Bitch, I'll peel your mutha fuckin'wig back, ya heard?! Keep fuckin'wit me. I'll put your stupid ass ta sleep just like that bitch ass Jake upstairs!!" I warned.

But it didn't do any good, the more I warned her to be quiet, the more the trick yelled and screamed. So I walked away quickly to the whip with Bunny right behind me, waking the neighbors all around. I couldn't wait to get into the car. Because I was sure that the cops would be on their way by now, when Bunny hopped passanger seat beside me still running off at the mouth, I reached over without hesitation, grabbed her around the throat angrily, and snapped her neck like a twig. I had no choice, the bitch had already probably drawn attention to us both by yelling out there in the dead of the night, plus she was a junkie on top of that. I spun out of the parking lot of the Byrdview and fishtailed across the wet pavement through the entrance gate and onto Route #31. Gripping the steering wheel, I sped along the lonely, leaf covered partially paved highway. A jumble of thoughts entered my mind all at once tearing at me. All the while my pager was buzzing out of control. Diamond, Kurtz, two coke clients from Savannah and the chick that waited on me and Kurtz at Big Momma's a while back. I turned the pager off because it begun to irritate me. I had a dead body in the car with me that had to be dumped. So I pulled off the side of Route #31 and hoisted Bunny's corpse onto my broad shoulders and carried her off into the woods as I'd seen my infamous uncle do dozens of times over during my teens. Her body was still somewhat warm when I tossed it down a steep ravine that was overgrown with wild vegetation. I relieved her of Rawbone's valuables in the car just before dumping her body into the ravine. I got back in West Peola about thirty minutes, heading straight to Kurtz's with the bittersweet news of both Rawbone and Bunny's deaths. The old Jew didn't take it well when I informed him of Bunny's murder. We yelled and cursed at each other for a while, but eventually The Hawk calmed down admitting that Bunny unlike his other girls had been a compulsive thief and had recently gotten hooked on Heroine, while away on one of her many month-long absences.

"Man, Hawk, I'm real sorry bout Bunny. Man, you know that's not now I usually roll, but I done my time in da joint, even if it was only a few months. I ain't gonna go back for nobody and Bunny sho nuff' a liability as far as I am concerned," I assured him. "But looka here dawg, I know a couple hoes down in Savannah and out in Ridgeland who'll be glad ta stop working solo turning tricks for lil' or nothing ta hook up wit a true pimp like yourself who'll provide them with an opportunity to make some real money, ya heard?"

Old man Kurtz looked at me with his steel blue eyes and chuckled ever so heartily as he lit up cigarette. "Thanks, but no thanks, Rae. I've been pimpin' probably longer than you've been here on earth. I just know how to keep things quiet. Bunny ain't the first whore I've lost. I had two nice looking dolls murdered in '71 and two more in '82. They were either police informants or trying to get me whacked for some rivals. So hey man, you do what you gotta do in this business...it ain't for everybody...so forget about it, life goes on."

That night I stayed over at Kurtz's crib leaving out early the next morning. I'd kicked a lot of ass in my day and I'd seen a lot of cats in the dame get killed, but never had I really murdered anyone before until now...but now I'd killed twice...I guess everybody gotta die.

XXI

Undercover

I was overjoyed when 1993 ended. It had been a fucked up year for me and my peeps. Shortly after the West Peola murders, a whole lot of unfortunate events began taking place. First off, Shawn attempted suicide twice once on Thanksgiving Day and again on December 8th. Aunt Melissa had no choice but to admit him to a psychiatric institution located in upstate Columbia, South Carolina. His depression and bouts of paranoia often turned violent, putting everyone in the general area around him including his own mother in danger. It was unbearable to see Shawn, rocking back and forth in his padded cell, mumbling and chuckling to himself, oblivious to anyone observing him from the window above. Aunt Melissa only made two trips to the Piedmont Psychiatric Institute once to admit him and the other to visit him on his 23rd birthday. Other than that the emotional strain was too much to bear for a mother who in essence lost both of her children. Uncle Snookey never visited Shawn, his reasons were never revealed. I could only guess that the pain and embarrassment of having to care for a mentally disturbed child was enough.

In early December, Donita and I got into a heated argument over the financial support of our three kids Ray Jr., Davon, and Chantel. The subsequent shouting match led to an angry confrontation between me and Donita's quarterback fiancée that quickly turned physical. I ended up with a broken nose and fractured left hand while Donita's new "baby dad" (Donita was four months pregnant by this dude) ended up with four broken ribs, a broken right ankle, and a deep gash across his right eye that needed twelve stitches to close. Both of us ended up in the hospital for a few days and later we were both thrown in a local Dekalb County jailhouse. I got out two days later after Kurtz posted bond for me.

On New Year's Day, the Georgia Tech Yellow Jackets faced the Wisconsin Badgers in the Peach Bowl...without him. I ended up warning Donita that if that fool ever disciplined any of my kids, I'd kill him as sure as my name was Rae Kwon Lake. Donita was afraid because she knew my family's reputation...so she had a restraining order issued against me. Now that hurt my heart, not being able to see my young'uns. I was able to communicate however with my children by the phone. Fortunately, I didn't have the same problem with Brandi as I did with Donita, in fact I saw my daughter Selena at least once a month, sometimes twice. During the end of the month, I visited Kurtz and celebrated Hanukkah with him and few of his family and friends. He always kept his prostitutes with him, even during the holiday celebration, though they dressed appropriately during the family visits. Kurtz didn't have any children but his two sisters and a host of nieces and nephews, and old friends visited him from Florida. After the celebrations and happy reunions came to a close later that night, Kurtz and I sat up well into the wee hours of the morning just joking around, drinking, and shooting pool.

"I don't know how the hell you do it? You've got a broken hand with a soft cast on it and here you are beating me like a drum. It's just not fair!" Kurtz laughed, referring to my pool playing skills that surpassed his, and Kurtz could really play the game.

"It's my knuckles that were fractured, Hawk, not my hand, besides I'm right-handed anyway so I can use my left handed cast to steady the pool stick, you feel me?!" I remarked while sinking three more pool balls.

Kurtz smiled and admitted defeat declaring that he would

turn in for the night; it was about 3:30 a.m. I noticed something strange about Kurtz. He seemed to have a lot on his mind, so I questioned him about it. As he had done so many times before, Kurtz attempted to downplay his somber mood, but I wouldn't take no for an answer. I must have harassed my old friend for at least twenty minutes before he fessed up. Kurtz suggested that we both sit down and have one final brew for the night before telling me what was troubling his mind. What he told me brought a lump to my throat.

"Yeah kid...I've got cancer. Lung cancer they tell me. Caught it too damn late. It's spread to both lungs and now it's running rampant inside of me. I should have known that eventually these fuckin' cigarettes would be the death of me. But hey, I've had a good run, made lots of money, met lots of folks...hell I can't complain." Kurtz flashed his trademark smile then took a deep drag off a smoldering cigarette before smashing the butt down into a full ashtray.

"Hawk, I, I...I don't know what to say..." I answered shaking my head pitifully.

"There is nothing to say kid, I'm gonna live out the rest of my days in style!" Kurtz announced with a broad smile. I nodded my head in agreement, smiling weakly.

But Kurtz would not be able to live out his life in style, he grew increasingly more ill with each passing month. By April '94 he was so bony he appeared skeletal. He'd given up his chemotherapy treatments because he'd said months earlier that he couldn't stand the extreme nausea and vomiting side effects.

Quietly, on May 14th, The Hawk passed away at 2:54 a.m. at his home surrounded by his family, friends, and, of course, his girls. I was on Hilton Head Island at the time when Nina, one of Kurtz's several prostitutes, contacted me on my cell phone tearfully telling me the sad news. Even though I was really sad, I was also happy that the old man was no longer suffering. Lionel Kurtz had a traditional Jewish memorial service and burial. He was buried in West Peola's Shalom Jewish Cemetery next to his mother, father, and infant brother who died at two months. Old Kurtz left most of his earthly belongings to the dozen or more whores whom he treated like daughters. The man was worth something like 2.5 million dollars. So you know that all those tricks were taken care of for the rest of their lives. Nina was chosen as the primary beneficiary and she was awarded the luxurious home that Kurtz loved. Nina later became sort of a 'Madame,' and operated a bordello out of Kurtz's crib. I'd visit the place a couple of times every few months just out of respect for Kurtz's memory and to offer Nina any type of assistance she needed if any of the 'customers' got out of line. Like the time I had to hospitalize these two cats who'd robbed Nina only a few months after Kurtz's death. They were two low life crack addicts from South Peola's Amherst Projects. Chuky and Percy Lee, I remembered that Dawn used to sell dope to them back in the mid-eighties when we lived there. Now, what they were doing across town in the high society area puzzled me, but after I got through beating the both of them half to death with a metal Louisville Slugger Nina never got robbed again. However, as Nina's sex-for-sale business grew she needed my services less and less, so though we remained close I stopped coming over so regularly.

During the summer of '94, Peola's Finest had discovered Bunny's skeleton remains thirty miles off of Peola's Route #31 near neighboring Crawford, Georgia. The ravine which I dumped the prostitute's body into was located in a three hundred acre stretch of forest known as 'the abyss' by locals because the wild, tangled underbrush made it damn near impossible for one to navigate out of the woods once deep inside of it. Nina alerted me that police chief O'Malley and his investigative staff had determined that the two murders (Rawbone's and Bunny's) were related.

"Ray, the cops were interviewing some folks out at Byrdview and one dude described your Ford Taurus and gave a description of you and Bunny saying that he saw you and her arguing on the night of the killings."

I was once again in some deep shit and I had to move quickly to silence this fool, who ever the hell he was. First thing that I did was to get David Ambrosia, Lee's uncle to destroy the evidence. I paid David a grand to have the car demolished at his Atlanta area auto junkyard. The young waitress I'd met earlier at Big Momma's kitchen had been fucking me since the first time we'd met now worked at the DMV. Kelly was her name. I had her pull some strings for me and she erased the license plate number from the computer system. Next, Nina owed me for policing her property, and feeding her all the free coke and weed that she could possibly want in exchange for an occasional blowjob. So by the end of June, I had main man's name, apartment number, the make, model and color of his ride and his hang out spots around town. I thanked Nina for her help by blessing her with a quarter pound of a potent strain of Hawaiian grown cannabis, which I'd gotten from David Ambrosia during my visit to Atlanta earlier in the week. Ever since I left Ridgeland, I was using Kelly's Toyota Corolla to get around until I could and myself a set of wheels; but when I saw what homeboy was pushing I made a decision that moment to not split his wig but to take over the phat ride he was rollin' in.

I determined that the off-white Suburban would be mine by the end of the week. On July 3, 1994, I successfully hotwired Christopher Mumford's Chevy Suburban driving away in it with Nina trailing behind in Kelly's Corolla. We pulled off the caper early one morning around four o'clock. The alarm sounded briefly but I worked fast deactivating it in a few seconds. From there I took it up the road to ATL where David Ambrosia and his home boys down at the auto junk yard refurbished the entire body at a local 'chop shop' for a kilo of coke that I'd been sitting on for more than two months. I got the Suburban back from David on July 10th. It was detailed so professionally that you'd think that it was fresh of the assembly line. I needed to have the truck a different color so I requested jade green exterior with a mint colored leather interior. Finally pimpin' it out with twenty-two inch gold rims. David threw in the J.V.C surround sound C.D. system for free. Now while I was away in Hotlanta enjoying my new ride, clubbing all week long and increasing my already extensive wardrobe with the credit cards I'd taken from

Bunny upon her death, Nina had gotten a pipehead to take Christopher Mumford out on July 12th.

"She just walked up to dude and shot him twice in the head as he stood at the bus stop that evening. When he fell to the street, that crack ho just kept on bustin' off dawg, shit I think she emptied the whole clip on that muthafucka," I remembered Nina laughingly saying on the phone.

"How do you know what happened?" I questioned Nina over the line.

"How do I know?...Shit nigga I was right dere watchin' da whole goddamn thing! That's how the fuck I know. Shit, I know you don't think that I'd ask a bitch ta do something like dat and not see da muthafucka carry dat shit out for myself, do you? Shit, Rae you got me fucked up, playa."

I laughed at Nina's irritation over my mock lack of trust. I knew better than that I was just fuckin' with Nina. "Don't make me come down there and put my dick in ya mouth, girl for talkin' dat ole bullshit!" I answered jokingly over the phone.

"Oh boy, shut da suck up, wit ya triflin' ass, always wantin' a bitch ta suck you off...ya hoss dick fucka! Bye!" Nina laughed as she hung up the other line in my ear, which left me and David Ambrosia rolling on the floor for several minutes after as we were listening to her comical tirade over David's speaker phone.

But July turned out to be a pretty bad month after all for me. On the 23rd, I was nabbed out at Fairmount Plantation, West Peola's largest, mostly wealthy community by undercover Federal agents. They'd wiretapped hours of conversations between myself, Big Gabby, Uncle Snookey, and various members of the Cellini crime family. Man, all I remember is these cats coming from everywhere dressed in dark blue suits, hopping out of a half dozen black sedans. All I could do was reach for the sky. It was sort of like getting' robbed, when they jumped put on me all of a sudden. After grilling me for at least two and a half hours at the West Peola County Police Department, the Feds offered me a deal.

"Listen up Rae Kwon, you've got very little options here my friend. You can either continue to portray this hardcore gangsta tough guy role like you're doing now and get thrown in a Federal pen for a shit load of narcotic and possible homicide charges for a very, very long time. That is if your uncle and his mob buddies don't whack you before you stand trial or get somebody to do it for them in prison, which I know and you know is gonna happen if you end up back in the joint. Option two, we've been trailing both you and your uncle, and Big Gabby for over a year now and we know all about your involvement with both men's narcotic distribution rings. We don't really care about you kid, you're small time. No offense, but we want the big fish, capeche?"

Even after all the things the late Lionel Kurtz told me about my uncle, I was still unwavering in my loyalty to the Lake family name. Until the Feds played a select number of recordings with my uncle and some other unrecognizable dude's voice plotting to murder me, behind my involvement with his old boss Lionel Kurtz. The recordings were authentic, more than a dozen, mentioning in graphic detail the methods, and times of planned murders of not only myself, but of Lionel Kurtz, Big Gabby, David Ambrosia, and several key members of Big Gabby's Jamaican Posse including Rawbone and Mr. Robbins both of whom ironically I'd already killed. I sat in a state of disbelief and pain as the tape played out letting me hear spoken testimony of my uncle's plan to rid Peola of every possible drug competitor and to cut ties 'permanently' with all those who'd been close to him, even his own flesh and blood.

"Now does that sound like someone you'd want to protect, and go out on a limb for?" the Middle Eastern looking agent asked noticing my disgust, anger and pain. They'd convinced me beyond a shadow of a doubt that it was in my best interest to help them bring both of the crews down. First of all, I wanted to know what my options really were…Federal Agent Mohammed informed me that I'd be placed into the U.S. Witness Protection Program. The Feds also assured me that my children and their mothers would be protected as well. That was all I needed to hear. It took a little over an hour for me to confess to more than two-dozen murders I'd witnessed my uncle and/or his henchmen carry out during the eighties. Afterwards, the Feds had me contact several buddies of mine who'd bought drugs from Uncle Snookey to fund their own illegal dope business when my uncle lived in Peola back in the day. But I was unsuccessful in catching up with any of them. By early August, Federal agents along with Louisiana State Officials recovered the skeletal remains of over thirty victims, who'd been murdered by Uncle Snookey and his henchmen during the eighties.

Several other witnesses, whose identifications remain concealed to this day, began revealing incriminating evidence of Uncle Snookey's extravagant lifestyle. With the recent confessions coming from myself and the other unknown witness, coupled with the gruesome discovery; the Feds had pretty much all the evidence they needed to take Uncle Snookey down for good. While working closely with the Feds under their Witness Protection Program even I was astonished at the sheer power my uncle wielded in just the last five or six years while living in Las Vegas. I'd learned that it was money from Uncle Snookey's Cellini mafia connection that bank rolled the Detroit based Motor City Mayhem Ecstasy crime ring, spear-headed by Jeremy 'Acid' Fawcett, which smuggled 521 kilos of X into the United States. However, it goes deeper because during the time and possibly earlier, Uncle Snookey operated his drug enterprises freely throughout the Southwestern United States under mafia ordered protection and bribery.

In 1990 alone, there was evidence that Uncle Snookey had laundered vast sums of money from New Mexico area banks, which both he and his girlfriend Madame DeLa Hoya purchased with the help of the Cellini Mob Family. Briefly in May of '89 according to a two page article in an Albuquerque newspaper the mafia owned Desert Sun Savings and Loan bank, which was co-owned by Uncle Snookey, received a little over 68 million dollars in cash deposits delivered over a span of three weeks by teenaged drug runners many of whom were high school dropouts from several of the Apache Indian reservation in the surrounding area. Federal agencies based in New Mexico could not determine where the funds originated. However the FBI knew that the funds were laundered in order to fund De La Hoya's illicit sex businesses as well as Snookey's booming drug operations. Even when key links to Uncle Snookey's drug ring fell victim to Federal drug agencies such as the 'Inland Regional Narcotics Enforcement Team' or IRNET, Uncle Snookey continued to flood Southwestern cities such as Dallas, Houston, Phoenix, and San Antonio to name a few with tons of narcotics each year primarily due to the inexhaustible amount of New Jersey mafia funds according to Agent Mohammed's accounts of the Marion Lake/Albert Cellini FBI Files.

On September 3, 1994 Federal Agents raided two A.M.E. churches in Peola and one Baptist church down in Savannah arresting Reverends Timothy Cauldwell and Leon McBride of New Zion A.M.E. and Spaulding A.M.E., both respectably located in West Peola and Pastor Loula Mae Harris of the Precious Lord Baptist Church located in Savannah, GA. Uncle Snookey's cash, sex, and drugs were being circulated throughout the three so-called houses of worship for years on end netting the ex-ABA star over 45 million dollars in drug sales between the three Georgia churches. According to authorities, when the raid was conducted a total of 2.6 million in cash was confiscated from offices between the three churches as well as high-priced TV home theatre system with a number of sexually graphic photos and videos exposing parishioners engaged in full scale orgies and a wide variety of other graphic sex acts, several semi-automatic weapons and 85 kilos of Ecstasy tablets (found in Reverend Leon McBride's cherry wood pulpit). Two parishioners of Cauldwell's New Zion A.M.E., evangelist Dottie Wiggins and choir director Patrice Fulsome were caught coming back from Atlanta with a million or more tablets of Ecstasy and about fifteen kilos of coke, concealed, ironically, beneath a mountainous stack of bibles. Once the two women were apprehended by the IRNET in the wee hours of the morning of September 8th outside of Broad Street, Patrice Fulsome dropped dime almost instantly on her pastor and other church leaders at New Zion A.M.E. Both women, teary eyed and terribly shaken by their unfortunate predicament, begun recounting disturbing allegations of gross misconduct and strong-arm tactics employed by Reverend Cauldwell and others within his church staff against members of his own congregation.

"I'd transport this mess for the reverend, 'cause I was just too afraid of what he or that God-awful Marion Lake would do to me or my family," Ms. Fulsome said sobbing bitterly as she sat at the small round coffee table in the middle of a makeshift interrogation room. When Wiggins and Fulsome had concluded their interrogations, they'd provided the Federal Agents with enough incriminating evidence to lock away Reverend Timothy Cauldwell and Uncle Snookey for life, which was exactly the sentence, the Feds were after regarding the two felons. Someone, somewhere must have tipped the good reverend off about the upcoming raid, because when the Feds accompanied by Peola's local police raided Timothy Cauldwell's swank 12th floor apartment over looking Peola's picturesque Lake McArdle, all they found was an abandoned apartment that Cauldwell had deserted about a week earlier in order to put as much distance between he and the authorities as he possibly could. For nearly a month and a half, the criminally minded pastor managed to elude and confound FBI Agents and various police departments across the country before he and a gun-wielding teenage love interest, Beverly Wilder, were finally arrested in Portland, Oregon exiting an area jewelry store. Although the reverend was able to summon his team of high-priced lawyers soon after his arrest, they were unable to prevent his deportation back to Guyana.

You see Timothy Cauldwell had never been processed legally as a U.S. Citizen, a fact hidden even from his closest friends. Leon McBride was apprehended on October 10th as he and two accomplices attempted to escape law enforcement officials as they closed in on the dope smuggling group while they were holed up in a rural Savannah farmhouse. That day federal agents recovered something like three hundred pounds of marijuana, as well as sixty-two assault rifles within the old dilapidated farmhouse. Shortly there after, Pastor Lula Mae Harris was promptly arrested as she and two female accomplices exited a seafood restaurant in downtown Savannah. Pastor Harris had a little over fifty thousand in cash on her person at the time of her arrest. A thorough search of her home revealed stacks upon stacks of compressed cocaine 'bricks' down in a cellar and crates of illegally smuggled firearms littering the floor of her attic. Harris who was by far the most ruthless of the three preachers, also kept homemade videos of various beatings and even footage of several murders taking place at her request. This and other evidence confiscated by federal agents landed Lula Mae Harris in a Federal prison for the remainder of her life. She ended up dying behind bars of breast cancer in 1999. Leon McBride attempted suicide twice while in custody as his fear for Uncle Snookey and Alberto Cellini was overwhelming.

"I'm a dead man walking," McBride explained, to the Feds. "No matter where you hide me, Snookey and Pretty Boy will find me...and that'll be my ass."

It wasn't until Agent Mohammed had me and several others under the Federal Witness Program reassure Pastor McBride of his complete safety within the program, that he finally relaxed enough to deliver over three days worth of detailed testimony as to the criminal enormities which took place between the three Georgia chapels during the six or so years that the church leaders became affiliated with Uncle Snookey and his underworld associates. I never did hear anything more about Leon McBride after that. Though some rumored that he was allowed to move out of the country; most of the Feds I'd mentioned that rumor to simply scoffed at the idea.

By 1994, David Ambrosia had resurrected his deceased brother's Bad Boyz drug gang, which numbered members close to a thousand strong. During my frequent travels upstate to Atlanta, David often spoke of wrestling South Peola's drug ridden housing projects away from the violent Jamaican posses which for several years now had become a scourge to the entire town. By the spring of 1994, David Ambrosia's Bad Boyz II crime syndicate arrived in South Peola with a vengeance. About five hundred heavily armed drug dealers made up of an assorted group of ex-cons, teen thugs and gang members. Bloodshed and chaos ensued throughout the months of March, April, and May. Once June arrived, the Rude Boys and most of the other Jamaican posses taking up residence in the projects of Amherst, Hemlock Hills as well as Geneva had been greatly reduced in numbers and power due in large part to the tremendous loss of life during the bloody turf wars of the previous three months. Yet still the casualty list continued to mount for the Jamaicans throughout the oppressively humid months of June and July 1994.

The arrival of August signaled the end of the Jamaicans reign of terror in Peola as the last dozen or so traffickers reluctantly but wisely relinquished control of South Peola's fertile drug markets. David Ambrosia took little time in establishing himself as the head drug lord of Peola, Ga. But unlike the ruthless, cold-hearted Jamaican dealers before him, the thirty something ex-mechanic turned dope man with the wind swept, fiery red hair, moustache and beard was quite the opposite in that he was instrumental in purchasing the real estate company which owned the three South Peola housing projects. Immediately Ambrosia went to work renovating the dilapidated apartments and holding late summer barbecues for the war weary tenants. By month's end Ambrosia had won the respect and admiration of every tenant in all three of the drug-ridden neighborhoods. The projects—though still very much active in drug trafficking— were totally free of violence and bloodshed. As a matter of fact any Bad Boyz member who was caught threatening, attacking, or raping any of Ambrosia's tenants was severely punished and sometimes killed depending on the offense.

"Dese folk don't need this bullshit, no more in their lives man," David Ambrosia would say in his lazy southern drawl. "Dem damn Jamaicans done took dese folk through hell and back and I'll be damned if anybody from my fuckin' crew will repeat dat punk ass shit!"

David Ambrosia was as loved by South Peola as the despised Jamaicans were hated. Even the oft times surly police chief O'Malley considered Ambrosia a personal friend since Ambrosia often donated large sums of cash to a number of local charities including the Fraternal Order of Police of which O'Malley was lodge leader. Ambrosia to this day remains not only Peola's one and only drug kingpin, but one of her favorite sons as well.

Triple Crown Publications presents

XXII

Oh, How the Mighty have Fallen

To me the Feds somehow seemed to turn a deaf ear and a blind eye to David Ambrosia even though they had more than enough proof that Ambrosia had ordered his criminal syndicate to overthrow Big Gabby Cantrell and his Jamaican crews. There was absolutely no doubt in my mind that David's hands were stained scarlet with the blood of countless Jamaican dealers whom he had murdered day in and day out throughout the spring and summer of 1994. Yet for reasons unknown to me as well as others in the witness protection program, they acted as though it didn't happen or either they simply didn't care.

"They aren't interested in a bunch of small time hoodlums offing each other...It's Cantrell, Lake and Cellini their after." I overheard a rookie agent say to another once in Peola's police station. "Ambrosia's Chief O'Malley's concern not ours," he continued on sipping a coffee, all the while watching me suspiciously. I felt like getting in on the conversation but my good sense warned me against sticking my nose in FBI business even if it did concern me indirectly. Once the South Peola slums were taken over by David's Bad Boyz II, Big Gabby didn't stick around to see the inevitable gunplay, but instead hightailed it out of town leaving his Caribbean 'friends' alone to deal with their fates. Big Gabby outwitted the Federal authorities for four months before an anonymous caller alerted police in Montpelier, Vermont after viewing a weekend episode of "America's Most Wanted" that featured Cantrell. The Feds cele-brated X'mas '94 heartily after taking Cantrell down on December 20th. It had been a long time coming and they had finally bagged at least one of the "Big Three" that they wanted so desperately.

Uncle Snookey was another story altogether. He was rumored to be living in Nevada still, unaffected by the arrest of Big Gabby in Vermont or the emergence of his own criminal profile on "America's Most Wanted." Communications between Federal Agents in Peola with those in Nevada continued on into the New Year. Secretly wiretapped hours of conversation between Uncle Snookey, Madam De La Hoya, and of course Don Alberto Cellini were building up. The Feds tried to appre-hend Uncle Snookey by having me set him up but it didn't work with Uncle Snookey making himself unavailable for each of the six times I attempted contacting him. Then finally on June 1, 1994, federal agents raided the mob-owned Maguey Bar and Grill, a dimly lit, yet lively watering hole in suburban Albuquerque, often frequented by notorious underworld figures, and assorted corrupt politicians. Uncle Snookey, Madam De La Hoya and Vito 'Guns' Lucci—Cellini's first cousin and premier enforcer—were seized as well as several other Cellini/Graciano mobsters. Don Cellini himself again avoided capture by vaca-tioning in Brussels for the summer. To this day the "Pretty Boy" remains at large. As for my uncle, he and his Latin Lover, Madam De La Hoya were both sentenced to 25 to life on a variety of charges ranging from racketeering, and money laundering, to drug trafficking, prostitution, and murder, while Vito Lucci was sentenced on murder charges dating back to 1972, he too received a life sentence from a federal grand jury. All three ended up in federal prisons.

Uncle Snookey and Ms. De Ka Hoya landed in Fort Leavenworth, Kansas, while Vito 'Guns' Lucci was sent packing to Attica back east where he and his family originally came from. Big Gabby Cantrell was locked up in a federal pen down in Alabama. I've since forgotten the name of the place, but I do know that it wasn't far from Montgomery. Gabby had three strokes; the first one in 97' another in 99' and a third which ultimately took his life on September 12, 2000. Tipping the scales at a walloping 555 lbs at the time of his death his remains had to be placed into a grand piano box that substituted as a coffin upon his burial. Having no close relatives to claim his millions in cash, property, and stocks, the states of South Carolina and Georgia divided the spoils amongst themselves after awaiting the emergence of any legal heirs. De La Hoya who was pregnant at the time of her arrest and conviction gave birth to an eight pound ten ounce baby boy whom she named Marion after my uncle.

Even though my uncle was no longer on the streets he was still pulling in a hefty income, the sales of his personal memoirs aptly entitled *Hate the Game...Not the Playa* sold several million copies during the first year of it's much anticipated release in 1998. Even as he did hard time behind bars in Kansas Marion "Snookey" Lake continued to make his storied mark on society whether they liked it or not. He earned a spot on the New York Times top ten bestsellers list for five weeks straight, finally reaching number one in its fourth and fifth week in July '98.

ABC's "Nightline" ran a thirty-minute segment on Uncle Snookey's erstwhile drug empire as well as CBS's "Sixty Minutes." His ruggedly handsome face graced the covers of such national periodicals as Ebony, Jet, Essence and Newsweek. Gangsta rappers, especially those hailing from the south paid homage to him through their lyrics and videos. In the end even captivity couldn't quell Uncle Snookey's successful 'bad boy' mass appeal much to the chagrin of his jailers and other police authorities nationwide.

Aunt Melissa continued her catering business on Hilton Head, which had grown considerably since leaving Peola and Uncle Snookey behind years earlier. We spoke often during the dark days of my ordeal and I thank God for her because she helped me cope during that tough time in my life. Aunt Melissa eventually removed Shawn from that psychiatric ward in ward in upstate South Carolina returning him back home. He'd put on a lot of weight from all the drugs the doctors gave him and was no longer the chiseled athlete he once was, but was instead a heavily medicated, dull-witted, shadow of his former self. It brought tears to my eyes to see him like that, but I was happy that his mom finally got him out of that nut house.

In 1995, Donita married her college quarterback sweetheart, only to end up in divorce court three years later. Through dude landed a spot on the Carolina Panthers roster as a second string quarterback his abuse of alcohol, and street drugs ended his NFL career after only two unproductive seasons. After her husband's pro football stint ended, Donita not only had to deal with his substance abuse, but spousal abuse and chronic infidelity as well. We are now better friends than ever before and share as much quality time together with our kids as we can. She resides in Atlanta with the children and manages a successful marketing firm downtown. Brandi, living off her nice little nest egg from the old geezer she used to date and take care of back in the day, invested her money into several Miami area beach properties and made damn good on her investments...so good that she owns property throughout Florida and in parts of Georgia. Our daughter Selena has grown up to be a gorgeous little girl who's at the top of her class in every subject. She travels abroad with her mother so often that she now speaks three languages fluently; Spanish, French, and German. I'm so proud of her, and I've got to give props to Brandi for raising her so well despite what people may have thought about her career choices.

I've since lost contact with almost everybody else from my drug-dealing past with the exception of Nina who continues to run her brothel in Peola even now in 2002. When I spoke to her a while back she claimed that she had not only one but five houses of prostitution, three in Peola and two in Savannah. She seemed happy with her life, so more power to her. Diamond has been perhaps the single most important person in my life, other than my own children and my aunt. She stuck with me through some of the darkest days of my young life. A lesser woman would have abandoned my sorry ass, a long time ago and shit. I would not have blamed her if she had. I was really stupid, money, power, and sex had corrupted me and I did not care because I loved every fuckin' minute of it. I owe Diamond my life because she gave me a reason to live. I've been in the witness protection program for over nine years now, and I can't wait to be free of all of this secretive, highly monitored living coming in April 2003. I can't really put down in writing where I live for obvious reasons however, I will say that I reside somewhere in the Pacific Northwest. It's quiet where I stay, lots of beautiful, untamed wilderness, mountains, forests, scenic lakes, wildlife...lots of clean fresh air.

I now live far away from any major metropolitan area, with the nearest town being about 35 miles away and that one town is truly small, population there is probably no more than eight or nine hundred people. There's like one hospital, one police station, one supermarket...you know what I'm sayin? Straight 'Mayberry' type shit. The people there are really nice always waving and/ or greeting one another. When I first traveled there for some groceries and auto parts I felt a bit uneasy because the town's population is predominately white. But soon the townsfolk took me in as one of their own, greeting and conversing with me eagerly whenever I made my way into town for supplies and/or groceries. I've even spent holidays over at the homes of several families in the community. But even still, I missed big city life; I yearned to be back down south where I belonged. Mrs. Dover a kindly old lady from town, once gave me $50. "Here you go young man. Here's fifty dollars try not to spend it all in one place, that's a whole lot of money you know."

The diminutive old lady said as she handed me a wrinkled fifty-dollar bill, smiling at me through glistening white dentures. I obliged the old lady by accepting her monetary gift smiling as I withdrew the crinkly bill from her outstretched hand. I thanked her warmly before loading up the Humvee and heading back up the mountain trail toward the lonely little log cabin that served as my temporary home. I couldn't help but laugh quietly as I put the fifty dollar bill upon the dash, remembering a time not long ago when I used to tip waiters and waitresses at least that much.

There'd be times when I'd be out in the yard chopping wood or in the kitchen cooking a simple meal for myself when I'd just stop and realize that I was actually living this way! 2002 was not a good year for me financially. No more expensive champagne or premium liquors, now I had to settle for Coors or Amstel Light. No more five star restaurants or hotel suites, now I had to accept T.V. dinners and a Lincolnesque cabin in the woods…and to add insult to injury the fifty dollars that Mrs. Dover gave me actually helped me out a great deal since I'd lived on a fixed income of about $200 a month provided by the Federal Government through the Witness Protection Program, two hundred fuckin' dollars per month! I'd blow $2,000 on the Las Vegas and Atlantic City black jack tables in less than thirty minutes! But Diamond would wire me money throughout the year, month after month, so I was never altogether broke, but still it was a major adjustment period for me. I had to order clothes via the Internet because the only retail store available to me out there was a Wal-Mart…I don't think so! I had to at least rock the latest athletic and casual gear. The Feds had a Special Agent assigned to me who'd check up on me at least twice a month. I never saw the same one twice, there was always different dudes checking on me. Usually they stuck around for a half hour or so asking questions, of which I can't reveal here on paper and they'd take a urine sample from me to ensure that I hadn't been taking any narcotics. My cabin was bugged; everything you can think of was wired. Two of the agents even told me that there were closed-circuit T.V. cameras inside the cabin as well as outside in the yard cleverly placed in surrounding treetops. I don't know whether that was true or not but I didn't care one way or the other. What could I do? I'd been totally stripped of everything that connected me to hustling, but I adapt well to any situation so I just learned to live without the luxuries that I once enjoyed on a regular. But other than the extreme boredom I experienced from time to time and the irritation of being monitored 24/7 by folks who weren't even physically present, I'd have to say, I learned a hell of a lot living out there in the mountains.

I became more spiritually fulfilled as a person than ever before because I had hours upon hours to simply look back on my young life and reflect. I soul searched deeply and found peace within myself through long evenings of quiet meditation and prayer. I even got up early on Sunday morning a few times and visited the quaint, little Methodist church down in the town square. Once I even turned down an offer to go on a deer-hunting trip with a couple of guys around my age from town. I just couldn't handle a firearm any more without dark memories creeping into my mind. Nightmares haunted my sleep from time to time causing me to awaken in a cold sweat, images of murder and blood shed, surreal visions of cemeteries, funerals, and bullet-ridden corpses. I'm glad that there was no one within miles to hear me scream out in terror or to see me reduced to pitiful sobbing soon afterwards. Diamond was allowed to visit with me whenever she could. She flew out west to see me at least once a month, those were the best times of my life. And it was during one of these visits that we both decided to get married. We tied the knot June 10, 2000, at the same tiny little church, within the same small little town below the mountainous ridge in which I resided. It was a wonderful celebration. All the townspeople made us feel like royalty because of their hospitality and warmth. The well-wishers numbered at least 250! As a wedding present, the mayor, Seymour Littleton, allowed us to spend the following weekend alone in the mayoral suite of the town hall building. That was really romantic. We were also given gifts in great abundance from half the town I'd imagine. Diamond and I have adopted the town and plan to visit here regularly and keep in touch with the citizens who showed us so much affection. As for me now, I will be able enrolling at South Carolina State University, where I plan to major in sports medicine. Well that's all I can say about my life so far in a book…at least about the bad things that I've done, ya know the stuff that I'm not particularly proud of. But hey…that was then and this is now. I've repented for everything I've done wrong, and no matter whether you or anyone else forgives me, I'm sure the Lord God will.

Triple Crown Publications presents

Conclusion

Rae Kwon Lake resides on Hilton Head Island with his wife Diamond and their three children: Lynette, age two, Lisa, age one, and LeRoi, age two months. He managed to maintain a 4.0 GPA throughout his four years at college and graduated Magna Cum Laude from South Carolina State University. He is now a team physician for the NFL's Carolina Panthers, while his wife continues her dentistry practice.

Triple Crown Publications presents

Epilogue

At the conclusion of Rae Kwon's taped recollections, a small contingent of students form the University of Kansas received permission from the Fort Leavenworth federal prison officials to come in and conduct a behind bars interview with Marion Lake that rendered the interviewer speechless upon the end of the taping. Here now we present the interview in its entirety.

Interviewer: So Mr. Lake, how old were you when you first started your criminal career?

Marion Lake: (Lighting up a cigarette) Ya mean selling dope?

Interviewer: Yes sir.

Marion Lake: Lemme see...I'd say bout eight or nine.

Interviewer: Your telling me that you were eight or nine years old when you begun your life of crime?

Marion Lake: You muthafuckin' right! Shit, I used ta steal shit from neighborhood homes and stores and I would bully neighborhood kids and take their lunch money.

Interviewer: When did you have your first run in with the law?

Marion Lake: Twelve years old. Bitch ass truant officer,

Oliver Petty, caught me playing hooky with some other lil' cats.

Interviewer: What did the truant officer do to you and your friends afterwards?

Marion Lake: Oh nuthin', not to me anyway cause I wasn't bout ta get in his car and go ta school. So I shot him a couple of times wit my pellet gun and my boys and me hauled ass.

Interviewer: (eyebrows raised) Surely that incident landed you into more hot water didn't it?

Marion Lake: Ya damn right it did, but hell it was well worth it.

Interviewer: You assaulted a man with a weapon, Mr. Lake at twelve years old didn't you have any sense of right and wrong or any feelings of remorse for your actions?

Marion Lake: Nope...not at all in fact later on that same year me and my boys jumped his son Max comin' home from school. We beat his punk ass so bad that day that he stayed in the hospital for a week. Oh yeah, I also remembered poisoning his two German Shepherds.

Interviewer: So I take it you and your buddies took pride in being menaces to society?

Marion Lake: Pretty much.

Interviewer: What did your parents think about your early juvenile activities?

Marion Lake: My father was always in and out of the picture, that no good nigga. Mamma say he was hexed with a root, but I don't believe in dat shit, anyway my moms spoiled me, it was my older brother who caught hell from her.

Interviewer: So what you are saying is that your mother

found it perfectly alright that you were a juvenile delinquent?

Marion Lake: (smiling) Other than an ass-whipin' every now and then...yeah.

Interviewer: (shaking her head) Unreal...Sooo, Mr. Lake, have you ever committed murder?

Marion Lake: I dunno...have you?

Interviewer: There has been numerous skeletal remains unearthed throughout the city of New Orleans, as well as other parts of Louisiana, and lab DNA has proven that almost all of those remains were those of your former associates.

Marion Lake: And?

Interviewer: Did you or any one you know have anything to do with those homicides?

Marion Lake: Looka here honey, I don't know who da fuck you think you talking to, but guess what I ain't da one. I don't give a fuck bout, you , dis muthafuckin' interview, or anybody else round dis here stinkin' ass prison! You think cuz a nigga behind dese bars he'll just freely tell you his whole life story, huh? Fuck dat move jack, ya lil' young ass gets Nathan, ya heard?! Cept a swift kick in da ass if you don't stop fuckin' wit me!!

(Interviewer appears uncomfortable, speechless)

Marion Lake: (leaning in closer toward the young college interviewer) Ya know what? I'm in here but y'all muthafuckas still, can't stop da flow!! Ya see, I got eyes and ears everywhere, ya heard? And if ya want some info about da Snook go buy da book...it's on sale all over da country. Ya gots ta pay ta hear what da fuck da Snook gots ta say. Right bout now I'm gonna knock off bout a thousand push-ups and a thousand sit-ups, then I'm goin' the fuck ta sleep, awiiight?!!

Sooo, I guess that means fa you ta get da hell on from round here 'peckawood' befo' I snatch ya lil' young ass cross dis table and piss in ya mouf!

(Sensing aggression, the interviewer quickly packed up his equipment and buzzed for a prison guard to release her Marion's jail cell. As the college student made her exit down the long narrow hallway lined by rows and rows of filthy jail cells, she was verbally abused by scores of rowdy inmates howling and clawing at her as she passed along. Marion stood at the entrance of his cell watching as the young woman literally broke into a run as she neared the exit door.)

Marion Lake: Punk ass.

Marion chuckled to himself as he watched with amusement. Slowly, Marion turned, approaching his bunk, stripping off his inmate jumpsuit until he stood naked except for his briefs. He smiled slightly as he admired his well sculpted physique in the mirror of his cell before he proceeded with his nightly exercise routine of multiple push-ups and sit-ups...channeling his pent-up frustration and aggression into his work-out, impatiently awaiting the day when he would walk through those prison doors a free man to once more take up his throne as drug lord of the dirty, dirty south...ya heard?!

The End

CPSIA information can be obtained at www.ICGtesting.com
Printed in the USA
LVOW121208030413

327365LV00002B/148/P